1st ed
/500
...end
Copy

CAME A
DEAD CAT

ALSO BY JAMES N. FREY

Fiction

A Killing in Dreamland
The Long Way to Die
Circle of Death
USSA
The Elixir
The Armageddon Game
The Last Patriot

Nonfiction

How to Write a Damn Good Novel

CAME A
DEAD CAT

James N. Frey

ST. MARTIN'S PRESS NEW YORK

Design by Judy Dannecker

Library of Congress Cataloging-in-Publication Data
Frey, James N.
        Came a dead cat / James Frey.
              p.   cm.
        "A Thomas Dunne book."
        ISBN 0-312-06314-8
        I.Title.
PS3556.R4474C3   1991
813'.54—dc20   91-19915
                                                                     CIP

First Edition: November 1991

10 9 8 7 6 5 4 3 2 1

To my daughter, Amy

ONE

■

Call me Odyssey.

Monday, April seventh, 10 A.M.

A young Filipino maid opened a set of sliding doors off the marble foyer and showed me into the luxurious living room. The off-white rug was thicker than my Beautyrest mattress. The brocade drapes hanging from a heavy rail were open and the morning sun filtered in through the slats of the shuttered windows. The couch and two wing chairs were upholstered in gray tones, subdued and fine. A copy of *Architectural Digest* lay on the brass and glass coffee table.

The maid said Mrs. Holmcroft would see me presently and went back out through the sliding doors, closing them behind her.

All I knew about Aletha Holmcroft was that she was the granddaughter of a U.S. Supreme Court justice, the daughter of a California governor, and the wife of a multimillionaire. I felt as if I were about to meet royalty. A tiny butterfly fluttered in my stomach.

I assumed she must have a big problem in need of a quick solution or she wouldn't want to see me. I'm a private eye.

I took a little tour around the room for no other reason than I'm nosy. A couple of paintings from the Flemish Renaissance hung on a wall; they were portraits of dark, brooding men in black with severe faces. No-fun kind of guys. In the corner, a globe of the world sat in a wooden cradle. Small ivory figurines lined the mantel: two elephants, a half dozen tigers, a man playing a flute. They were Asian, probably Burmese. The place felt like a museum where they let in only about two visitors a year.

Suddenly the doors slid open and Mrs. Aletha Holmcroft came in. She was slender, stately, manicured, about fifty. She was wearing a plain black dress with a single string of pearls. Her shoulder-length hair was gray and lustrous. She seemed unhurried and calm and perfectly in control, but when she put her hand out to shake mine I could see something tense in her eyes, something that told me she was scared.

She looked at me unblinking for a moment. "I don't know why, I guess I assumed Mr. Frampton would be sending a man."

"If you like, I could smoke a cigar." I smiled.

She didn't smile, but her eyes softened. "I'm sorry. I suppose women are into all sorts of professions. I don't know why I should be so surprised that one is a private investigator. I hope I haven't offended you, Miss Gallagher."

I said, "I'm not offended. Please, call me Odyssey."

"All right. Odyssey. Please, won't you be seated?" She gestured toward the couch.

The Filipino maid brought us some yellow finger cookies and a pot of steaming coffee, all on a large silver tray. The maid had a smile that seemed as fake as a TV preacher's. While she poured, Mrs. Holmcroft kept looking me over. Most people don't trust private eyes, that's why I always try not to look too slick. I was wearing charcoal gray slacks and a light gray blazer. I have auburn hair cut shoulder length, tied in a knot that morning, and I wore large, heavy-framed glasses that make me look serious. Just a touch of lipstick.

When she finished pouring the coffee, the maid floated silently

2

out of the room, quiet as smoke. She closed the sliding doors behind her again.

Mrs. Holmcroft lifted the little silver spoon out of the little sugar bowl. "Sweetener? Sugar?"

"Just black."

She passed me a cup with a saucer and a linen napkin. She spooned some sugar into her coffee and doused it with cream, then stirred slowly, delicately.

"My husband—I think—has been threatened with death in a grotesque way," she said. I waited for her to go on, but she didn't. She just kept stirring her coffee and looking me over. Then she said, "Before I tell you more about my problem, I wonder whether you'd mind if I ask a few pertinent questions as to your qualifications." She had one of those deep silken voices, not phony. It was just part of her.

"Ask away."

"How long have you worked with Mr. Frampton?"

"Two years, two months."

"And before that?"

"Six years with All American Alliance Insurance Investigators. We did mostly Inland Marine, which covers jewelry, art, bullion, stamp collections, that kind of thing. Occasionally we'd investigate an accidental death or fraud. Call Harvey Thorenstein in their Oakland office if you'd like references."

"I may do that," she said. She paused and stirred her coffee again, though I doubted it needed stirring.

"I feel somewhat ill-equipped to ask you the right questions," she said. "I've never interviewed someone in your profession before." She smiled for the first time. A pleasant little smile that warmed the whole museum.

I smiled in return.

"Where did you go to school?" she asked. "I'm sorry to be so, so—I'd just feel better, I guess, if I thought I knew you better."

"I went to the University of California at Santa Cruz," I said. "I have a Ph.D. in English Literature." I took a finger cookie and bit into it. A buttery taste. Nice and crunchy.

She looked at me out of the corner of her eye as if she didn't quite believe me about my doctorate.

"A fact," I said. "I'm smart as a whip. My dissertation topic was Mary Wollstonecraft and the impact of her 'A Vindication of the Rights of Woman,' on women writers who followed her: George Eliot, Edith Sitwell, Edith Wharton, Virginia Woolf, Stevie Smith, Doris Lessing—all very boring stuff. I couldn't stand the quiet of academia, and I couldn't stand grading freshman English papers, and I couldn't stand playing the game—so I became an investigator. I wanted to have an adventurous life, not read about one. It's a rough business, but last year I earned a brown belt in aikido, so I know a little bit about taking care of myself."

I had the distinct impression she didn't know aikido from Mary Wollstonecraft, although she nodded as if she were impressed, and I felt she was halfway convinced I could handle the job.

I took a sip of French Roast coffee, good and strong. I said: "My time is costing you fifty dollars an hour, but if you like I'd be happy to tell you my whole life story. I'm thirty-five, never been married, I have a boyfriend who's a computer programmer, I never take bribes, and I'll give you a true accounting of the time I spend on your case. Unlike the Mounties, I don't always get my man. But I always give it all I've got. Now, you mentioned your husband is being threatened, maybe we should get on with putting a stop to it."

"Since you put it that way," she said, "I suppose we should." She seemed to relax a little, but the fear was still giving a hard cast to her eyes.

I took out my leather-bound note pad, the kind you see TV cops use. Makes clients feel they ought to tell you something you can put in it.

She took a long sip of coffee from her cup. "My husband," she said, "is a philanderer." She said it matter-of-factly, but I could tell it hurt her to say it. Something in her voice.

"You want to know who the woman is?" I asked.

She shook her head. "I already know who the woman is. The

4

latest one, anyway. Rachel Collins, her name is." She took a breath. "All I want you to do, Odyssey, is to find where she lives. That's all. Just find her, my lawyers will take it from there."

"Can you give me her last known address? Last place of employment, that kind of thing?"

"She's listed in the phone book, but there's no address given and the phone has been disconnected. I know she used to work at a place called Lemming's Cocktail Lounge downtown. My lawyer sent someone down there. She had left their employ and Mr. Lemming would not give out her address."

"Do you have a description of her?"

"She has curly—almost frizzy—bright red hair, and knowing my husband's tastes in these kinds of women, she probably has a lot of curves. Age, about twenty-eight, maybe younger, but not older."

"You said your husband was threatened in a grotesque way."

"Maybe I'd better tell you the whole story." She pressed the flats of her hands together and peered off into space. "We belong to the Marconi Club. It's rather exclusive. It seems she somehow got in there and, well, attacked my husband." She looked at me now. "Not that he didn't deserve it, he probably did. He no doubt promised her the sun and the moon and all the stars in the sky. That's his usual practice. And then when he tires of his little . . . bimbos he just sends his chauffeur over with an envelope with some money in it and a note wishing her luck. I suppose that's what he did with Miss Collins and she became incensed. I have no idea how she got in the club, their security arrangements must be abysmal. Fortunately, no one was hurt."

"When was this?"

"Friday night. Three weeks ago."

I turned to the calendar in the front of my notebook. "March fourteenth?"

"Yes, that's right."

"What time?"

"Eight, eight-fifteen. I wasn't there, you understand."

"Your husband told you about it?"

5

"No, I heard about it from friends. Fifty people saw it. Ever since this . . . unpleasantness, we've been getting strange phone calls. Nobody there. I've had the number changed, of course, but the calls continue."

"You should notify the police."

"My husband says he's taking care of the matter, but I don't trust him to do it. I want it very clear, you are working for me, not for him."

"You may be dealing with a very sick woman here."

"I know. It's not just the phone calls. Come with me, please."

I followed her out through the foyer and into the formal dining room—sixteen Queen Anne chairs, a huge chandelier over the Chippendale table, a corner vitrine displaying Imari porcelain—and through a set of swinging doors into a kitchen that seemed big enough for a hotel. At the back of the kitchen was a small stairway. We went down the stairway to a sort of utility room lined with white cabinets and shelves full of canned goods, about enough to feed the Russian army for a month. A lean young man was wire-brushing some gardening tools in a sink.

He was about sixteen, a lanky bag of bones and pimples. His hair was mussed and he had on jeans and a brown shirt. He was wearing gloves, the kind used for gardening. They had big green stripes and gold stars and his thin arms looked funny sticking out of them.

"This is Miss Gallagher, Conrad. Miss Gallagher, my son, Conrad Winter."

He looked me over with eyes as sharp as pruning shears.

"Miss Gallagher is a detective," Mrs. Holmcroft said.

"Yeah?" His eyes got even sharper.

"I want to show her the present we received last night."

Something flickered in his eyes, I couldn't tell what. Not fear. He bowed slightly, the way a stage magician might before sawing a woman in half, then he walked over to a large food freezer and opened it. It was full of packages of frozen foods, everything from broccoli to veal parmigiana to duck à l'orange. There was something else too, wrapped in a large piece of clear plastic.

6

Conrad took it out, holding it as if it were precious and breakable, and brought it over to a table.

The plastic was stuck together, but Conrad managed to pull most of it away. Inside was a large, fat, black cat. Conrad got the cat's head clear of the plastic and pointed to its throat. It had been slashed through to the neck bone. Conrad looked grieved.

"Enough, Mother?" Conrad asked.

"Thank you, Conrad," Mrs. Holmcroft said. Conrad returned to the sink and went back to work. I thought it odd she treated him as one of the help, but then again, perhaps it was the way she treated everyone.

The sight of the cat sickened me. I braced myself and started examining it. It had no collar and no identifying marks, but it had a nice healthy coat and no scars, defects, or deformities. He hadn't spent his life scraping around in an alley; this was a pampered house cat that passed its time on somebody's lap being stroked.

Mrs. Holmcroft wasn't looking at the cat, she'd turned her back to it. She said, "That animal was left on our doorstep last night by that Rachel Collins woman."

I said, "Did she leave a note?"

"No."

"Anyone see her?"

"No one saw her, but I know it came from her. I'm as sure as I can be."

She was a client. I was paid to take her word for it. "Had you ever seen the cat before?"

"Never."

"How about you, Conrad?" I wondered if he were listening.

"Nope." I guess he was.

I wrapped the cat in the plastic and tucked it under my arm. Mrs. Holmcroft looked surprised that I'd want to take it with me.

"I'll take it to a lab—might tell us something."

"Whatever you say."

We went back upstairs. She accompanied me to the front door. I said, "Would you mind if I spoke to your husband?"

7

"I don't mind, but he might. You can find him at his office in the Transamerica Pyramid." She smiled what I took to be an ironic smile. Then she said, "My husband can be a most difficult man." She opened the door for me. "Bring the cat back when you're done with it, please," she said.

I looked at her.

She said, "When you find this Rachel Collins, I intend to give her back her cat."

TWO

∎

A heavy rain earlier that morning made the streets smell clean; the air was clear and fresh. The Holmcrofts' house was in Pacific Heights, on Pacific, between Steiner and Pierce. As I went down the walk to the street I could see the Golden Gate Bridge to the north, and the bay, blue and shimmering in the morning sun. To the west, beyond the bridge, was a fog bank like a huge comforter that would come sliding in and cover the city in the afternoon.

I put the cat in the trunk of my old, bright yellow Camaro I call the "Banana Slug," which just happens to be the mascot of my old alma mater, as well as the State of California's official mollusk. I got in behind the wheel and took my time log from the glove box and marked the start of the case at the moment I'd entered the house.

I paused and thought about revenge, and I remembered a quote I read once. Francis Bacon, I think it was: *A man that studieth revenge keepeth his own wounds green.* I had a feeling

9

Mrs. Holmcroft's wounds were green enough to glow in the dark.

Oh well, that's what keeps us in business.

I turned the key and the Banana Slug rumbled to life. My Camaro has a beefed-up Cadillac engine that one of my old boyfriends gave me for a birthday present. Besides going from zero to sixty before you can inhale, it has a special overdrive that gears it way up, so the top end is maybe one-sixty.

The closest I've gotten to the top end was ninety-five once on the way to Reno, where I was anxious to try out this system I worked up to win at blackjack. I needn't have hurried.

Okay, so I headed down Pacific. I drove a few blocks and turned right and went toward California Street, which a lot of people avoid because of the cable cars, so usually the traffic's not too bad. But this morning, as I made a left onto California, the traffic was terrible. I was in the left lane and decided to go right, so I cut a guy off and made a right on Van Ness, and that's when I saw it in my mirror: a black Nissan Z car.

I changed lanes. It changed lanes. I slowed down. It slowed down. I sped up. It stayed with me.

Van Ness is divided, three lanes each way. I cut to the left and hit it; I sailed through the yellow at the next intersection and kept watching in my mirror. The Z came after me, running the red. I pulled over into the center lane and slowed down behind a huge green furniture van. The Z was hanging back, in the right lane now behind an Oldsmobile station wagon. Whoever it was, he knew what he was doing. There was no way to get his plate number.

Well, if he wanted to play games, it was okay by me.

I hung back from the furniture van a bit, swung to the left again, then stepped on it. The Banana Slug shot forward, smoking rubber. At the next intersection I made a U-turn and headed right back up Van Ness, passing the Z coming the other way. The plates were mud covered so all I got was a K, and the glass was tinted so I couldn't see who was driving. Whoever it was, I hoped he had his seat belt on.

I made a left and shot up a hill past a couple of car dealerships, then made a left on Gough, tires screaming, and when I looked in my mirror he was still with me. I crossed Bush, Sutter, Post, and Geary, making all the lights cleanly. I headed down toward the freeway, cutting in and around traffic. Up ahead, at the Turk Street skyway entrance, I could see the light turning, but the right lane was open. A couple of taxis and a sports car had the Z hemmed in. The light was red and cross traffic started to move. I hit it hard, sounded the horn, and flew through the intersection at sixty miles an hour as cars to the left and right hit their brakes.

I was on the freeway and there wasn't any black Z to be seen. And no cops. My lucky day.

I let out a long breath and put a cassette into the stereo. Charlie Parker, a little mellow sax. I sat back and wondered whether my being followed had anything to do with the case and thought probably it did. This was going to be a good one. My heart felt as if it were trying to beat its way out of my chest. I was lightheaded. An adrenaline high.

Exhilarating.

I took the freeway south to Army Street, came back up Potrero, and found my way over to Rhode Island. I parked in front of a modest little white stucco house sandwiched between two three-story apartment buildings. The apartment buildings had all the charm of packing crates. The little stucco house wasn't much, either. The grass was overgrown and the paint was peeling. I got my camera out of the glove box, got out of the car, opened the trunk, and retrieved the cat. Then I walked up the front stairs of the house and rang the bell. Then rang it again.

Irving Tredich opened the door. He was sixty-five, balding, his shirt not tucked in. "To you I am not speaking," he said.

"Uncle Irving!"

"Ten months you don't come to see me, I'm not speaking." He shut the door.

I rang the bell again. He opened the door. "What's under your arm?" he asked.

"A dead cat."

11

"For me, a present? Ten months I don't see you, and you bring me a dead cat."

"Somebody sent it to a client of mine. I want to know more about it."

"Come in, Odyssey. About not speaking I was only joking. You look so flushed, must be you're in love."

"I've been road racing."

"Such a life."

Irving Tredich was retired from teaching at Cal Tech, where he worked in the Biology Department with my father for twenty-five years. My father and Irving Tredich never got along, but I always called him Uncle Irving because I was best friends with his daughter Nancy.

"So how come you don't ship this to your father?"

"He's in Greece."

"I should be in Greece."

The house was cluttered, but homey, with antique clocks everywhere. He lived alone. He'd been widowed for twenty years. I followed him into the kitchen. He cleared away some dirty dishes and laid the cat out on the table on some newspapers. He pulled some rubber gloves out of a drawer and put them on.

"How's Nancy?" I asked.

"Getting a divorce."

"Again?"

He shrugged. "Already she has number four picked out, I think." He looked at the cat's claws. "Cat's had a manicure."

He showed me where they'd been clipped. Then he looked at the wound. "After the cat was dead, this cut was made. Look, this is an artery, blood would gush like a fountain. Tell me more about the animal."

"All I know is that it showed up on my client's front door step."

"And you want me to tell you what?"

"What killed it. What it had for lunch. Who owned it. Anything you can find out. This time you might even be paid. Send a bill to Frampton Investigations."

12

I took some pictures of the cat from every angle. "Well, thanks, Uncle Irving. I guess I've got to go."

"So how much time do I have?" he asked.

"Soon as possible."

"Some retirement I have. Cutting up dead cats. Going to weddings."

At the front door, he said: "You don't wait ten months again, you hear me?"

I kissed him on the cheek. "Promise."

I took the freeway back toward downtown and exited just before the Bay Bridge. Traffic was breezing along. I kept an eye out for a black Z, but didn't see one.

I drove down Mission and made a left on Main and crossed Market. When I got to Battery, I made an illegal left turn, and took a parking space at the curb. There's a goddess up there in the heavens in charge of parking spaces and she usually looks out for me.

I took off my glasses and brushed my hair back, unfastened the top two buttons of my blouse. Appearances are so important in this business.

I put two quarters in the Banana Slug's parking meter, which made me good for an hour, and headed over to Lemming's Cocktail Lounge, where Aletha Holmcroft said Rachel Collins had worked.

It was just a little before twelve when I walked into Lemming's Lounge. Dim and cavelike inside, the place had an ebony bar, red leather stools, and glassware and mirrors everywhere. It was supposed to look classy. It looked tawdry. Some business types, four men and a woman, were seated at the bar chatting together. The woman was midthirties with a beak nose like a chicken hawk's. The men were a little older. Flabby. Bags under their eyes. Over-worriers, over-eaters, over-drinkers, overdue for cardiac problems.

I sat at the bar near the door; from there I could see the door to Lemming's office. The bartender was a fat man in a red apron. He was busy at the moment mixing martinis for the business

13

types. The woman paid the tab. One of the men protested, but not too vociferously. Then it was my turn. The bartender came over and pushed a cocktail napkin in front of me.

"What'll it be, Miss?"

"Soda and lime," I said. I never booze it on the job. Well, almost never.

He poured me the soda, looking none too happy. Soda lovers never tip. A bartender I used to date told me that. He'd never let me order it when we went out.

But I tipped the fat bartender a buck, which brought a smile to his lips. "Mr. Lemming in?" I asked. I used my sugar voice on him. Sweet, sort of low. Faintly southern. The kind of voice that makes men want to do things for you.

His eyes narrowed. Suspicious. Bill collectors often use that sort of voice.

"A personal matter," I said. "Mr. Lemming said he'd buy me a drink."

He glanced at the office door, then gave me a long look-over and shook his head. "He ain't in."

I gave him a sexy smile and handed him my card. Not my P.I. card, the one that reads: Are you ready for an Odyssey? Below was printed my name and P.O. box. High-class hookers have cards like that. The bartender took the card, wiped it on his shirt, and read it. He cocked an eyebrow. "Wait one," he said.

"Sure."

The soda and lime tasted good. I guess road racing made me thirsty.

I watched the bartender go to the office door, knock, and be let in. He came out a moment later and went back to the bar and smiled in my direction. Lemming came out of the office a moment later. He waved to me from just outside his office. I headed over to him. He was balding, thin, nervous. He wore a light blue sportcoat, his shirt collar open at the neck.

When I got close to him, I realized I'd seen him before—at a Security Services Seminar on crime prevention for small businesses. He called himself "Bobby." He waved me into the office with a grin and flourish.

14

"Hi, Bobby," I said.

He looked me over like I was a good used car he was thinking of buying.

"I remember you," he said. "Do I ever!" The veins on his neck stood out and his face flushed. He shoved my card back at me. "I wanted to buy you the best dinner you ever ate in your life and what did you do? Spit in my face."

"I didn't exactly spit in your face."

"Metaphorically speaking."

"I just said I'd rather have dinner with a pig."

He bared his yellow teeth. "Yeah, that was it."

"I want to apologize for that," I said, sugar voice. "Honest. I guess I was just having a bad day. You know. Forgive me, Bobby, please."

He peered into my eyes trying to decide whether I was telling the truth. I guess he decided I was.

"Apology accepted," he said at last. "You're a P.I., right? Something like that. Never let it be said that Bobby Lemming ever held a grudge. So what you want? How about we go grab some lunch?"

"No thanks."

"A drink?"

"No."

He scowled suddenly and went behind his desk and sat down. Then he nodded as if he'd finally figured something out. "Okay, so give it to me."

"Give what to you?" I honestly had no idea what he was talking about.

"The papers," he said.

"What papers?"

"You are a P.I. aren't you?"

"Yes."

"Don't P.I.'s serve papers?"

"I'm not here to serve any papers."

He let a long breath out slowly, then he put his hands on his desk and smiled. "In that case, have a seat."

"I'm here about Rachel Collins."

15

"Rachel? What about her?"

"I want to know what you know about the scam she's running."

"What scam?"

"Don't pretend you don't know, Bobby. The way I hear it, you and Rachel are practically partners."

He looked bewildered. Sometimes you have to fabricate a little to get a little. Like in aikido, you're supposed to lead your opponent's mind. I was leading his, getting him worried.

"Partners, what partners?" he said. "She hustled drinks in my saloon. Just that, nothing more. She's my goddamn employee—rather *was* my goddamn employee. Look, about three weeks ago on a Friday evening a Mr. Holmcroft's chauffeur went over to her house and gave her a letter from his boss—the kiss-off. She comes over here, has a few drinks, gets madder and madder, and finally storms out of here. I ain't seen her since. I heard she went over to some swank club and threw a drink in Holmcroft's face. Hey, I'd have loved to have seen that. Holmcroft, he's a real shit."

"The way I hear it, you're the one running the show."

"What show? What the hell are you talking about?"

"You know damn well what I'm talking about." I kept my eyes dead on him. "She's going to take you down with her, unless she can be derailed quickly."

"She really got herself into the soup this time?"

"It looks bad."

"I knew she was trouble," he said, shaking his head. "What's she been saying about me?"

"I think you know," I said. I said it as if I knew the big secret. Nothing like sharing secrets to get what you want from a man.

He said, "Look, okay, she used to date guys from the bar. Sometimes she'd go with them during working hours and leave me short. I figured I let her do that, she should compensate me. Is that a crime? How the hell could that be a crime? I had nothing to do with who she picked up or where they went or what happened. She say different? What the hell am I being accused of here?"

16

"You're not being accused of anything. Not yet. She gets nailed, she's going over for some heavy time. The Alcohol Beverage Control Board, if they figured you were in with her, could shut you down without even blinking."

"But I ain't got nothing to do with her! She hustled drinks for me, that's all!"

"I believe you," I said.

He exhaled slowly. "That dumb fucking bitch. She'll dry up like a prune in the can. Looks is all she's got, don't she know that? Who's she extorting from? Let me guess. Holmcroft? She take him down, did she?"

"Looks like she's trying to."

He shook his head as if it truly mystified him. "I can't understand it. She's got a body men would jump off a bridge for. I told her ten jillion times, she ought to marry one of these birds, take him for enough in two years to retire for life."

"Maybe she likes to live on the wild side."

"You're goddamn right she does. She's hot-tempered. In here one night some guy grabbed her ass. She put a cigarette out on his forehead. She's a fire-eater, that one. Loves to party. Toots a little snow up her nose now and again. Extortion wouldn't seem to be in her bag."

"She ever do time?"

He nodded. "Once, down in Louisiana. Used a derringer on a guy. Got three years for manslaughter. Heat of the moment stuff. That's the way she is."

"She got any friends you know about?"

"She had lots of friends, past tense. Half the guys who come in here. Holmcroft was her fling of the month."

"Any women friends?"

"Nope."

"Give me her address, Bobby, I'll keep you out of it if I can."

"You'd do that for me?"

"You help me, I'll help you."

It took him ten minutes to find her address in his files. The way he kept records, he had to have trouble with the IRS. The poor dumb slob. What a way to go through life, wading through a

17

mess. I wrote her address down in my coplike leather-bound notebook.

When I got back to the Banana Slug I still had ten minutes left on the meter and Rachel Collins's last known address. I was doing okay. I made myself a bet that she'd be there, and if she wasn't, I could find her in two days. A chocolate eclair at Just Desserts if I did it. I'd clean out my closets if I didn't.

I made a couple more notes in my notebook about Rachel—a hot temper, doing tricks, did time in prison. Quite a gal, this Rachel Collins. Shooting people, killing cats.

I started up California Street, keeping a sharp lookout for a black Z, or anyone else who might be following me. I didn't see anyone, so I was feeling optimistic.

I should have remembered what Havelock Ellis once said: *The place where optimism most flourishes is the lunatic asylum.*

THREE

■

I bought an apple, a Diet Pepsi, and a hard roll at a little mom and pop store for lunch and ate it in the car on the way to Rachel Collins's place.

The traffic was bad, creeping along at five to ten miles an hour, stopping, starting, honking. I had plenty of time to finish my lunch and listen to half a Charlie Parker tape.

I finally pulled into the parking lot behind the Fresian Towers. The Fresian Towers are twin octagonal buildings set on what they now call Cathedral Hill. I guess they call it that because St. Mary's Cathedral is across the street. St. Mary's is one of those oddly shaped modern buildings, all white marble and glass, surrounded by parking lots. It would make a nice indoor basketball court.

The Fresian Towers are nine stories of semi-swank. Lots of glass, and every apartment has its own little balcony. Nice views. A one-bedroom would go for $1,200 a month or thereabouts.

Rachel Collins was the only name on the index for tower A,

apartment 8C. I took a peek inside her mailbox. It was empty. Her mail had to be going somewhere. Everybody leaves a paper trail. You're in this business two days and you figure that out.

You can't get into the Fresian Towers without a key or some-body to buzz you, so I stood around pretending to be looking for my keys in my shoulder bag, waiting for someone to go through the door. An elderly gentleman came by and opened the door with his key, then held it open for me.

"Thank you so awfully much," I said, sweet as hell. He beamed and touched his hat. What a nice man.

The old guy tipped his hat again as he got off the elevator on seven. I blew him a kiss. Least I could do. He beamed. I took the elevator up to the eighth floor.

I found apartment 8C. I knocked. No answer. I tried the handle. Locked. There were two locks on the door. One a dead-bolt. To tell you the truth, I'm not too good at picking locks. I practice a lot, but it's a tricky deal, you've got to work that little pick into just the right notch.

I got out my lock-picking kit and fumbled around with the deadbolt for a few minutes. You have to move the tumblers with one pick while holding the retractor with another and it's a bitch. I finally managed to get the dead bolt open. I was working on the lock in the door handle when a guy got off the elevator and headed in my direction.

This guy was about six ten and half beer belly, wearing a blue blazer with a patch over the pocket. A rent-a-cop. By the dull look on his long face, I guessed he probably had the intelligence of an amoeba. Hidden surveillance cameras had alerted him, no doubt.

"What ya think you're doing?" he said, surly as hell.

"I'm trying like hell to pick this lock, what does it look like?"

Honesty always gets people. He didn't know what to say. He squinted and breathed hot breath on me.

I said: "You wouldn't happen to have a pass key, would you?"

"Who are you? Identify yourself."

I reached into my shoulder bag and fished out a copy of a P.I.

license. Not my real one. A fake one, one that says my name is Debbie King.

"You a private eye or something?"

Gad, this guy was dumb.

"That's what it says, doesn't it?"

He read it again, moving his lips. Then he nodded like he finally got it.

I snatched back my fake ID and said, "When's the last time you saw Miss Collins?"

He shrugged. "Two, three weeks ago."

"Where'd she go?"

"I dunno, nobody knows. Nobody's seen her—far as I know—since the day she says she was shot at."

"Shot at?"

"Yeah, she claimed somebody shot at her down in the garage. The police came, but they couldn't find any bullet or nothing. I don't think they believed her."

"Who's picking up her mail?"

He shrugged again. He folded his arms. "She don't get no mail here. She's got a box down at the post office."

"You wouldn't happen to know the box number, would you?"

He scratched his head. "Nope."

I put away my lock-picking kit. "You'd better open this door."

He scratched his head. "I can't let you in there, you gotta have a search warrant or something."

I pinched the bridge of my nose like he was causing me great pain in my sinuses. "Look," I said, "this apartment is rented by Rachel Collins. She has not been seen or heard from for three weeks. Her mother, Mrs. Floria Cox of Middlefield, Vermont, has hired my firm to find out what's happened to her. There might have been foul play. At this very moment Rachel may be in there tied up and starving to death. Open it up."

He looked as if I'd asked him to solve the riddle of the Sphinx. He scratched his head again. Dandruff snowed down onto the shoulders of his nice blue blazer. "I'll call the police," he said. "They'll know what to do."

"Wait a minute," I said. "Hold it. Sometimes a man must

21

make a command decision on his own, right? Emergency situations call for quick thinking. A delay could be disastrous."

He didn't move. He just didn't seem to get it, so I said:

"And I'm sure you're the kind of man who can make command decisions." I smiled at him, the big hunk. Then I added: "You do have the key?"

He nodded dumbly. I could see in his eyes he was still thinking it over.

"If she's dead in there," I said, "it'll be you who they interview on the TV tonight." I was guessing he was a big TV fan. I was right: his face brightened.

"You don't want some dumb cop to get all the credit, do you?"

He shook his head.

"So why don't you just get out your key and we'll take a quick look inside. I promise, I won't touch a thing. Girl Scout's honor."

He pulled the keys from his pocket. It took him a couple of minutes to find the right ones. He smiled like he'd smile for Barbara Walters as the door came open.

We stepped in. A yellowish light filtered through the curtains. The place had that dusty, closed-up smell. The rent-a-cop rushed in and made a quick sweep of the place calling, "Miss Collins, hello?" No one answered.

I checked out the living room.

The furniture seemed all in place. Pretty nice stuff. Modern wood and glass. A double recliner. A sumptuous, down-filled couch. Polished inlaid floors. A small serving bar. Stereo disc collection, mostly "easy listening" sort of pap. A TV and a VCR. Nice collection of tapes. *Maddie's Magic*, *Debbie Does Detroit*, *Wild Stewardesses*, *Leather Tails*. Get her boyfriends in the mood, no doubt.

Everything seemed neat and orderly. I opened the drapes and the door to the little balcony and let in some fresh air.

"Okay, she ain't here and there's no body," the rent-a-cop said. "Let's go." He seemed brutally disappointed he hadn't found a body.

22

I put one of Rachel's X-rated tapes in the VCR and turned it on, then clicked on the TV. "Better check this out," I said.

"What for?" he said.

"For some kind of clue, maybe she was kidnapped."

The picture came on. His eyes locked onto the screen. A man and a woman naked in a bubble bath. Not much of a plot, but it had the rent-a-cop held in thrall.

I went into the kitchen. I checked the cupboards. Cereal, sugar, instant coffee. Rachel seemed like just regular folks. The refrigerator was empty except for the stuff that wouldn't spoil. Mayonnaise, ketchup, stuff like that. No milk. Nothing in the garbage can. In fact it had been scrubbed clean.

She'd planned to go; her disappearance was not hastily done. She was planning to come back.

Next, the bathroom. Lots of bubble bath, some combs. No hair dryer. No toothbrush.

I went into the bedroom. What a bed. A super-king-size with a shocking pink comforter and huge red pillows. I couldn't resist sitting on it. It was like sinking into a pile of cotton balls. In the bedroom was another sound system; this one could play a long tape, and next to it was another TV with a VCR and another collection of tapes.

The princess phone by the bed had no dial tone. On her dressing table she had all the blushes and creams and stuff to do a hundred women. A hundred shades of lipstick, at least. Not many scents. Dreamtime and Chanel No. 5 seemed her favorites.

The underwear drawers were empty, but she'd left behind a few nighties and some sweaters. Some nice sachets.

I checked the closet. A lot of clothes and a lot of empty hangers. The clothes had labels from Nordstrom's and Saks, places like that. She sure liked nice things. The colors were a little loud, I thought. She went in for bright yellows and lavender.

In the back of the closet was a chest and inside the chest were some whips and heavy leather thongs. Nice toys. On the top shelf of the closet were half a dozen dummy heads for wigs, but no wigs. An advertising sticker was glued to each one: Fantasy Styles with an address on Sacramento Street.

23

She had a little desk in the corner. I opened it up. No address book. No checkbook. No bills, no correspondence.

I went back into the living room. The rent-a-cop was sitting on the edge of the couch, his eyes glued to the TV. I figured I'd just leave him there. He seemed to be happy. On the way out I noticed a picture of a woman on the wall by the door. A rather stunning-looking woman sitting on Santa Claus's lap. I took the picture off the wall and walked over to the rent-a-cop. I held the picture in front of his face.

"That her?"

"That's her."

"Thanks." I took the photo out of the frame. I put the frame down on a table and headed out.

The rent-a-cop yelled: "Hey! Put that back!" He lunged for me.

I ran out the door and down the hall. Someone was just getting off the elevator.

The rent-a-cop almost caught up with me as the elevator door was closing and I just had time to give him a little wave as the elevator door slammed shut in his face. Poor guy. Wasn't going to be on TV, and now this.

Well, I hadn't found her yet, but I knew more than when I'd gone into the place. I knew she didn't leave in a panic. I knew she was planning on coming back. I knew she used two kinds of perfume, Dreamtime and Chanel No. 5. I knew she got her wigs at a place called Fantasy Styles. And I had her picture. I was doing okay.

Next, I planned to see what Morrison Holmcroft, the skirt-chasing husband, had to say for himself.

I drove back downtown.

Holmcroft's office was in the Transamerica Pyramid, not far from Lemming's Cocktail Lounge.

The Transamerica Pyramid is the building shaped like an elongated pyramid you see on all the postcards. It's louvered at the bottom. When they were building it, they had the largest concrete pour in the history of man for the foundation. A hundred cement trucks worked around the clock for three days. Something like that. When we get an earthquake, the pyramid is supposed to stay upright. Somebody's theory says so, anyway. We'll have to see when the big one comes if the theory holds up. In '89 it didn't even shiver.

Holmcroft Financial Services Corporation took up half of the tenth floor. What financial services they were offering I had no idea. All I saw when I got off the elevator was a glass door and behind it a lot of people at desks talking on the telephone and tapping away at computer keyboards.

The receptionist was twenty and blond; her lipstick was too red and her blouse was too tight. She showed me a perfunctory smile. I was wearing my glasses, had my hair combed back. Businesslike.

"Mr. Holmcroft," I said. "Odyssey Gallagher."

She dialed the phone. "A Ms. Odyssey Gallagher to see Mr. Holmcroft." She listened for a moment, then hung up. "This way, please."

As I followed her back to Holmcroft's office, I noticed her jiggling rear end drew a lot of lustful stares from the boys at their computer terminals. She seemed to appreciate them.

The receptionist turned me over to Holmcroft's secretary, Hillary Hoyle, one of those supremely competent types in a tweedy business suit. Mousy brown hair, big round glasses, pursed lips.

"Mr. Holmcroft has to be at a meeting in five minutes, Miss Gallagher," she said. "He cannot be late."

"Okay, five minutes," I said.

She gave me a businesslike nod and showed me into Holmcroft's office. It was on the north side of the building, with a great view of the Ferry Building, the bay, Alcatraz. I could see fingers of afternoon fog had already reached Angel Island.

It was a spacious office, with one huge plexiglass desk and matching plexiglass chairs. Miss Hoyle pulled one up for me.

"Miss Gallagher, Mr. Holmcroft," Miss Hoyle said, and headed back to her work station.

Holmcroft himself looked a little older than his wife; mid-

25

fiftyish, I guessed, graying hair, a square, tanned face; pinkish, drinker's eyes. He gestured for me to sit. He sat down, leaned forward, and folded his hands on his desk.

He waited a moment for the door to close, then said: "Stay out of it, Miss Gallagher. Completely out."

So, Mrs. Holmcroft must have let her husband know she'd hired me, which was something of a surprise.

He stared at me coldly. Like most executives, he knew how to project an air of menace. He took his glasses off.

"I've been hired by your wife, Mr. Holmcroft. If I'm to stay out of it, I shall do so only if and when she so directs."

He put his glasses back on and glared at me, I guess, because I didn't fall on my knees when he gave me an order. "I'll have my lawyer get an injunction," he said angrily. He straightened his tie, as if all this blustery talk had rumpled it. It hadn't.

Executive types are so used to having people bow and scrape to please them, it's generally a bad idea to confront them head-on. Not if you want to solicit their cooperation. So I figured I'd try a little silk:

"This is hardly the reaction I expected, Mr. Holmcroft. Naturally my firm and I don't wish to cause you any embarrassment, we are trying to help you out of a . . . a bad situation."

"I'm not embarrassed by anything," he said. "It's simply that my business is my business, and I want you and your firm and my wife to stay the hell out of it."

"It just seems that in the light of what happened, I mean, when someone sends you a dead cat, it might portend worse to come."

"I don't believe for one minute that Rachel had anything to do with that cat."

"If she didn't drop it on your doorstep, who did?"

"Kids in the neighborhood—as a prank."

"No, Mr. Holmcroft, it was Rachel Collins. If she didn't do it, why has she disappeared?"

"She's probably just taken a trip. Look, I know the woman. I know what she's capable of and what she's not capable of. And

26

what she's not capable of is slitting a cat's throat. It was more likely my wife's idiot son."

"Conrad?"

"Yes, Conrad."

"Why would he do that?"

"You've got me there. Okay, it wasn't Conrad. But that doesn't mean it was Rachel. It definitely was *not* Rachel."

I smiled and nodded, to let him know I was being open-minded about it. Then I said, "Your wife explained your relationship with Miss Collins, so I understand how you feel. Do you have any idea where she might have gone?"

His face reddened. "Didn't you hear what I just said? I want you out of this. Tell my wife you spoke to me and I refused to cooperate. Look, tell you what. I'll give you a thousand dollars right now to call her up and quit." He reached for his checkbook. The great problem solver.

"Sorry," I said.

"Two thousand." He scrawled out a check and signed it. "Here you go." He shoved the check across the vast expanse of plexiglass.

"No, thank you. That wouldn't be ethical." I stood up to leave.

He chuckled suddenly. "I find people guided by ethics refreshing," he said. "Often misplaced, but refreshing."

I just smiled.

"Really," he said. "I admire people with ethics. Not having any myself." The hardness drained from his face. "I hope I haven't offended you, Miss Gallagher."

"Not in the least."

Since bullying me hadn't worked, he was turning the charm on full blast. He said, "Is there no way short of getting hold of my lawyers I can get you to drop the case?"

"No."

"Look, Miss Gallagher, a man in my business, if he doesn't have enemies, he hasn't made any money. And I've made a lot of money. I've stepped on someone's toes and they've sent me a dead cat. I've hired a very good man to look into the matter.

27

So you see, Miss Gallagher, you're not really needed. There's no sense in having two detectives on the same case, you'll be stumbling over each other."

"Who is this other detective?"

"Sorry, that's confidential."

"Does he drive a black Nissan Z?"

"I don't know."

"Who are these enemies you mentioned?"

"Sorry."

"Do you know why anyone would want to shoot at Rachel Collins?"

"Has she been shot at?" This seemed to worry him.

"Allegedly."

"You think I did it?"

"Did you?"

His eyes narrowed slightly. A blush came to his tanned cheeks. "Your time is up, Miss Gallagher."

FOUR

■

At a pay phone in the spacious, gleaming lobby of the Pyramid, I called home to speak to Martin Roberts, my computer programmer boyfriend and roommate.

"So how's it going?" I asked him.

"Okay," he said.

"Still love me?"

"Uh huh." He was talking to me and working at the same time; I could hear him clacking keys on his keyboard. He was working on a new accounting program for a shipping company and it was driving him crazy.

"King Kong tried to rape me in an elevator," I said.

"That's nice. What time are you going to be home?"

"I don't know. Not too late, I hope. Want to go out for dinner?"

"I got to keep at this."

"Okay, see you later."

"Okay. Take care, Od. Love you."

29

"Love you too, Martin."

The phoning-home ritual over, I went out into the street and got back in the Banana Slug and made some more notes and filled out my time log for the day so far. Mr. Frampton, my boss, insists we keep track of every moment of our time, so just in case clients think they've been cheated we can go back and show them exactly where we went and what we did. Then I started the car and pulled out from the parking lane and drove over to Sacramento Street to Fantasy Styles where Rachel Collins had her wigs made, but it was closed Mondays.

So I drove down to the Bryant Street Station of the police department and saw Mrs. Rodriguez in the records section. Last year I found her runaway daughter, and ever since she's been doing me favors. The daughter left again and is now doing time for petty theft in Santa Rosa Jail, but Mrs. Rodriguez is still grateful.

The computer was down, so I had to wait almost an hour before Mrs. Rodriguez gave me Rachel Collins's rap sheet.

Rachel had been arrested twice for prostitution when she was a teenager in New York, once for assault, and that time down in Louisiana for second-degree murder. In California she had one conviction for assault. Nearest living relative: none. Contact in case of death: Sara Williams. Her address was given as 101 York Court.

I thanked Mrs. Rodriguez, thinking this had to be a hot lead. York Court was in the outer Mission District. I drove out there. It was a mixed neighborhood. Blacks, Hispanics, whites. On the court were a dozen small white clapboard houses in need of paint. The small yards were barren except for patches of weeds. A lot of cars sat around looking like they could no longer move. The old Plymouth in the driveway of 101 was up on blocks. I went up on the porch and knocked. A black woman about twenty-five came to the door carrying a baby wrapped in a blanket.

"I'm looking for Rachel Collins," I said.

"How you find me?"

"Are you Sara Williams?"

"Who wants to know?"

"I'm a private investigator, my name's Odyssey Gallagher. Rachel Collins put you down as a reference once when she was in jail. Her mother asked me to find her. There's an illness in the family."

I gave her my card. She scanned it and passed it back.

"We were in the same cell once," she said. "She was in for hooking, me for fightin'." She grinned. I guess she liked fighting.

"Where is she now, do you know?" I asked.

"For her mama, you say?"

"Yes."

"She live in the Fresian Towers, they called. High class. Near Geary, you know. Up above that big hotel."

"She's gone from there."

"Then I can't help ya. I get a card from her now an' again, that's about it. We don't exactly move in the same circles." She chortled. She had a gold tooth in front.

"Do you know any of her friends? Relatives?"

"Nope. Sorry, I don't know nothing 'bout her, except we pass some long, lonely hours together."

"Then maybe you could answer something for me. Do you think she's the kind of person who could slit a cat's throat and leave it on somebody's doorstep to scare them?"

She thought about it for a long moment, then nodded. "She a tough lady, don't take no shit from nooooobody."

"Thanks," I said. Her answer had disappointed me for some reason. "Thanks for your time, Ms. Williams." I started to leave.

She said, "Somebody else been lookin' for her."

"Who?"

"Some white dude."

I figured that had to be the private eye Mr. Holmcroft hired. So he, too, must have gotten her rap sheet. "What did he look like?" I asked.

"The babysitter here, so I didn't see him. He drive a black car, real sleek. He call back today. Real smooth, he was. He say he give me a hundred dollars to find her, but I don't know nothin'."

31

That had to be the guy who followed me from Mrs. Holmcroft's place in the Nissan Z. "He have a name?"

She shook her head. "I forget. He say is he want Rachel so he can give her some money he owe her, but I don't believe that, do you?"

"Not for a minute."

A martial arts teacher is called a *sensei*, a teacher, but he's more than just a teacher. He's a role model, a spiritual guide, a priest. *Dojo* is Japanese for a school where martial arts are taught. But a dojo is more than just a school. Aikido is not just a way to fight, it's a spiritual path. It's a way of learning to be at one with the world. Hard to grasp if you're an American.

Roland Matsumoto, my aikido sensei, was not pleased I showed up twenty minutes late for class at the dojo. I bowed to him when I came onto the mat; he bowed in return and gave me a disapproving look. He's short and dark, a serious-looking Japanese man, past fifty, but looks more like thirty-five.

In aikido you wear a gi, which is a sort of heavy white cotton jacket tied with a cloth belt. With it you wear black pants, sort of like pajama bottoms. There were a dozen other students in their gis and black pants there that night doing practice throws when I arrived. Our dojo is upstairs in what used to be a grammar school but is now used for community activities. A barbershop quartet was practicing in the room next door.

I did my warmups and stretching exercises, then I did some practice throwing with my fellow students. There are about twenty students in all, white-belt beginners, brown-belt intermediates, and black belts. I'm a brown belt. The only other brown belt there that night was Nick Pirano. Nick is tall, olive skinned, with slicked-back hair, always smiling. I worked out with him.

Aikido is also an art form. It has balance and harmony and grace, more like a dance than a fight. Nick Pirano has a way of doing things in a quick, artless way that always irritates me.

We worked on the throwing technique called *ushiro ryote-dori*. You use it when you're grabbed from behind. You throw

32

your attacker over your shoulder. I used it once on a bus when a guy smelling like cheap gin tried to get a little too friendly.

For some reason Pirano and I couldn't get it right and we looked like the Keystone cops trying to jitterbug. He kept stopping and saying, "What the hell you doing, you're not supposed to resist!" Things like that.

Maybe it was my fault. I couldn't keep my mind on aikido. I kept thinking about Rachel Collins and the dead cat. I wondered what it meant to send someone a dead cat. Was it an insult, or a warning? And who was the guy in the Z and why was he after Rachel Collins? Was he Holmcroft's private eye?

Pirano tried again to throw me, but I reflexively bent my knees and he couldn't make it. He pulled me into his back and stumbled forward.

"Damn it, Odyssey!"

The sensei could see Pirano and I weren't doing very well. He put us to work on fencing techniques using Japanese wooden swords. Kendo, it's called. It helps breathing and concentration, and builds up your wrists. Aikido depends a lot on the wrists. Into our third exercise, I missed with a thrust, and whacked Pirano on the head.

He waddled around in a little circle rubbing his head for a moment. "That does it!" he snapped, and stormed off the mat and disappeared into the locker room.

After he was gone, I worked with the beginners on some falling and rolling techniques until nine-thirty, when the session was over. Then I went into the women's locker room and showered and was on my way out the door when Sensei Matsumoto asked to speak to me for a moment.

"I have been watching you," he said.

Oh, oh, I thought, here it comes.

He said, "You have not been directing your ki."

Ki is what makes aikido aikido. Ki, according to the founder, Morihei Uyeshiba, is the "stuff" of the universe. It is what makes a rock a rock, a tree a tree, it's what makes gravity and electricity. It's the power that energizes a ninety-pound grandmother to pick up the front of a Cadillac her grandchild

33

is pinned under. Aikido teaches you to call up and direct that power at will. It's all sort of mystical and Eastern, and it's one of the most difficult things to grasp, even after you've spent half a lifetime studying it.

"I guess I've got other things on my mind, Sensei."

"Keep your ki flowing outward," he said, "at all times."

A trick of aikido practitioners. As long as you keep your ki flowing out from the center of your body, which you can do by concentrating on it, the power of the universe flows through you.

He smiled at me. "Aikido in its spiritual aspects is often elusive, but you are on the verge of grasping it."

"It would be nice," I said.

"Lead your opponent, keep your mind always ahead of your opponent's." He bowed.

I bowed and told him good night. Rachel Collins, I figured, was my opponent. How was I going to lead her? Somehow, I thought, that idea was going to help me in this case. Weird, but the feeling was a powerful one.

I live in what's called Cow Hollow, in San Francisco's Marina District, which is in the northern part of the city. San Francisco is shaped like a thumb stuck between the Pacific Ocean and the San Francisco Bay. I live on the nail part, a little down from the edge.

I rent from a Chinese-Portuguese guy named Fernando Chin, who came over from Macao in the late sixties and started as a dishwasher, saved his money, bought a house, gouged his tenants, bought another house, gouged more tenants, and became a multimillionaire real estate mogul.

My apartment is over a garage. It was once a storage area. To get to it, you go down a driveway that runs between Rudy's Discount Liquors and Dr. Cat, a vet. He's partners with Dr. Dog, across the street.

At the end of the driveway, there's a grove of trees surrounding the garage and my apartment. Behind it is a fence, and on the other side of the fence is an apartment building. It's urban, yet secluded. Quaint. There's a deck built on stilts out back and bird feeders and I like it a lot.

The only problem is the little cottage to the south and its nosy occupant, Mrs. Eversole. As I drove up, she was sitting at her rear window, as usual, nothing more on her mind than minding my business.

I parked the Banana Slug in the garage next to Martin's BMW 325i and headed up the stairs lugging two bags of groceries I had bought from the Arab bandit who runs the convenience store on the corner. Why is it the gods have decreed that women do the shopping? Vestiges of woman's slavery past. My grandmother had to grow her own food, so I shouldn't complain, I guess. At least I don't have to walk behind a mule.

I found Martin in the half of the living room we had partitioned off for his study, staring into his glowing screen full of numbers and symbols. His work area was crammed with shelves full of books and computer magazines and piles of papers and computer printouts.

Martin was fortyish, a little fleshy, but had a rather nice face, square jaw, deep blue eyes. He wore wire-rimmed glasses that were cute as hell. He thought they made him look like John Lennon. When I came in, he turned to me and said:

"Shit."

"Hello to you, too."

"I'm sorry, sweets. But you couldn't have come home at a worse moment."

"Sorry."

I went into the kitchen and put down the groceries. I made some meatloaf sandwiches and put them on a tray with some potato chips and Bud Lights and carried them into the living room and put them down on the coffee table. Then I went into the study and asked Martin if he'd like to eat. He clicked off the screen and sat back, took off his glasses, and rubbed his face.

We sat down in the living room on the old couch my parents had given us. I had to make room on the couch because that's where I'd dumped the laundry that morning. I turned on some big band music, which Martin loves.

35

"Well, how was your day?" he asked.

"I told you about my getting raped, didn't I? King Kong?" I took a bite of my sandwich. I love meatloaf sandwiches with lots of ketchup.

"Yeah, King Kong. I heard you, I just don't want to dignify that kind of stuff with a comment. I've got a problem."

"Oh?"

"I can't get the subroutine to run through the accounts receivable and index the dailies correctly. I keep coming up with function errors."

"You'll work it out, you always do."

He chewed on his sandwich. His body rocked gently with the music. Moonglow, something like that. Syrupy. After a moment he said, "What's your case?"

"A weird one. My client's husband got what may be a death threat—sort of—from an ex-mistress of his." I didn't want to tell him about the dead cat. Too gruesome for him.

"Death threats from an ex-mistress. Sounds thrilling."

"The husband thinks the threat came from a business associate. It's all very mysterious."

"You should quit that job," he said. Whenever anything looked as if it could get dangerous, he wanted me to quit.

"And then what do I do? Go back to teaching young morons how to write moronic term papers?"

"Every professor has to teach freshmen. You'd get to teach advanced students eventually."

"Like showing sophomores the blood symbolism in *The Red Badge of Courage*. Maybe even teach seniors the basics of structuralism in literature. Whoop-dee-do."

He gulped some Bud Light. "You're not exactly getting rich doing what you're doing," he said.

"What's that supposed to mean?"

"I don't know. I guess I was thinking I make enough for both of us."

"And what would I do, sit around here all day?"

"You could improve your mind."

"I find my mind so improved already it frightens me. Let me

36

get this straight. You want me to be your kept woman, is that it?''

"I want you to be my wife."

I stared at him. "A *married* wife?"

He wasn't looking at me. He was leaning forward on the couch rolling his Bud Light can between the palms of his hands. "People do it," he said. "Normal, everyday, work-a-day people get married all the time. They get married and they have babies and they're normal. What do you say, yes or no?"

"Can't I have a few minutes to think about it?"

He glanced at me and smiled. "Sure. I guess it's a pretty important step."

"How come all of a sudden you want to get married, Martin?"

He shrugged.

I said, "You didn't think of it just now, I mean."

"Angela's getting married. She called today."

Angela was his first wife.

"What does Angela getting married have to do with our getting married?"

"Betty Sue is already married."

Betty Sue was his second wife. That's all the notches he had in his belt so far.

"I still don't get it," I said.

"I'm the marrying kind," he said. He stuffed some meatloaf sandwich into his mouth.

"But maybe I'm not."

"Sure you are. Once you try it, you'll like it."

"You know what Mary Wollstonecraft said about marriage? It was the end of improvement. In other words, a woman stopped growing after marriage. Of course she changed her mind and married William Godwin, but that's another story."

"Mary Wollstonecraft has been dead for two hundred years. Look, I love you. I want to make a commitment to you. I want to get married. Do you want to or don't you?"

"If we do get married, will you ask me to quit my job?"

"I'd want you to."

"Why?"

37

He shrugged. "It's dangerous, and . . ."

"And what?"

He looked at me. "It's not fit work for a woman. Or anybody else for that matter."

"But I like it."

"Okay, you like it."

"I want to keep doing it. What do you say to that?"

"Married people talk things over," he said. He took a swig of beer and wiped his mouth on the back of his hand.

"If I won't quit, is the wedding off?"

He smiled. "Why is it I'm always attracted to headstrong women who walk all over me?"

"If you want to marry me, you've got to take me as I am, not as how you want me to be."

He nodded sadly. "All right. Keep your job. Do you want to get married or don't you?"

"All right, let's get married."

He leaned over and kissed me. "I've got a few minutes' work to do before I knock off," he said. "Make yourself beautiful."

He took the rest of his sandwich and went back to his screen.

Funny, I'd been proposed to before, but had never said yes before. Thirty-five, biological clock ticking loudly. Maybe it was time, I thought. We'd been living together for a year or so and well . . . we got along okay and he was a hell of a nice guy and we cared for each other. So what if it isn't torrid, torrid, torrid, I thought. That's imaginary anyway. Teenagers with hormones raging look for torrid.

I had a quick shower, put on my favorite powder-blue teddy and doused myself with Madness at Midnight, and slipped into bed. I could see the light of Martin's green screen monitor reflected on the ceiling on the other side of the partition. I heard a groan and the clacking of keys.

"Okay, Martin, I'm ready," I called to him.

"In a minute."

A few minutes later I said, "Martin?"

"Damn it, I've almost got it!"

I looked through a book. *Aikido in Daily Life.*

38

At one in the morning I called to him and asked him when he was coming to bed. He said, "I think I've got it, I'm running the final check."

I tried keeping my eyes open, but finally I drifted off.

I woke at seven-fifteen, light streaming in the window. I reached for Martin. He wasn't there.

"Martin?"

No answer.

I got up and went into the living room. He was asleep in his chair, slumped over his keyboard.

I just stood there and stared at him for a long moment, a large lump forming in my throat. He had his arm up around his monitor, the way a man might put his arm around a lover. I wasn't angry, I was sad. Sad and disappointed, and even though I tried like hell I couldn't hold back the tears.

FIVE

■

Frampton Investigations, where I work, is located on Market Street just above Laguna on the second floor over Weldon Sporting Goods. It's been there for twelve years.

I arrived at ten after eight and parked my car around back in one of the parking spaces reserved for operatives. I went up the back stairs and down the hall and into the reception area. Mrs. Kentfield, our secretary, looked at me over her granny glasses.

"Trouble," she said.

"Bad trouble?" I asked.

She nodded and pointed a pudgy finger in the direction of Mr. Frampton's office. "His Lordship requests the honor of your presence forthwith."

I went down the hall to Mr. Frampton's office. The door was open, so I went right on in.

Mr. Hampton Frampton was sitting at his desk surrounded by his high-tech equipment: a Macintosh CX, a laser printer, a fax machine, a color copy machine.

Mr. Frampton is a fifty-four-year-old black man, medium height, slightly overweight, slightly balding. He was, as usual, impeccably dressed. This day he was wearing a three-piece blue serge suit, white silk shirt, striped rust-red tie, gold wristwatch, gold bracelet. Mr. Frampton has a round face and large, curious eyes that seem to take in everything. When he smiles, he looks friendly as a Bible salesman. At the moment, he was not smiling.

"Good morning, Miss Gallagher," he said.

"Good morning, Mr. Frampton."

"Somebody shoved this through the slot in the middle of the night." He handed me a padded envelope. My name was misspelled "Odyseey G." on the front.

I opened it. Inside was an audio tape.

"What's it say?" I said. I knew he would have already opened it and played it.

He lit a cigarette with a gold lighter and blew a cloud of smoke upward. Then he put his lighter back in his vest pocket. A place for everything, everything in its place. "A truly thankful employee would overlook her beloved supervisor's peccadillos."

"You would think that, wouldn't you," I said. I poured myself some coffee from the pot he kept on his desk. I'm sure he kept it there to keep track of how much coffee I, Eddie, the other operative, and the secretary drank. "So what's the message?"

"I think you should listen to it yourself." He reached into his desk and took out a small cassette player and passed it over to me. I put the tape in and pressed the play button. The tape scratched for a moment, then a graveled man's voice came on:

"If you know what's good for you, bitch, you'll get off the Holmcroft case."

That was it. A tingle of fear crawled up my back.

"What do you make of this threat, Miss Gallagher?"

"I don't recognize the voice."

I rewound it and played it again, twice. Then I looked over the tape, a perfectly normal tape you can buy anyplace for a buck.

"Well, Miss Gallagher?" Mr. Frampton asked.

"It might have come indirectly from Morrison Holmcroft. He

wants us off the case. In fact, he's threatened to get his lawyers to have a judge order us to stay out of it.''

Mr. Frampton dismissed that with a wave of his hand. "We're on legitimate business for a client. We have a license. No judge would enjoin us.''

I took a sip of coffee, hoping it would steady me down some. As usual, it tasted like tar. He makes it that way on purpose I think to discourage his three employees from drinking it to excess. Every office has its little games.

"I was followed yesterday as well,'' I said.

"Followed?''

"Someone in a black Nissan Z car. I couldn't get the plate, but I managed to lose him.''

"I hope you weren't road racing.''

"Maybe just a little.''

"The firm does not pay traffic citations.''

"Want to know how I lost him?''

"Spare me.''

He looked thoughtful for a moment. He cleared his throat. "What do you think, Miss Gallagher, should we quit the case? I don't want to see any of my people hurt.''

I felt my face warming. He never took a man off a case in his life. Gad, how I hate to be patronized.

"Well, Miss Gallagher?''

"It's something to consider, I guess.'' I didn't want to seem defensive.

"Where there's smoke there's fire,'' he said. "Let's get another opinion.'' He pressed a button on his desk and a moment later the other operative, Eddie Fisk, appeared in the doorway. Eddie's tall, thin, midforties, wears cheap and flashy sport coats that hang on him like burlap bags. He spends most of his time at the track and chews gum every waking moment. He has a habit of not looking at you when he talks to you. But when he's on a case he's tenacious as a tiger, and he knows every cop, crook, whore, and junkie in the city, and it seems like they all owe him a favor.

"Yeah, boss, you called?''

42

"You heard the tape?"

"I heard it."

"How do you appraise the situation?" Mr. Frampton asked.

"Anonymous threats are always bad. Dinks who make them are scared. Scared people are always dangerous."

"You think we should pull out of the case?"

"Eddie Fisk never pulls out of a case." So said Eddie Fisk about Eddie Fisk.

"Odyssey Gallagher never pulls out of a case either," Odyssey Gallagher said about Odyssey Gallagher.

"Seriously, Mr. Fisk," Mr. Frampton said. "Would you be given pause over such a warning?"

"Naw, but then I'm not the 'dickless dick.' " He was referring to me. He grinned as if that was the first time he'd said it. Actually it's the scum's favorite witticism.

"How'd you like it if I shove yours in your ear?" I said.

"Like to see ya try," Fisk said, smirking and chomping on his gum. One of these days I'm going to lose my aikido cool and show him a *ushiro ryote-dori* out a window.

"Now, now," Mr. Frampton said, suppressing a grin, "let's be civil." He enjoyed watching Fisk and me go at it. He wanted us combative so we'd try to outdo each other.

"I'm staying on the case," I said.

"Least she's got balls," Eddie Fisk said of me. What a wit.

"Look, Fisk ole bean," I said, "instead of you standing around waxing poetical, why don't you do some good? Find out what you can through our network of gutter rats who Rachel Collins might have hooked up with. She's been a hooker, maybe she's gone back to work."

"Okay, I'll ask around." He didn't look too happy about it, but Mr. Frampton insists his operatives help each other out.

"Anything I can do?" Mr. Frampton asked.

"I'd like to know more about the Holmcrofts. Mr. Holmcroft's of the opinion some unnamed enemy sent the dead cat. I'd like to know who hates him."

Mr. Frampton made a few notes on a large legal pad. "I'll run the usual background stuff, see what I can come up with. Meanwhile, what leads have you generated?''

"I had a look at Rachel Collins's apartment. She took a lot of clothes with her, but it looks like she's planning to come back.''

"Get a lead?''

"I think so. Her wig maker.''

Eddie Fisk laughed. "Going to see a wig maker, you ought to carry something for protection.'' He reached into his pocket and pulled out a small automatic. "Take it, I got lots of 'em.''

I didn't touch it. I don't like guns much.

"Maybe you should be armed,'' Mr. Frampton said. "I mean, about the threat and all.''

"I haven't got a ticket,'' I said. Meaning, no permit.

"I know,'' Mr. Frampton said. "But under the circumstances, I'd feel better.''

"Okay,'' I said. Not that I had any intention of using it. If I'd refused, I would have looked wimpy. Who the hell wants a wimpy P.I.?

So when I left the office that morning, I was armed and dangerous.

I came down the stairs and out into the parking lot and headed for the Banana Slug. Someone wearing jeans and a red parka was leaning on it and when he saw me he turned and started walking away, shoulders hunched. Although I didn't see his face, I thought I knew who it was—Mrs. Holmcroft's son, Conrad Winter.

I called to him: "Conrad!'' He stopped, but didn't turn. "Conrad!'' I called again, and started running after him.

I caught up with him. It was Conrad, all right. He had the hood of the parka pulled up tight around his head.

"Good morning,'' I said. "Were you waiting for me?''

He nodded. He kicked something invisible with his foot.

"What can I do for you?'' I said.

He shrugged.

"It's about the cat, isn't it?'' I said.

He looked at me with a hollow gaze that gave me an eerie

44

feeling. "I just thought I'd like to bury it," he said. His voice was barely above a whisper. "I mean when you're through with your investigating."

"Sure. Did you know the cat?"

He shrugged. "I got to go." He ran out of the parking lot and around the corner.

I got in my Camaro and started it up, wondering what it was he wasn't telling me.

I drove back over to Fantasy Styles on Sacramento. It was nine-fifteen. I had a hell of a time finding a parking space only to find the place didn't open until ten. I went and had a cup of coffee at a mom and pop coffee shop and thought about my future with Martin. I always thought that if I ever said yes to a marriage proposal I'd be dancing on the ceiling. Funny, but I didn't feel like dancing in the least. Maybe that's why I hadn't mentioned it to Mr. Frampton.

The truth of the matter was, Martin was not ready to marry. He was already a two-time loser at the marriage game and the only reason he wanted to marry me now, I thought, was because he thought we *ought* to be married. His mother wanted it that way and he never liked letting his mother down.

I shouldn't have said yes. We needed more time. Time to decide if we want children, a house. Time to decide if we really love each other.

Yes, that was the only thing that really mattered. That is why I had felt so sad. Martin's failure to come to bed wouldn't have meant a thing if I felt he really loved me. But the truth was, Martin didn't really love me.

And maybe I didn't love Martin, either.

That thought hit me hard. If I didn't love him, why did I say I'd marry him? Why was I living with him?

I had a second cup of coffee and puzzled over that one. Was it just because I was fond of him? That we were somewhat compatible? That we didn't fight? That we both enjoyed the same kind of films? Tennis? Bicycling in Golden Gate Park?

I was getting a headache. I had to work this out somehow. What was the big hurry, anyway? I'd tell him I needed time to think it over. A month or two, at least. Give us both a little time to make sure we had the same expectations.

Then I had to ask myself, was I just putting off the inevitable? I didn't know. And at the moment I didn't have time to work it out. I was on a case. I paid the waiter and went back to work.

At ten sharp I was standing in the doorway of Fantasy Styles. An older man with long white curls and wearing a white smock opened the door. I showed him Rachel Collins's picture.

"Can you make me one like you made for her?"

He looked at her picture as he backed into his salon. It wasn't much of a salon: just one chair, a wall full of wigs, a mirror.

He asked me to sit in the chair, which I did. He ran his fingers through my hair.

"Hair like this, you shouldn't cover it up. This is beautiful. You should be on your knees thanking God every morning and night for hair like this."

"Sometimes I just want to look different. Something in a strawberry blonde."

"Can do."

"Then again, maybe I ought to restyle it. It needs to be cut just right, by someone who really knows what they're doing," I said. "Somebody like Rachel uses."

He said, "Like Rachel?"

"Who does her hair, do you know?"

"Oh, I know, but I can't say."

"Please," I said, with a little bit of southern breathiness.

He pulled back and looked at me with suspicious eyes. "I've got a feeling you didn't come in here to have a wig made."

I sighed. "Actually, no, I didn't."

"Who are you and what do you want?"

I got up out of the chair and gave him my card. The real one that uses my real name and says I'm a private investigator with Frampton Investigations.

"What's Rachel up to?" he asked.

"Her mother hired us to find her."

"She's missing?"

46

"For three weeks. She's depressed, her mother's afraid she might do something to harm herself."

"You mean you think she might commit suicide? Not the type."

"Still, her mother's worried. Will you help me?"

"How much is it worth to you?"

"You would ask for money in a case like this where a poor mother—"

"Skip the soap. I'm in business."

I offered him a twenty. He turned his nose up at it. I doubled it.

"Three more," he said.

"That's a hundred bucks!"

"Business has been slow."

I gave him the hundred. He went to a card file and looked up the name of Rachel's hairdresser. "Mr. Michael, on Union Street. Very exclusive."

Mr. Michael turned out to be a Hindu. I watched him through the window working wonders on a very large matron with short white hair. He was well on the way to making her thinner and younger when I walked through the door.

I asked the anorexic receptionist, who had a garish modern cut that looked like a Roman centurion's helmet, whether I could have a moment with Mr. Michael. He could not possibly be disturbed, she said. The artist in the throes of creation. I asked her when I might have a few moments with The Great One and she said I'd have to catch him between appointments.

So I had a seat and watched Mr. Michael try like hell to please the matron, who wanted to look even thinner and younger than he had made her. Mr. Michael had a high-pitched voice that made him sound like a petulant four-year-old. Finally he threw up his hands and said it was the best he could do. She took one more look in the mirror and must have decided it was the best anyone could do. She fished around in a big purse and pressed a bill into his hand and then marched out.

The receptionist told him I wanted to see him. He asked me to come with him out back, he'd talk to me on his smoke break. Three other hairdressers were hard at work snipping, tinting, shampooing, gossiping.

We stepped outside into what was a sort of patio. A small picnic table was cluttered with styrofoam coffee cups. Mr. Michael had brought his shoulder bag with him. It looked something like mine, only a little more petite. He opened it up and took out a cigar and lit it up.

"You hear what that *focking* old broad said to me?" he asked, his high-pitched voice gone. It had turned low-raspy. "Said I'd butchered her! Ahhhhh, if it weren't for the hundred grand a year, I would tell them to shove this job up where the sun don't shine." He reached over and ran his hand through my hair. "Now here is something I could work with. With this, I could create a masterpiece."

"You know this woman?" I showed him Rachel Collins's picture.

"What about her?"

"You see her often?"

"Every two weeks. She phones in, I set her up as soon as I can. She's big with the tips."

"She come in with anybody?"

"An older guy, real natty dresser. Silver hair, drives a Jag. I don't know him from George Bush. What's this all about?"

I gave him my card. The real one.

"A shamus, eh? Come and get it, copper!" He said it in very bad Cagney. Meeting a P.I. often brings out the worst in people.

"This silver-haired guy, he wouldn't be Morrison Holmcroft, would he? He has white hair."

"Naw, this guy's hair is real silver. Shimmers in the sun."

"Look, it's very important that I get in touch with Rachel as soon as possible," I said. "Some very nasty people are looking for her, and if they find her first . . ." I drew my finger across my throat.

He looked at me out of the corner of his eye and let some smoke out his nose. "Tell you what, sister," he said, still in Cagney, "you give me a big pile of dough, I put you onto her—as

48

soon as she calls in for her appointment. Which she should do any day now.''

"How big a pile?''

"Five hundred.'' This he said straight, looking me in the eye. He dropped the Cagney.

"A hundred is the best I could do.''

He shook his head. "My conscience would bother me. I don't buy it for one minute that you're doing her any favor. Four hundred.''

"Lao-tse, the great Chinese sage, said there is no greater disaster than greed.''

"He didn't have a wife addicted to charge cards.''

"Lao-tse called lavish desires a calamity. How about one-fifty?''

"Two-fifty.''

"Split the difference?''

"Okay, two bills. You got a deal. When she phones in for an appointment, I'll give you a call.''

"When she phones, get her in for an appointment as soon as you can.''

"For that, you've got to go another hundred.''

"Thief,'' I said.

"What thief?'' He held out his hand. "Pay in advance.''

I gave him one-fifty. "Half now, half on delivery.''

"Agreed.''

Mr. Frampton was going to squawk like hell if this didn't pay off. First a hundred to the wig man, now this.

I gave him my other card, the one with my home phone number. I also showed him a picture I carry in my wallet where I'm standing beside Pedro Lampo, the three-hundred-fifty-pound wrestler, a very scary-looking guy. "Before you think about selling me out, this is my boyfriend, the president of the Hell's Angels motorcycle club. I might not be able to restrain him, if you get my drift.''

He swallowed hard. I guess he got it.

49

S I X

■

I left Mr. Michael's place and crossed the street to a phone booth on the corner. I called Uncle Irving to see if he'd found out anything about the cat.

"Odyssey, wonderful you're calling. Good news I have. X-rays show that the cat had a metal pin put in its right rear leg at one time. Expensive surgery for an animal. And just like I told you, the cat did not die of the wound in its throat. It was drugged. Barbiturates."

"Thank you, Uncle Irving. Was the cat suffering from anything? Was there any medical reason the cat should have been killed?"

"Not that I could tell. If you want a more complete autopsy you should get an expert in pathology. Nothing else I can tell you—except you should find a husband and get married."

"Thank you, Uncle Irving. I'm working on the problem."

"And when you see that schnook of a father of yours, tell him I said he was a schnook, but I wish him well. Come and get your cat whenever you want, I'm keeping him in my freezer."

We said good-bye. Next, I called Mr. Frampton and told him what I'd found out.

"Now all we have to do is find the vet that did the job on the leg," I said.

"Okay," he said, "but so what if we find out who owns the cat?"

"Maybe they'll tell us who killed it and why."

"Okay, Miss Gallagher, I'll get something in the mail today to every vet in the Bay Area."

He could do it because he had a vast data bank of professions and could easily get a letter out to every vet, every financial institution, every pharmacy, you name it. He loved using his Macintosh CX. The modern P.I. at work.

I had him switch me to Mrs. Kentfield for my messages. She had just one; Martin wanted me to come home immediately.

"He say what the trouble was?"

"No, but he sounded very angry."

Angry? Not repentant? Angry didn't sound like my Martin. Depressed, sullen, sulky, withdrawn, peeved, maybe. Rarely angry.

I gave him a call. Busy. We have call interruption service, so he had to be on both lines at once. I fidgeted for a minute and tried him again. Still busy.

I was less than a mile from our place, so I decided what the hell, why not run by, see what the flap was about. On my way over I tried to figure out what Martin's state of mind might be. He was probably all upset because I'd left him asleep at his computer and he would pretend to be angry because he'd think I'd be angry, and by his pretending to be angry he could counter my really being angry.

Why oh why do we play such games?

Traffic was light. It only took five minutes to get over Divisadero and down into the Marina District. The closer I got to home, the tighter my stomach became. How was I going to tell Martin I wanted more time to think about getting married? What would he say if I said I wasn't sure if we really loved each other?

Then again was I so sure that we didn't really love each other?

51

Martin had so many great qualities. A hard worker. A brilliant programmer. Easy to be with. A dry wit. So Roman candles didn't go off when we kiss. So he isn't the most romantic man on the West Coast. We did have a great vacation in Mexico a few months before. Hunted seashells. Went sailing and surfboarding. Drank piña coladas in the moonlight, listening to a mariachi band. Danced under the stars.

Why can't there be a test you could buy at the drug store? You pee in a bottle and shake it up, if it turns pink you're in love. If it turns red, get married immediately.

As I pulled into the driveway I saw a sleek and shiny Z car parked in my parking stall. Well, well. I thought it had to be the one that had followed me the day before from the Holmcrofts' place. Morrison Holmcroft's P.I., perhaps. Or his hired thug. I took a close look at the car. A man's sunglasses on the dashboard and some *Handgunner* magazines in the back. The doors were locked.

The license plates still had mud on them and weren't readable. I scratched at the mud; it wouldn't come off. It was fake, permanent mud. Very sneaky.

I went up the stairs with my hand inside my jacket pocket, firmly wrapped around the grip of the little automatic Eddie Fisk had given me. Dumb, I know. You shoot somebody with an unregistered gun in San Francisco, you won't see sunshine for ten years.

I eased the door open and took a peek inside. Martin was seated on the couch reading—or pretending to read—a thick book, a petulant look on his face. A large, muscular man, his back to me, was talking on the phone. He had on a checkered sport coat and his hair was in need of a trim.

Even without seeing his face, I knew him. He was Charlie Gore, a P.I. with a reputation for doing anything short of murder for a client. I'd met Mr. Gore just before I'd met Martin, about a year and a half ago. I'd had a few too many tall Bloody Marys and went to bed with Charlie Gore and the next morning he was gone and I hadn't seen him since. What fools we mortals be.

I felt anger rise in me, remembering how I'd felt that morning, hungover and abandoned at the Holiday Inn in Oakland. There's only one way to handle the Charlie Gores of this world, and that's to attack. I shouted: "Who said you could use my desk!"

He swung around, a smile coming to his boyish face. He'd lost a little weight since I'd seen him last, and had a tan. He looked like Robert Redford at his roguish Sundance Kid best, and had the bluest eyes I've ever seen on a human being. "Hellooooo, Odyssey," he said. "Good, you're home. Be with you in a minute." He went back to talking on the phone.

"Hang up that phone!" I snapped.

Martin came to his feet, his face as red as ketchup. "Odyssey, you've got to do something about this man! He pushed his way in here saying you said it was all right, then he made himself a sandwich like this was his house. Who is he, what does he want?"

Charlie hung up the phone and came over to me to give me a hug. I pushed him away. "Go bite a lemon," I said.

"Is he a friend of yours or isn't he?" Martin asked.

"Tell him what great friends we are, sweetheart," Charlie Gore said.

He was blackmailing me. He grinned.

"Martin, this is Charlie Gore," I said. "A former colleague of mine."

"Not *just* a colleague," he said with a smile. "There was a little more to it."

"A gentleman wouldn't mention that," I said.

"Mention what?" Martin said. He could be dumb sometimes.

"Never mind, Martin," I said. "Charlie is leaving, and taking his bad manners with him."

"Isn't she sweet?" Charlie said to Martin.

Someone else appeared from the kitchen, cramming his mouth full of a meatloaf sandwich. He had Charlie's shape and size, but he was an ex-boxer and had a scarred, puffy face. He wore a rumpled gray suit. I recognized him, Charlie's gofer.

"Well if it isn't Mickey Fingers," I said. "When did they let you out?"

53

"That was just a little misunderstanding, I didn't mean to hurt the guy that bad, but he insisted on it."

"The man has paid his debt to society," Charlie Gore said. "Ninety days, is all. It was not a big deal."

Fingers grinned. A tooth was missing. He opened a beer.

"Did I say you could have that?" I said. I took the beer away from him. "You don't take things around here unless they're offered to you, get it? It's called 'manners.' "

"I think you should get these people out of here," Martin said. "I mean, this is our home, after all."

"You live here?" Charlie asked Martin. Martin ignored him. Charlie turned to me. "You mean you two are, ah, like living together?"

"Soon to be married," Martin said.

Charlie Gore laughed a false laugh. Martin's nostrils flared.

"You followed me yesterday from the Holmcrofts' house, didn't you, Mr. Gore? And you left that tape at the office—you ought to be ashamed of yourself trying to scare people like that. Mr. Frampton took you seriously."

"Odyssey, Odyssey, would I do something like that? Me? Charlie the Gentleman?"

"Get out, Mr. Gore," I said. "Our landlord is making war on cockroaches, you might be gassed any minute. And take your pal who's paid his debt to society with you!"

"Look, sweetheart," he pleaded, "I didn't mean to get your boyfriend all excited, I just wanted to see you. I didn't even know he was your boyfriend. I admit I'm a little abrasive at times and I sincerely apologize."

"A little abrasive? Try incredibly rude."

"What can I say except I'm sorry? I thought we were friends. I see we're not. Sorry for the misunderstanding, Martin. I'm a big enough man to admit it when he's wrong."

Charlie put out his hand to Martin, but Martin refused to shake it. Instead he grabbed his coat out of the closet. "I'm going to visit Mother. Don't wait dinner."

"I've got something I want to talk to you about, Martin—about last night."

"What is it?"

"We can discuss it after Mr. Gore leaves."

"I don't wish to wait for *Mister* Gore to leave."

Martin left, slamming the door behind him.

Charlie flinched as the door slammed. "Hothead, isn't he?" Charlie said to me.

"Not usually. You just bring out the worst in him."

Charlie turned to Fingers. "Take the rest of the day off, okay? See you back at the office in the morning."

"Sure, boss." He lumbered out.

"Your boyfriend's already talking like a husband," Charlie said. He shoved a cigarette in his mouth.

"We don't allow smoking in here," I said.

"Sorry." He put it away. He smiled that damn boyish grin of his. I found myself looking into his blue, blue eyes. He straightened his coat, which was stretched across one shoulder. He lifted weights and his muscles were bulked up so his clothes never seemed to fit. I could smell some aftershave on him, spicy. Just nice.

"You're a perfect ten, Odyssey," he said.

"You're a perfect jerk. What do you want?"

"Are you really going to marry Dumbo?"

"Damn right I am. He's a computer programmer. One of the best, most creative, most dynamic men in his field. He has a hell of a future."

"And you could have had me."

"You used me like a Kleenex."

"Maybe you scared me off."

"I didn't know you scared so easy. Look, I've got to get back to work, why don't you state your business? I'm sure you didn't come to whistle 'Oh Remember When.' "

"I do want to say I'm sorry for taking a walk that morning. I had every intention of coming back. I really am sorry."

"Okay, you're sorry. I'm sorry, we're all sorry."

"Would you like to hear my explanation?" He brushed a shock of hair out of his eyes.

"No."

55

"I was afraid."

"So you said."

"Not just of your smarts. I was afraid I was falling for you."

"Well I wasn't falling for you, so you were in no danger. Now what are you doing here?"

"Okay, I'm here on a case. Seems you and me have husband and wife as clients."

"I deduced that much."

"He wants you to tell me what you know about this woman, what's her name?"

"Rachel Collins."

"That's her." He snapped his fingers.

"You know I can't give anyone confidential information. Any leads I uncover as to the whereabouts of the subject legally and ethically belong to my client and no one else. My client is Aletha Holmcroft, not her husband."

That brought him to his feet. "Of course you can't tell anyone. But *anyone* doesn't include me." He came over to me and ran his fingers through my hair. The strangest tingling sensation percolated through me. I swallowed and backed away from him.

"Not anyone," I said, "especially including you."

"I really was scared of falling for you," he said. "I was terrified."

"For you, I was nothing but a quick piece." His hand was back. I moved farther away. "You did leave that tape at my office this morning, didn't you? Don't deny it, you couldn't even spell Odyssey right."

He moved closer to me. Damn, he smelled good.

"I didn't do it."

"Like hell you didn't."

"Honest, it wasn't me. I'm sorry for what happened in Oakland. Let's kiss and make up."

"I'd rather kiss a dog."

"I've missed you."

"You could have called. Don't give me that stuff about being afraid of involvement. That doesn't cut it."

"You come on with all that intellectual stuff sometimes, it

scares a guy off. No guy likes a woman who can do the *New York Times* crossword puzzle in half an hour. It freaks them."

"I have never done the *New York Times* crossword puzzle in half an hour in my life. I don't even like crossword puzzles."

"You could do it if you tried." He kissed my neck.

"Stop it!" I backed away from him again. I closed the drapes. If somebody saw into the room they could get the wrong idea. Especially nosy Mrs. Eversole. Or Martin. Or anybody. At least that's what I told myself at the moment. Sometimes I can kid myself about things like that.

The room was dim, so I switched on a light. He went over to the stereo rack and started going through my CDs and tapes.

"Stay out of there!" I said.

"Relax." He switched on the machine and a crying, mournful sax poured out into the room. "Sweet Nothings" by Lonnie Tubs.

Charlie came over and put his arms around me.

"What is this?" I said. "A seduction? Eleven o'clock in the morning?"

"No seduction, just trying to put you in a better mood." He squeezed me tight. The aftershave was stronger now, spice and musk. Something about musk does it to me. The tingling enveloped me, but I wasn't going to let it get the best of me. Henry Brooke said it: *The worst of slaves is one whom passion rules.*

Then I turned toward Martin's computer and I remembered Martin. The man I supposedly loved but didn't know if I loved or not.

I eased Charlie away from me. "Time to go, Charlie."

I clicked on the floor lamp. He clicked it off.

"You're going to get me angry," I said.

"You forget what we did that night?" he asked.

"I don't want to remember."

"You were terrific. The whipped cream was your idea."

"I've totally blanked it out of my mind."

"You said I was the best lover on earth."

"I say that every time. The truth is, you were nothing special."

"It's not nice to fib."

I was circling around the room, keeping a step ahead of him. I bumped into the coffee table. Charlie bumped into me. He kissed me. His lips felt warm. He tasted nice.

His arms went around me again and he kissed me again. I had my arms around him now too, feeling the tight muscles in his back. A swimming feeling came over me. Like my backbone was going soft.

He drew back. "Very, very, very, very nice," he said.

"I hate you," I said.

He kissed me again.

"This isn't right," I managed, his lips still pressed against mine. My damn heart was thundering in my chest. My throat was closed up.

We were moving with the music. Suddenly he picked me up. I put my arms around his shoulders, but then I saw Martin's computer again and it snapped me back to reality. I just couldn't complicate my life like this right now. Not until I decided exactly where Martin and I stood.

"Hold it, Charlie, put me down."

"What's the matter?" We were heading for the bedroom.

"Hold it, damn it!"

He kissed my neck; we were almost to the bedroom door.

"Wait! Halt! Stop!" I grabbed his ear and pulled like hell.

"Yeow!" He put me down.

"This has gone too far," I said firmly. I screwed up my resolve and looked deep into his eyes. "Read my lips: I am engaged to Martin. I love Martin. You will have to leave. Now."

"Can't we, you know, just once? Just for old time's sake. What Martin doesn't know won't hurt him."

"Get out of my home, Charlie Gore, and I mean right now!"

He stepped closer to kiss me again, but I jumped away. "No. I mean it."

He reached out for me; I grabbed his arm and gave him an *irimi-nage*, landing him on the couch upside down.

"I'm sorry I had to do that, but this is not the time to . . . ah, for us to, ah, you know what."

58

He rolled off the couch, took off his sport coat, and folded it over a chair. He undid his tie and loosened his collar.

"Want to play, do you?" he said.

"I just want you to leave."

"You didn't have to throw me. That was incredibly rude."

We started circling each other. He had an awkward, kung-fu sort of style. He obviously hadn't had much training.

"You're out of your class, Charlie," I said.

"We'll see who's out of whose class. Tell you what, I make you say uncle, you make love to me. You make me say uncle, I make love to you."

"No lovemaking, Charlie. Just go quietly."

"Not until I've taught you a little lesson."

"Leave while you can still stand erect."

He made a couple of feints, then I had his arm; I twisted it, but he made a quick move to the side, and I found myself flipping over and landing on my seat on the floor. Hard.

"A Marine taught me that," he said. "Ready to call 'uncle'?"

I gave him my hand so he could help me up. When he did, I grabbed his wrist, pulled down and in with a twist, and sent him somersaulting across the floor and rolling into the bedroom with a loud bang. He hit his head on the dresser.

I hurried over to him. He started writhing on the floor, holding his head, blood appearing between his fingers.

I knelt over him, pulling his fingers apart. It was only a slight gash; blood was trickling out into his hair. He looked at me and shook his head. "Ooooooooo, it hurts," he said.

"Don't be such a big baby," I said. I stared at him. He was grinning now, blood running down his face. He laughed and I laughed, and I suddenly wanted him badly. I don't exactly know what happened. I threw my arms around him and kissed him and he pulled me to him, pressing his lips against mine.

"You're going to get blood on my blouse," I said.

"Then you'd better take it off," he said, flicking the top button open.

He peeled back the folds of my blouse and kissed the tops of my breasts above my bra. His hands were on my thighs and I felt my belt buckle being undone.

"We need protection," I said.

"Taken care of," he said.

And suddenly I was pulling his shirt up over his head and my blouse flew off and my bra and my pants and panties and he was kissing me on my neck and my breasts and he was lifting me onto the bed and I could smell his sweat . . . he paused for a moment while he undid his pants and got the protection on, then he bent over me, the blood still running down his forehead, he was kissing me, caressing me . . .

Damn, damn, damn. It was good.

After, he just lay there and smoked a cigarette, his arm around me. Dorothy Parker had it right: *There's nothing more fun than a man.*

I ran my fingers through the fur on his chest. "I hate you with my whole heart and soul," I said.

He just sighed with satisfaction.

Then I heard the front door open. We froze. Martin? Couldn't be. He never came home from his mother's place until well past midnight.

Martin's voice: "Od? You home?"

"Oh no!" I said. I pulled the blanket up to my chin. Martin appeared in the doorway. His eyes seemed to glow, and he was shaking all over.

"What have you to say for yourself?" he said.

Everything I could think of to say sounded dumb. "I'm sorry, Martin," was all I could manage.

"Sorry doesn't make it. I'll send somebody for my things. We're finished, Odyssey. Finished forever."

Martin turned stiffly and disappeared from the doorway. A door slammed. Silence followed. The sword of guilt sank deep into me.

After a moment, Charlie said: "Oh, good Lord."

"I hurt him, Charlie, I didn't mean to."

Charlie didn't say anything for a long moment. Then he said, "I shouldn't have done it."

"Done what?"

"Taken advantage. If you two were planning to get married, what business did I have to butt in?" He did seem bothered by it. He put out his cigarette and sat up, rubbing his hands through his hair.

"You didn't take advantage. I wanted you."

He lay back down and put his arm around me. We were quiet for a while. We were both feeling guilty, I think. I was feeling sad, too. Sad for me and Martin and maybe for Charlie, too.

Then Charlie said, "You know deep down under it all, Odyssey, you're just like I am. You and me, we're soul mates."

"How do you figure that?"

"We're in this crazy business because there's something of a knight in shining armor about us. We see something's wrong, we got to fix it. We're not everyday people. We're something special. All those books you read and all those degrees you got on the wall don't change what you are underneath. Underneath, you and me, we're the same. That's why you want me so bad and why I want you so bad."

If he was right, I figured I was in a lot of trouble.

SEVEN

■

André Malraux once said: *We owe to the Middle Ages the two worst inventions of humanity—romantic love and gunpowder.* And when you think about it, gunpowder isn't all that bad.

Charlie and I got dressed without speaking, then he went over to my serving bar and poured himself a drink and sat leaning back in a chair, staring into the glass like it was a crystal ball.

"Look," he said. "Since we're both working on the same case, why don't we share information? No use both of us tracking down the same clues and suspects."

I froze.

"What's the matter?" he asked.

"Damn it all to hell," I said.

"What? What?"

"You really had me going, you know that? I actually started thinking maybe you were right, that we were meant for each other."

"We are meant for each other!"

"What you want isn't me. It's what I know."

He gaped at me. "Genius, I may be a rat, but I'm not that much of a rat." He put his drink down and looked away from me, shaking his head.

I didn't believe him. I'd been conned. "I have to go," I said.

"Me, too," Charlie said. He grabbed his coat. "Look," he said, looking as earnest as a congressional candidate. "I'm sorry if that's what you think. The truth is, you do something to me, Genius. I mean you make little earthquakes inside me. I'd do the decent thing and marry you myself, but I'm not the kind a kid with your class ought to marry. But we got chemistry between us."

"Sure. Chemistry."

"Really. I mean it."

He came over to me and kissed me on the neck. I pushed him away.

"I know and you know we could have something really great," he said. "You think I'd trade that for a case? You want, I'll call Morrison Holmcroft right now and tell him I quit."

"Watch it, I might call your bluff."

"I mean it. Say the word, I make the call."

"Okay, make the call."

He went over to the phone, picked it up and dialed. He waited a moment, then said, "Mr. Holmcroft, please."

"Hold it," I said. He looked at me. "Hang it up, I believe you."

He hung up. "Thanks, Odyssey, I need the bread."

He came over to me and put his arms around me.

"I swear to God it's you I care about, Odyssey. Maybe I came over here to get info, but once I saw you, all that stuff went right out the window."

I wanted to believe him . . . and looking into those eyes of his, I *did* believe him.

He said, "Let's try it and see if we can't make it together. How about I stay here with you for a while? Just a couple of days to see if we can get along?"

"You're a dog, Charlie Gore," I said with a smile. "And I don't

63

like living with a dog. I can't have you here, Charlie, there's things I have to work out with Martin.''

"He said you were finished forever.''

"I know, Charlie, but I can't let it end like that. He's still got his things here . . . besides, you and me—it's just happening too fast.''

"I know you can take care of yourself, Odyssey, but I'd feel a hell of a lot better about things if you'd let me stay. Holmcroft may have been playing with some pretty rough boys.''

He kissed me and I felt warm all over. It would be so nice to have him around. And I would feel safer.

"I'll sleep in my car in the driveway,'' he said. "Now that we're back together, I'll be damned if I'll let anything happen to you.''

"You won't have to sleep in the car, Charlie.'' I took a spare key to the place and handed it to him. "No loud music after ten if I'm not back. And don't block the driveway with your car.''

He kissed me, gave me a pat on the rump—for which I gave him a shot in the arm—and started to leave, whistling "Happy Days Are Here Again.''

"One thing, Charlie,'' I said. "Can you get a sport coat that's, well, got a little more style?'' His had big checks on it. It made him look like a cereal box.

"You don't like this?''

"No class.''

"Okay, soon as I can, I'll get a new wardrobe.'' He gave me a wave and left.

I tossed the gun Eddie Fisk had given me in a desk drawer and locked up the place. Damn but I was feeling strange. Light-headed. Charlie Gore knew how to light my fire.

Oh well, isn't sex nine out of the ten great mysteries of life? The Internal Revenue Service being the other one.

So I went back out into the field, determined to keep my mind on my job and not to think about my mixed-up love life.

What had my investigation turned up so far? Not much, except that, according to Mr. Michael, Rachel Collins was going around with a guy with silver hair who drove a Jaguar. Next step: find the identity of Rachel Collins's silver-haired companion.

I drove downtown and parked in the Sutter Stockton Garage and walked four blocks to Lemming's Lounge. Lemming wasn't in, the fat bartender told me. I knocked on his office door anyway. He didn't answer it.

"Told you he wasn't here," the fat bartender said with a grin.

Next stop: Morrison Holmcroft's office. It was a long shot, but I thought he might know who Mr. Silver Hair might be.

I walked over to the Transamerica Pyramid. A bunch of Berkeley types were picketing out in front, chanting, shouting, making a show for the TV cameras. A couple of bored-looking cops watched. Something about an oil spill. At least they care. I signed their petition to ban off-shore drilling and gave them a few dollars.

I went on into the lobby. The security guard was reading a newspaper. I took the elevator up to Holmcroft Financial Services on the tenth floor.

"Mr. Holmcroft isn't in," the receptionist said.

"When will he be in?" I asked.

"I don't know."

"Can I make an appointment?"

"No."

I said, "He's left orders I'm persona non grata, hasn't he?"

She shook her head in bewilderment.

"Not wanted," I explained.

She nodded with a tiny grin.

"Is he in or isn't he?"

"He's not in, really."

"I'll have to check for myself," I said.

I vaulted the counter and headed for his office. The receptionist backed away from me as if I might attack her and grabbed a phone. As I marched down the aisle between the desks, I could hear her yelling: "Security!"

Holmcroft's secretary wasn't at her desk and Holmcroft's office door was open, so I just waltzed right in. Holmcroft and his secretary were busily stuffing papers into a briefcase. He looked at me and groaned. "What the hell do you want?"

"A few moments of friendly conversation, covering facts you may find a valuable addition to your vast store of knowledge. Can I have five minutes?"

He didn't answer and he didn't stop what he was doing. He handed the secretary a bundle of papers. Their eyes met as if they had a guilty secret, then she took the bundle of papers and left. As she was going out, a security guard—tall, beefy, stupid-looking—barged in. He hiked up his pants and snorted at me, jerking his thumb in the direction of the door.

"Escort this lady out of here," Holmcroft said. The security guard put his hand on my shoulder. That was a big mistake on his part.

I made my move on him, took his wrist as I dropped down on my right knee, twisted his arm, and sent him flying across a corner of Holmcroft's desk, scattering papers like a snow storm. He made a loud crash when he hit the floor.

Holmcroft looked at me wide-eyed, then a slow smile appeared on his lips.

I said, "How about you answer just one question, then I'll leave, Mr. Holmcroft. Who's Rachel Collins's silver-haired friend? He drives a Jaguar."

He shook his head. "Sorry, I have no idea."

The security guard scrambled to his feet, trying to steady himself against the desk. He started to go for his gun. "That better be made of chocolate, friend," I said. "Because if you pull it, you're going to eat it."

He kept his hand on his weapon, but he didn't pull it out. Holmcroft turned to him and said, "You're fired." Then he turned back to me. "I've got to be in my attorney's office in ten minutes. Walk along with me?"

"Sure."

He picked up his briefcase and we walked through the office and into the hall.

"Where did you hear about this friend of Rachel's?" he asked, pushing the button for the elevator.

66

"I found someone who knows Rachel Collins well, and this person claims she's been seen recently with him."

"I don't know him, but there can't be more than five or ten thousand Jags in this town." The elevator door opened and we got in. He pressed G and the door closed. I guessed he'd put Charlie to work checking on automobile repair shops that work on Jags.

That would keep him busy for a while.

"Good work, Miss Gallagher," Holmcroft said.

"I thought you weren't interested in finding her."

"Only to clear up this mess. I suspect her of nothing."

The elevator stopped, the door opened, and we stepped into the lobby.

"Good day, Miss Gallagher," he said. He went through the glass doors into the street. I stayed with him, just a few steps behind. There were a lot of pedestrians on the wide sidewalk. That's when I saw this strange figure standing by the curb: thin, wearing a hat and trench coat, frizzy red hair sticking out. It looked like a woman, but I couldn't be sure.

Suddenly the figure pulled what I thought was a gun. I stepped up and kicked Holmcroft's legs out from under him and dropped him from behind and fell on him. Holmcroft bellowed, waving his arms. I rolled off him and looked up and saw that whoever had been standing there was gone.

I scrambled to my feet and ran to the street and made a right. I could see someone in a trench coat running toward the far corner. I sprinted after her or him—threading my way through pedestrians. I was closing the gap. My quarry turned the next corner. I was half a block behind.

I made it to the corner and looked around. It was a narrow one-way street. The sidewalks were crowded with business types going to lunch. A small red Toyota pulled out of a parking space and it looked like someone with red hair was at the wheel. I ran down the middle of the street, but the car sped off, ran the red light at the far corner, turned right, and was gone.

I couldn't get the license number, but I did see a large dent in the right side toward the back. I stepped onto the sidewalk and

67

headed back the way I came at a walk. My hands were shaking. I took a few deep breaths and calmed myself down.

Around the corner I found Holmcroft coming toward me, shaking with rage.

"Who the hell you think you are, Miss Rambo?"

"I may have just saved your life, Mr. Holmcroft."

"You've ruined my suit, that's what you've done. You've made me a laughingstock."

"Didn't you see the gun?"

"No, I didn't. You must have a feverish imagination."

"Was that Rachel Collins?"

"No," he said. "It definitely was not Rachel Collins."

"Then who was it?"

"How the hell should I know? Listen, Miss Gallagher, from now on, just stay the hell away from me. If you don't, you'll be hearing from my lawyers."

He crossed the street and got into a cab. I turned and headed up the street thinking what I needed most in the world right now was a double martini.

EIGHT

∎

Two double martinis at a Battery Street businessmen's bar called
the Onion Eater didn't help much, I was still trembling. A lawyer
with wavy golden blond hair bought me the second one. He said
I was looking shaky. When I told him I always got that way when
people pointed guns at me, he stared at me for a few moments
trying to decide whether I was loony, then excused himself to go
to the john and I didn't see him again.

I took a walk and went into some bookstores feeling light-
headed. I browsed through the art section. I love the French
impressionists. Gauguin, Renoir, Monet. Waving grasses, shimmering water, sun-dappled buildings, and people who seem to
belong to it all, like forms fitting within forms, yet it is all so
formless. Goethe said something to the effect that art imposes
the illusion of higher reality. The impressionists, I think, do that
best.

I finally stopped trembling and after a while the lightheaded-
ness left me. I went back out into the street, walked up Stockton,

ransomed the Banana Slug and drove home to have a hot shower and get some lunch.

When I drove down my driveway there was a beat-up old pickup parked by the stairs and Charlie's flunky, Mickey Fingers, was unloading boxes and carrying them into my apartment.

I parked and got out of my car. Mrs. Eversole was, as usual, sitting on her porch watching everything. I waved a greeting to her. She nodded and smiled, and rocked in her rocking chair. The old witch.

I went up the stairs and into my living room. Mickey Fingers grunted some kind of greeting. His shirt was untucked and sweat had soaked the armpits down to his belt line. On his right arm was a tattoo that said MOTHER with a red heart. Hard to think of a lunk like Fingers having a mother.

"What the hell is all this?" I said.

"Charlie told me to bring his stuff."

Charlie was not thinking of spending a few days; he was moving in. "Oh, no," I said. "He wants to bring a few shirts and some underwear, okay, but not all this. No way."

Fingers shrugged. "Charlie say . . ." He gave me a stupid expression. Then I noticed that some of Martin's clothes and other belongings were piled in the corner, including his computer and printer.

"Charlie say to get rid of it."

"You never mind what Charlie says. You don't touch anything in this apartment, you got that?"

"You say so. But Charlie say—"

"Never mind what Charlie says. This is my place and I'm telling you."

"You better talk to Charlie. I don't want to know anything."

"I'll talk to Charlie all right."

"Please. Just a few more things to bring in, okay?" He had a pathetic hurt look on his face. "Just a little more, then you speak to Charlie. Please? So he don't get mad at me."

"Oh, all right, you've gone this far."

He headed for the door. I headed for the shower.

70

The hot water felt good cascading over my body. I lingered there, letting my head clear.

After a few minutes I began thinking about what I was going to do next. I really had no clear line of pursuit, so I planned first to check in with Mr. Frampton and see if he'd come up with anything through his research.

Then I could always check with Rachel's old parole officer. Former parolees sometimes kept in touch with their old parole officers—also that might be a clue as to who her friends were. Maybe even get me a lead to Mr. Silver Hair. Maybe Charlie would know who he was. Getting information from Charlie wouldn't be too difficult.

Having a plan always gets me energized. I got out of the shower, dried off, and put on my robe. I took the blow dryer and that's when I heard the phone ring. I thought the answering machine would get it, but when I stepped out of the bathroom I could see Mickey Fingers hanging up the phone.

"Who was it?" I asked.

"Some guy. Michael something. Didn't say no last name."

"Mr. Michael? What did he want?"

"He said somebody was on their way over. Something like that."

"Rachel? Did he say Rachel Collins?"

His usual dull expression got even duller. He shrugged and said, "Maybe."

I called Mr. Michael, but the clerk said he was busy doing a tint and perm and couldn't come to the phone. I hung up and got dressed in a hurry.

On the way out, I told Mickey Fingers not to be there when I got back.

Fifteen minutes later I parked the Banana Slug across the street from Mr. Michael's. I decided to wait and see if Rachel showed up. Two minutes later a Jaguar drove up with a silver-haired gentleman at the wheel. He got out. He wore a blue blazer with a handkerchief tucked into the breast pocket; his shoes gleamed. He looked like something out of a Fred Astaire movie.

He went around the car like a perfect gentleman and opened

71

the door on the passenger side. Rachel Collins got out, wearing what looked like a leopard skin jacket and a green skirt. Her hair was red, flaming red, and sort of stylishly unkempt and curly. Not quite like what I had seen in the alley, but then again it could have been uncombed or fluffed out. She went into Mr. Michael's.

I'd found her! And in less than two days. I was sure going to have a great chocolate eclair at Just Desserts.

Mr. Silver Hair locked his car and went into the shop after her.

I waited a few minutes, then got out and opened the trunk of my car. I went into my tool box and took out a piece of flat iron an old boyfriend made up for me. The same old boyfriend who modified my car's engine. It's about two feet long with a hook gizmo on the end. I use it to get into cars when I don't have a key.

I put on a kerchief which hid my hair and most of my face, then I put the piece of flatiron up the sleeve of my jacket and walked across the street and approached the beauty salon. I wanted to check on Mr. Silver Hair and make sure he wasn't watching his car. But just as I got to the front window of Mr. Michael's, Mr. Silver Hair suddenly came out, nodded to me with a nice smile, and walked on by, leaving the air scented with cologne. Nice.

His silver hair shone brilliantly in the sunlight. I could see him wearing an admiral's uniform in a liquor ad in a magazine, something like that. He must have been a model or an actor. Somebody who makes his living by his looks.

He went down the block and into a deli. He was probably going to have a cup of coffee while Rachel was getting her hair done, so I went over to the Jaguar, slipped my flatiron out of my sleeve, slid it down between the glass and the outer metal skin of the door, found the cross bar for the locking mechanism, and lifted it. The door swung open, just like it was supposed to.

The blasted glove box was locked. I fished around in my purse for my Swiss army knife and used the big blade to pry it open. Inside were the usual accumulated receipts for tires, battery guarantees, a box of Kleenex, a small bottle of aspirin, a couple

72

of Band-Aids, a cocaine inhaler—everything you need to get through the day. And the vehicle registration.

The car was registered to Raymond Pendergast, 1010 Hickock Drive, San Francisco.

I sensed someone approaching the car and looked up right into Pendergast's face. Damn.

"Hey, there! What do you think you're doing?"

"Doing?" What a dumb thing to say.

He swung the door open and grabbed my arm. I wrestled it away from him. I could have grabbed his wrist and broken it in several places, but instead I pushed him backward with my foot, then slid across to the other side and opened the door into the street. A car screeched to a halt. I scrambled out and dashed across the street and down the block. I stopped at the corner and looked back.

He hadn't come after me and he wasn't running for a phone to call the police. I took a deep breath and took off my kerchief.

I circled around the block and waited for a while before going back. No cops around. The Jaguar was still there. I got into the Banana Slug and waited, listening to tapes. The history of jazz. I was almost through Thelonious Monk when Rachel and Pendergast came out of Mr. Michael's. Pendergast showed her how he'd found me. He still seemed a bit angry as he demonstrated how he grabbed me. She seemed amused. Then they got into the Jaguar and drove off and I started up the Banana Slug and went right with them.

I hung way back behind a produce truck and followed them west on Geary. They weren't doing anything to make sure they weren't being followed, which I found a little strange. If I were sending people dead cats, I'd be a little wary.

They turned off on Hickock and headed south, up the hill overlooking the Cliff House and the ocean. They pulled up in front of a large stone house on the corner. I stopped up the block by a small park. Kids were playing on the swings. An old man was walking his German shepherd. The two subjects I had under surveillance went into the house. That's P.I. talk.

I sat there and thought about duty. One of my problems in life.

73

I believe in being ethical. Lacordaire said, *Duty is the grandest of ideas, because it implies the idea of God, of the soul, of liberty, of responsibility, of immortality.* My father made me memorize that when I was in tenth grade because I hadn't done my French homework for a week.

In this case, my duty was clear. I should immediately turn around and call the office and tell Mr. Frampton that I'd found Rachel Collins and where; he would then tell me to come in, make a written report, then I'd hand-deliver it to the client.

Know thyself and do thy own work, said Plato. And that's just what I intended to do.

First, I'd have a look around her place. Why? Just a feeling I had that this all didn't add up somehow. I wanted to see if she drove a red Japanese sedan with a dented rear fender. And I wanted to talk to her, woman to woman, without Mr. Silver Hair around (who could have me arrested for breaking into his car). I wouldn't tell her who I was, of course. I just wanted to dig into this a little and get a fix on what was really going on.

Or I could have made my report and walked away from it. It is true that the client had hired me to find Rachel Collins and no more, but I felt I had a higher duty to the truth. Had she sent the dead cat? Was she a threat to my client? These were questions that needed answering.

So I sat and waited. I made some notes in my log. I chewed some Beechnut gum. I listened to a radio talk show. They were talking about sugar and how it might not be as bad for you as we've been led to believe. Wouldn't that be nice.

The news came on. Someone had blown up fifty people in Paris and six different extremist groups had claimed credit. A plane with six people had crashed into a shopping mall. The talk-show host came back on with a guest to talk about aliens from outer space. He said they had taken over the city government in Berkeley. He seemed to have a lot of proof. Pretty weird place, Berkeley. They had seceded from the Union in 1969 and still called themselves the People's Republic.

An hour and fifteen minutes later, Mr. Silver Hair came out alone, got into his Jaguar, and drove away. Time to go to work.

74

NINE

∎

I waited a few minutes, then got out of the car and walked down the block. An elderly lady was coming the other way with a Pekingese on a leash. I said, "Nice day," and she gave me a look reserved for suspicious strangers and hurried on. And San Francisco used to be such a friendly town.

Pendergast's place was made of gray stone with ivy growing all over it. It had two floors with a large porch that ran along the front. Not typical of San Francisco. It looked like something you'd find in Philadelphia or Pittsburgh.

It was on a raised corner lot and had a garage under it, around the side. A woman across the street holding a bag of groceries was letting herself in the door to her house. I waited for her to go inside, then I went over to Pendergast's garage and checked the door. Locked. Frosted windows.

I wanted to know if a little red Japanese car with a dent on the right rear side was in there. I was betting it wasn't. If it was, I had my culprit and I might as well go back to the office, write up a report, and get on with my next case.

I got out my lock-picking kit and set to work. It was an old-fashioned lock with only a couple of worn and easy tumblers and I had it open in a few seconds. I raised the garage door and slipped inside. There was a red Toyota parked in one of the stalls. The license plate read: RACHEL C. I closed the door.

With the door closed the garage was almost dark. It smelled of oil and gasoline. I clicked on my penlight. I moved around to the right side of the Toyota. There was the large dent right where it was supposed to be.

I froze. A cold chill came over me. Perhaps she was the woman with the gun that I'd chased down the block. Perhaps she was dangerous and I was an idiot to be sneaking around her basement. I went around to the driver's side and opened the door. I was going to open the hood and see if the engine was still warm. It takes almost four hours for a car engine to completely cool off. As I groped for the hood latch, I heard a noise.

Footsteps.

I eased the door closed and went around to the other side of the Toyota and crouched in front of it. I was armed with aikido, but even aikido isn't much good against a gun.

The door opened. A woman's voice: "Who's in here?" She sounded shaky.

I didn't make a sound. I didn't breathe.

The woman's voice: "I saw you in the street. I've called the police."

Damn, I thought. Mr. Frampton was really going to be mad. The last time he bailed me out he lectured me for two and a half hours about the necessity for obeying the law, blah, blah, blah.

"I have a gun," she said. "And I know how to use it."

I stood up and said: "You won't need a gun or the police. I'm harmless."

The lights clicked on. I put my hands in the air.

Rachel Collins was standing in the doorway pointing a double-barreled shotgun at me. She had on the jacket and skirt she'd worn to the beauty parlor and her hair looked fabulous, long flowing waves. Mr. Michael was no hack.

76

Even though she had the gun, there was fear bordering on terror in her eyes.

"Just take it easy," I said, my tongue feeling stiff.

"Who . . . who are you?" The shotgun trembled in her grasp.

"I've been hired to find you," I said. "I'm a private detective. My name's Odyssey Gallagher."

"Are you the woman who broke into Raymond's car?" Her mouth tightened.

"Yes."

"Who hired you?"

"I'm not allowed to divulge the name of my client."

"You are when I'm holding this." She raised the shotgun a little higher, pointing it directly at my head.

I said: "Mrs. Aletha Holmcroft."

My policy of protecting my client has limits.

"Why would she want you to find me?"

"I don't know the real reason. She said it's to give you back your cat."

"What cat? What the hell are you talking about?"

"The dead cat."

"What dead cat?" That's when I noticed tears running down her face. She sniffed and said, "When is this nightmare going to end?"

"Please put the gun down," I said. "I'm not armed. I won't hurt you."

She kept pointing it at me for a long moment while she studied me. I tried to look as harmless as I know how to look. I even gave her a sheepish little smile. Finally she put down the gun. "I'm just not cut out for this," she said.

"Thank you," I said.

She sniffed again. "You can go, if you want to. I didn't really call the police."

"Okay if I ask you some questions?"

"About what?"

"Well, for one, have you used your car today?"

"Yes—just to the store."

"When was that?"

"A little before noon."

"Too bad."

"Why?"

"A car's engine holds heat for four hours. I was hoping it would be cold as ice."

"Why?"

"Because I saw this car—or one very much like it—downtown this morning."

"It wasn't this one. This car has been right here except for one trip to the Seven-Eleven."

"No one else could have taken it?"

"No one else has a key. Why don't you come upstairs, Miss Gallagher, and tell me more about this."

She turned and put the gun over her shoulder and went into the basement adjoining the garage. I followed.

Off to the right was a huge wine cellar. I guess she figured I wasn't going to murder her. We went upstairs into a huge kitchen and down a hall to the living room. A chandelier hung from a vaulted ceiling. On one wall was a tapestry depicting a medieval hunt. There was a large stone fireplace. The mahogany floors gleamed. The furnishings were red leather, solid, masculine.

Rachel put the gun up on a rack with a couple of others, even larger ones. Elephant guns.

"Shouldn't you unload it first?" I said.

"It's not loaded. Raymond said they've been fixed so they won't shoot anyway."

"Don't you have a handgun?"

"No. I'm not allowed to have one. I've had trouble with the law. They catch me with a gun, I'd end up doing about five years."

"You really weren't downtown this morning, were you?"

"Lady, I don't know what the hell you're talking about."

I believed her. I'm not sure why. It was something in the way she said it, I could tell she wasn't trying to snow me. She really wasn't there. I said, "Call me Odyssey."

"I was supposed to be downtown with a gun this morning?

78

This is getting weirder and weirder. You want a drink, Odyssey?" She wiped her eyes with the tips of her fingers.

"I would like a drink." I showed her my trembling fingers. Having guns pointed at you twice in one day wreaks havoc on your nervous system.

I followed her through the house to sort of a small family room with a fireplace and a cozy little bar at one end. Behind the bar was a picture window and out the window you could see the Great Highway running in front of the Cliff House, and, beyond, the beach and Seal Rock, and beyond that, the wide, endless, gray Pacific.

We sat at the bar and she mixed us a couple of strong margaritas. I noticed my hand was shaking, too.

"Now," she said, "it looks to me like you're operating under a lot of misconceptions. You said you had some questions. Ask away."

"Where were you this morning? Just for the record."

"I went to the store for some things, like I said, then Raymond and I took a ride down the coast in his car. Just the two of us. We came back here for lunch, then I had my hair appointment."

"Anybody to verify this story?"

She shook her head. "Just Raymond. Who saw me downtown?"

"Me, for one. Morrison Holmcroft was the other. But whoever it was wore a trench coat with the collar way up, and a hat. But the hair was sticking out. It could have been you. Same general build."

"It wasn't me, Odyssey. Honestly it wasn't."

She seemed so sincere, and so scared.

"It's absolutely not possible that my car was anywhere." She said this looking me dead in the eye. If she was lying, she was damn skillful at it.

She tipped her head back and drained her glass. Then she started mixing some more. She sure seemed to like margaritas. But then, who doesn't?

"Did you get the license?" she asked. "Mine has my name on it."

79

"I didn't get the license."

"That's because it wasn't my car. Lord, this has been just the strangest month. So many weird things have been happening."

"What do you mean?"

"Somebody tried to kill me! The day after the thing that happened at the Marconi Club. I came home from aerobics class and parked my car in my slot and bang, a shot! All I saw was this person running away. Wearing a trench coat, just like what you saw. I called the police and they came out, but they couldn't find any bullet. I don't think that they thought it really happened. But it did."

I finished my margarita. Rachel brought out some fresh glasses and salted the rims, then poured us a couple more. Such a civilized drink, the margarita. My hands had stopped shaking. My legs felt heavy.

"So you're hiding from whoever shot at you?"

"You bet I am."

"You think it was Morrison Holmcroft?"

"No, I don't."

"You claim you know nothing about the dead cat."

"This is the first I've heard of it."

"Somebody left it on Holmcrofts' front porch, its throat slit."

She shook her head vigorously. "I don't even know where the Holmcrofts live and I don't care. Look, here's all that happened. I'd been seeing Mo Holmcroft—and yes I knew he was married and I didn't give a damn. It was just fun and games. And then he started making promises and I started to dream the big dream—you know how that is, I'm sure. I mean the white picket fence and everything. His wife was a bitch and he was going to dump her and he whispered to me over long candlelit dinners all that crap that moony teenagers tell each other, and I bought it. Then all of a sudden a couple of months ago he starts acting real weird."

"Weird? How?"

"Moody and strange. Like he had something on his mind. Suddenly he'd lost interest in me. He came over a couple of times and we didn't even have sex. Anyway, three weeks ago on a Friday night we had a date. I get all dolled up. His chauffeur drives up and I think it's him. The chauffeur comes to the door. I open it and start down the stairs. 'Mr. Holmcroft sends his apologies, Madam,' he says, with this gawd-awful smirk on his face. It was that smirk that did it.''

"Did what?"

She gulped her margarita. "I lost my mind. Sometimes I get this pressure in the back of my head. Like a bomb goes off, and my whole body fills up with like this rage, and I gotta do something. First I went to Lemming's and had a few. Then I went looking for the snake and I found him, too. At the Marconi Club. And I walked up to the son-of-a-bitch and threw a drink in his face.''

Hurray for her, I thought.

She poured us some more margaritas.

"So there you have it," she said, "the story of my life. I actually believe it when a man says he loves me—I guess I just want it too bad."

"I guess we all do," I said. My head was buzzing most pleasantly.

"You've been stung, too?"

"Hasn't everyone?"

She looked at me with deep brown eyes full of sympathy. I was beginning to understand what men saw in her, and it wasn't just her looks. She cared about people.

"Tell me," she said. She said it as if she really wanted to hear it.

I told her about Martin's proposal and how he stayed at his computer and forgot all about me, then I told her about Charlie, and how I wanted him and at the same time I found him so obnoxious.

"I know exactly what it is with his type. It's his *animalness*. The truth of it is, the female sex drive is supposed to be less than the man's, but it's not, not when a certain kind of man triggers it."

She hit it right on the head.

"What can I do about it?" I asked.

81

She eased back in her chair. "There's nothing anyone can do about it. You have to go with your emotions and don't let your head get in the way."

"But Charlie Gore is such a . . ."

"Animal."

"The word exactly."

She smiled, staring off at the ocean. "Sometimes a woman gets over a man like that. But more likely he'll leave you one fine day. Then you can get on with your life."

I had a couple more drinks with Rachel and we talked about what terrible creatures men are, and had some laughs and were feeling no pain. After we'd finished another pitcher of margaritas, she said:

"Odyssey, please do something for me. Don't tell the Holm-crofts where I am. I haven't done anything to them, and I won't do anything to them. Something's going on real funny with those two. I swear to you, all I want is to stay out of it."

What she was asking was just not possible. How could I take an assignment to find someone and then not report back to a client? That would be a terrible breach of ethics.

I shook my head.

She clutched my hand. "Please."

I was trying to be careful not to make any big decisions. I knew I had a buzz on. I thought about it for a moment, then I said: "Will you let me take a look around?"

"Why? What for?"

"Let's just say I'd like to satisfy my own curiosity about some things."

"All right, search the whole place, top to bottom, what do I care?"

I looked through the hall closets, the cabinets in the living room, the cupboards in the kitchen and the pantry, the trash, the laundry bins. Upstairs were three bedrooms, two bathrooms, and a study. Closets packed with clothes. A dressing room packed with more clothes. Raymond Pendergast must have had fifty pairs of shoes. Rachel had half a dozen.

Then I went down into the garage and checked out her car, glove box, under the seats, in the trunk.

I found no gun, no trench coat, no barbiturates to drug the cat.

I went back to the little room at the west end of the house. Rachel was sitting at the window, a margarita glass in one hand and half a pitcher of margaritas in the other. She was staring out at the ocean; a syrupy red sun was cutting into a huge fog bank.

She held up her glass, sloshing her drink. "What a wonderful drink, the margarita. It's the only thing I ever drink. Never get a hangover with a margarita. Never ever. It's the salt and the lime juice. Besides, when I drink them, I hear Mexican music playing—well, what did you decide? You going to keep my secret?"

"I can't promise you anything, but I'll do my best. My boss may force me to tell her. I'll call you and let you know."

She gave me the number there at Pendergast's place.

"Who is this Raymond Pendergast?" I asked.

"Someone who loves me," she said. "Someone who I'm fond of."

She smiled a crooked smile. "Have another. I've been sitting here thinking, Odyssey. Something happened that maybe you ought to know about. The morning after I was shot at, when I was packing up, I got a call."

"From who?"

"From somebody who said I should never mention his name. What if it was that somebody who sent the cat, and that same somebody fired a gun at me?"

"Who?"

"Man named Preston Chang. He used to be Mo Holmcroft's partner. They had a falling out, oh, about three or four months ago. Then he completely disappeared. About a week before Mo dumped me, Preston Chang showed up at Lemming's Lounge. He tried to put the make on me. Even though things with me and Mo weren't going so hot, I thought it was funny him trying to make time with me, know what I mean?"

"Go on."

"I gave him the old buzz off, and so he tried a different tack—

he tried buying some information. He wanted to know why Mo was selling this property and that stock, and liquidating everything. I didn't even know what the word meant, I had to look it up later. Means 'turn to cash.' What do I know from that stuff? I told him again to buzz. He got real mad and called me a name. You want to know what I think?"

"Preston Chang shot at you so that you'd run and not be around to deny sending Holmcroft a dead cat, shooting at him, and so on."

"That's right. And so you know what else I think? I think he and Mrs. Holmcroft are in on something."

"What makes you say that?"

"When he was asking me all this stuff, he kept saying, 'That property belongs just as much to his wife, so if he tries to leave the country that would be stealing.' If the two of them are in on something together, then she might have hired you to find me, so it would look like they really wanted me, see, when really they're planning something big and they want to blame it on me."

"Like what?" I wasn't buying any of this.

"Like I don't know what. That's why I'm so scared. I don't know anything that's going on. I tell you what, Odyssey. I've got a few bucks saved. I can sell some of my good jewelry. I'll pay you to find out the truth. Chang's a regular customer of a friend of mine—Molly Tens. She's—you know—in the business. She lives on Bush Street near Franklin, up over a pizza shop. She'll tell you what a weird number he is. He's setting me up for something, I can feel it. Find Preston Chang and make him tell you the truth."

"I can't take two clients at a time, it wouldn't be ethical."

"Is it ethical for you to tell them where I am so they can come and kill me?"

She had me there. "No," I said. "Not if that's really what they want to do."

I checked my watch. It was after six. "I have to go," I said.

She walked with me to the front door. She was a bit unsteady.

I was pretty sober by then. Tears were coming down her cheeks again.

At the door she said, "Don't betray me, Odyssey. In a couple of days I'll leave town and nobody'll ever see me again. Just give me two lousy days."

"I'll try," I said.

She gave me a little sisterly hug. I went down the steps and up the block and got into my car and started her up. As I pulled away from the curb, I caught a glimpse of a black Nissan Z in my mirror at the intersection behind.

Good old Charlie Gore.

I crested a small hill, made a quick U-turn, and hit the gas. I shot back over the hill and saw the Z pulling up in front of Pendergast's house. He must have seen me, because he suddenly accelerated, tires squealing, and shot around the corner.

I went after him. It took me maybe fifteen seconds to make it to the corner. I made my turn and shot up a hill and down the other side, heading toward the ocean. But he had already made the turn onto the Great Highway that runs along the beach. He could have gone right or left. I guessed he'd gone right, made the turn on a yellow light, and headed up toward the Cliff House.

But there was no black Z to be seen.

TEN

∎

I stopped and had some strong black coffee at a coffee shop behind the Opera House. Then I called Mr. Frampton at home and said I'd like to meet with him as soon as possible. I told him I'd found Rachel Collins and before I made my report to Mrs. Holmcroft, I wanted his advice. He said I should file my report and go and see her. I said I had to talk to him first. I said it was urgent and I couldn't say what I had to say on the phone. He grumbled, but said to come on up.

Mr. Frampton lives in an apartment high up on Twin Peaks. He bitches about the rent, but I always suspected he owned the building. I parked my car on the street. A strong, cold, gusting wind was bringing in the fog.

Mr. Frampton's building had a dozen apartments. Out in front was a little fountain with blue water gurgling in it. A circle of bird-of-paradise plants surrounded it. They look like long-necked birds with orange heads. I pushed the button to 2A and Mr. Frampton buzzed me in. I stiffened up and tried to look as sober as I could look.

I took the stairs to the second floor. Mr. Frampton was waiting for me in the hall wearing an embroidered robe over his silk shirt. He had his curved pipe in the pocket. He smoked a pipe only when he was trying to look intellectual, so I knew he must have a visitor. Someone he wanted to impress.

"This better be important, Odyssey," he said.

He showed me into his apartment. Mr. Frampton had the place done in Art Deco, very stylish and expensive. A black woman in a tweed suit, about fifty, was admiring his collection of African art. I happen to know the whole collection was made by a white kid who turns them out by the hundreds in his garage, but they do look authentic. Mr. Frampton has made up little stories about each one. How they're, say, used to cure diseases even Western medicine can't cure, or find water, or predict the weather with unfailing accuracy.

The woman was nicely proportioned, oval face, intelligent eyes. She had that well-groomed, professional look Mr. Frampton admires in a woman.

"Miss Gallagher, Miss Johns," Mr. Frampton said perfunctorily. Miss Johns gave me a cold look. "Very pleased to meet you," she said in a polite voice.

"This way," Mr. Frampton said to me, and led me into his study and closed the door.

The study was jam-packed from floor to ceiling with books on every subject from growing prize peaches to the history of gypsies in Brazil. Mr. Frampton took a speed-reading course in the late sixties and had since read over twelve thousand books. Or so he claimed.

"Well, what is it?" he said, folding his arms across his chest, half-sitting on his desk. He didn't invite me to sit down.

"Sorry to intrude like this, Mr. Frampton, I see you have a guest." A piece of concrete had formed in the pit of my stomach.

"Yes, yes, just get on with it."

"Well, as I told you on the phone, I've found Rachel Collins."

"Yes, and?"

"She had nothing to do with sending the dead cat."

"Is that so?" He always said that when he didn't believe you.

87

"It is so."

"How do you know that it is so?"

"I interrogated her."

He had a sour pucker on his lips. "And she told you she didn't do it?"

I nodded.

"And you believed her?"

"Yes."

His lips grew tight across his teeth. "We were hired, Miss Gallagher, to find her, not to let her know that she'd been found."

"I, ah, well you see, sir, I felt I should in this case."

"You felt. Miss Gallagher, you are a *professional*, and as a *professional* you have a code, and that code says that you will fulfill your contract with your client to the best of your ability in the most efficient manner possible."

He shook his head and looked toward the floor, as if it were painful to lay his eyes on a dolt like me and he didn't want to go on wasting his valuable time trying to straighten me out.

"But Mr. Frampton, you don't understand. All Rachel Collins wants to do is forget about Mr. Holmcroft and the whole mess. She said she's leaving town for good in a few days. I can assure Mrs. Holmcroft that I've found her and that she poses no threat. There's no reason for us to give her Rachel Collins's whereabouts. All Mrs. Holmcroft will do is cause a lot of trouble."

He raised his eyes and stared into my eyes for a long moment. "Have you been drinking, Miss Gallagher?"

"Drinking? Me?"

"You have been drinking, haven't you?"

"A little. Just to become more friendly with Rachel Collins, to get more information out of her."

He shook his head with disapproval. "Look, Miss Gallagher, we were hired by a client to do a job, a job we are licensed to do by the State of California. Our mission is to serve the public. We are not serving the public if we do not fulfill our contracts, is this clear?"

"It's clear," I said. I dreaded what was coming next.

"Now then," he said. "Here's what I want you to do. Go and report to the client immediately and tell her everything. Tell her you spoke to the woman. We must not try to conceal anything, but try to make it sound like it was *accidental*. Perhaps you had her under surveillance and she discovered you, or you knew she was in the neighborhood and you were canvassing and ran right into her—something like that. But you must give Mrs. Holmcroft Rachel Collins's address, that is what she paid for. Am I making myself clear on this?"

The concrete felt like it was rolling around. "It's perfectly clear."

"Go now, Miss Gallagher. Don't waste one moment." He opened the door.

On the way out, Miss Johns said, "Do you work for Hampton?"

"Yes. I'm an operative," I said.

"Oh." Her face brightened. I guess she had thought I was a girlfriend or something.

"Well, it was nice meeting you," she said cheerfully.

I stepped close to her and whispered in her ear, "Those masks are fake."

"I know," she whispered back.

I drove down Market Street to the office and called Mrs. Holmcroft from there. I told her I wanted to see her, that I had something important to discuss with her. She said she had to go out in an hour, but would be back by ten. I said I'd see her then.

I went over to the aikido dojo and had a light workout and tried to focus on what I was going to tell her and exactly how I was going to say it. My sensei said I seemed preoccupied, and that was not the way to do aikido. He put me to work with a high school student, Naomi Quade, a moody, intense girl who was getting ready to be tested for her black belt. She was smooth, efficient, artful, and I envied her grace and concentration. Spiritually, she was getting there. Spiritually, I was not.

I showered and put on my street clothes and left at nine-thirty. I drove over to Uncle Irving's. He wasn't home, but I knew where he hid his key, so I went in and got the dead cat out of his freezer, wrapped it in newspapers, and put it in a shopping bag. I left a note thanking him and promised to do my best to find a husband.

I arrived at the Holmcroft mansion exactly at two minutes after ten. The maid met me at the door and said Mrs. Holmcroft phoned and said she'd be a few minutes late. She showed me into the living room and closed the sliding doors. Someplace in the house someone was playing rock and roll music, sounded like the Grateful Dead. The kind of stuff I was crazy about when I was in college.

A moment later the door opened again and Conrad was standing there. He was wearing a plaid bathrobe over a black T-shirt with a skull on the front.

"Well, hello," I said. "I brought you the cat. You said you wanted to bury it."

He nodded and took the shopping bag with the cat in it and started to leave.

"Wait a minute, Conrad. Do you know whose cat it is?"

He shook his head. "I got to go," he said.

"Can't we talk for a minute?" He looked scared. He was shivering and I was trying not to spook him.

I said, "Can I speak with you, just for a minute?"

"What do you want?"

"I was wondering if you might have seen the cat before around here. Do you know who owns him?"

"I got to go," he said.

"Please, just a moment. Why won't you talk about the cat? Do you know who killed it?"

"I don't know anything."

"I want to help you," I said. "Something is bothering you. Can't I help?"

He just stared at me.

"You do want to find out who killed this poor animal, don't you?"

He nodded.

"Then tell me what you know."

"I d-don't know anything," he stammered, and ran off toward the back of the house.

I sat on the couch and wondered just what might be going on in the kid's head. Was he covering for someone? Or had he killed it himself? If he was covering, who was he covering for? His mother? If she had killed that cat, why had she called me in on the case?

I was still running all this around the labyrinth of my mind when Mrs. Holmcroft showed up, apologizing for being late. I rose to greet her, we shook hands, and we took our seats. I noticed a little ache forming right between my eyes.

Mrs. Holmcroft seemed ill at ease, as if she'd just had some worrisome news.

"I take it you've had some success," she said with a wan smile.

I said, "Rachel Collins did not leave that dead cat on your doorstep."

Her smile faded. She waited for me to go on.

"I ask you to trust me on this," I said. "She will not bother you or your husband again."

"You've spoken to her?"

"Listen, Mrs. Holmcroft—yes, I've spoken to her. She told me the whole story. She received a note from your husband via the chauffeur, just as you said. She has a temper, she went directly to the Marconi Club and confronted your husband. She fully admits it. But she knows she overreacted. She's very explosive, but she cools down quickly. As far as she's concerned the affair is over. If you wish to sue her, I will serve the papers on her. But I'd feel better, really I would, if you'd just let the matter drop."

"What else did she tell you?"

"That she and your husband are through for good. That she's going away and will never come back."

"She's a liar." Anger flared in her eyes.

"She said that one of your husband's business associates probably sent the cat."

"Which one?"

"Preston Chang."

"Believe me, Miss Gallagher, Preston Chang would not send a dead cat. He and my husband have had a falling out, but I know Preston Chang, and he definitely would not bother trying to scare us with a dead cat."

"I'm only reporting what she told me."

"How did you find her?"

"I located someone who knew her and I paid him a few dollars."

She gave me a cool, polite smile, with just the corners of her mouth. "I want her address."

An image of Mr. Frampton, bloated with rage, ushering me out the door of Frampton Investigations flashed through my mind. But then I thought of Rachel Collins, and there was really no point in Mrs. Holmcroft's knowing where she lived unless she wanted to make trouble and I just couldn't do it. I just couldn't.

"I'm afraid," I said, "I'm going to have to know more about why it's so important for you to find her."

"What do you think, Miss Gallagher, that I want to physically harm her in some way? That I'm going to get a gun and go over there and shoot her?" She laughed a coarse little laugh.

"No, of course not," I said.

"The reason I want to know her whereabouts is frankly none of your damn business." Her face turned hard as flint.

I said, "I can positively assure you she isn't any threat to either you or your family."

"I demand you give me that address, Miss Gallagher, or I will have my lawyers take your two-bit detective agency apart."

"I'm sorry, I can't tell you."

She stood up suddenly. "Then our association has ended," she said.

Better to be poisoned in the blood than in one's principles, some great genius once said.

Having stuck by my principles, I felt good. Heroic, almost. The trouble was, Mr. Frampton might take exception. I had one chance to prove that I was right, and that was to find the person

92

who had sent the dead cat, and the only good candidate I had at the moment was Preston Chang.

I drove over to Bush and Franklin and found the pizza joint and the apartment where Rachel Collins said I'd find Molly Tens, Preston Chang's "girlfriend." On the door to apartment A it said, "Molly" with one of those happy face smiles. I rang the bell.

A moment later I heard a woman's voice:

"Fred? I told you I can't see you this week."

"It's not Fred," I said. "I'm a friend of Rachel's."

Nothing. I knocked. "Hello. Did you hear me?" I called.

"I can't see anyone right now. Go away."

"Here's my card," I said, slipping it under the door. A moment later: "What do you want?"

"I'd just like to ask you a few questions. It'll only take a minute."

"I don't want to see anyone right now. Come back next week."

"It's important that we talk now."

"I'm sorry."

I knocked on the door some more, and called out her name, but she wouldn't answer. A young woman across the hall opened the door. She wore a sweatshirt and a pair of shorts and was rubbing her eyes like she just woke up.

"What the fuck you doing there?" she said.

"Molly won't open the door."

"Leave her alone. Some dude gave her a going-over."

"What dude?"

"Some john, how the hell should I know? I'm sure she'd appreciate it if you just went away."

She went back into her apartment.

I got out my lock-picking kit and went to work on the lock. It took me a couple of minutes, but it finally popped open.

I stepped into the darkened apartment. A woman in a robe appeared in a doorway, the light behind her. She had a large kitchen knife in her hand.

"Get out of here."

"Not until you answer a few questions."

93

"You sure don't take no for an answer, do you?"

"Rachel Collins is terribly frightened. She said you were a friend. She needs your help."

"If it gets back to him that I've been talking to people, there's no telling what he might do to me."

I couldn't see her well in the dim light, but I could tell she was lowering the knife.

"Listen, Molly, Rachel thinks Preston Chang might have tried to kill her."

"If he had tried to kill her, she would now be dead. He's a very efficient man."

"Did he beat you?"

"You want to see?"

She clicked on a light. Her face was a mass of black and blue lumps. One eye was swollen shut. It look hideous. She clicked off the light.

"Why did he do it?" I said.

"He wanted to know where Rachel is. He's got it into his head that she's about to run off with Holmcroft. He thinks Holmcroft is going to take some of his money with him. He's a madman when it comes to money. I couldn't tell him where Rachel is because I don't know. But if I had known, I'd have told him. You bet I would have."

"I'm so sorry. Did you call the police?"

"Somebody like me gets beat up, what do they give a shit?"

"Just one more thing—where can I find him?"

"Nobody knows. He's afraid people are trying to get him. But if you keep looking, he'll hear about it. Then watch out, he'll find you."

ELEVEN

∎

Charlie's black Z car was parked in the driveway. I went up the stairs and into the apartment. Charlie was sitting at my kitchen table eating a plate of spaghetti, a paper towel covering his chest, his mouth smeared with tomato sauce.

"Welcome home, Genius," he said. "Want some spa-gett?"

He gestured toward a large bowl of it already mixed with tomato sauce and meatballs the size of oranges. I picked the bowl up, balancing it on my palm. He looked at me with a quizzical expression. As if he didn't know why I might be ticked off.

"What's this?" he said. "What?"

"Your flunky was here when the call came in from Mr. Michael."

"Yeah? So?"

"So your flunky called you and told you, and then you followed me from Mr. Michael's to Rachel's." I raised the bowl up over his head. "Don't try to deny it."

"Come on, Genius, so I followed you, so big deal. We're practically going steady. We shouldn't have no secrets."

Whoosh, I dumped the bowl on his head, covering his eyes and ears. He sat there unmoving. Spaghetti and sauce dripped down into his lap. "This is not a kindness," he said, his voice hollow, coming out of the bowl.

I went into the bedroom. He'd brought in half a dozen boxes of junk and his clothes were in a large pile in the middle of the room. I picked up one of the boxes, took it out on the deck, and dumped it into the driveway. When I turned around, he was standing in the doorway wiping his face with a towel. His shirt and pants were stained red.

"What are you trying to say, Genius? You mad at me?"

I marched past him and took another box. It was full of *Playboy* magazines. I headed for the deck.

"That's a very valuable collection," he said.

I dumped them in the driveway. When I turned around he was blocking the way back into the bedroom.

"Don't make me hurt you," I said.

He smiled a crooked damn smile. "You gonna throw me off the deck or what? Look, Odyssey, sweetheart, we're both on the same side here. How you think it feels that you know where this Rachel Collins chick is and you don't tell me, your lover and roomie?"

"Get out of my way."

He stepped aside and I went on in. I picked up another box. More magazines. *Penthouse. Male. Oui.* The man was a voyeur.

He said, "If making a mess of my property makes you feel good, go right ahead and destroy away, but before you do you ought to stop and think that maybe what I found out about this case might be of some interest to you."

I stopped. "Like what?"

"You going to act like a civilized person here?"

"What about the case?"

"Let's have a drink and calm down, then I'll tell all."

I didn't say anything. He went out into the kitchen and got a bottle of red wine off the table and came back into the bedroom

96

with two glasses and poured us each a little. I put down the box of his magazines.

"*Salud,*" he said. We drank.

"Okay, I'm calm," I said. I wasn't the least bit calm, but I can act calm as an oyster when I want to.

He smiled a sheepish little smile and said, "After I saw you leave Rachel's I had to make sure that was her place, so I went up and knocked on the door. I gave her my real estate salesman card and told her I was trying to make a listing. She was a little sloshed, and told me to take a hike. So I went to my car and got on my cellular and called Mrs. Holmcroft."

"Why'd you do that?"

"Because I was supposed to report to her if I ran into Rachel Collins."

I didn't believe a word of this. "Mr. Holmcroft told you to report to *Mrs.* Holmcroft?"

"That's right."

"That's odd."

"I thought so, too. I think he wants her and Rachel to mix it up, I don't know why. The guy's a schemer. He's really worried about someone else—only I'm not supposed to say who that someone is."

I had the distinct impression he wanted me to ask him who that was, so he could play games with me. I wasn't playing. I said: "Preston Chang."

"Oh, so you know?" He seemed disappointed.

I smiled. I put down the glass and picked up another box of his junk and headed for the deck.

"Hey! Haven't we made up?"

"What made you think that?"

I dumped the stuff off the deck and when I turned around he was standing in the doorway with his chest bared, beating on it:

"Aaaaaaaaaa, Ahhhhhhhhh, aaaaaaaaaa."

"Tarzan, right?" I said. "You're crazy, know that?"

"I love you, I want you, I must have you!" He started for me, hunched forward, his arms outstretched.

I said: "You want another bump on the head?"

He halted.

"Just one kiss," he said.

"I don't kiss jerks."

"Wait. Hold it a minute here. I'm a jerk because I took advantage of some information Fingers just happened to overhear, huh? Is that what makes me a jerk? You've got to admit you'd have done the same thing I did, things was vice versa."

I said nothing.

"Tell the honest truth. Some info just falls in your lap, you're going to take advantage, yes or no?"

He had me there.

He grinned. "Okay, so I took advantage. By way of apology, I should have brought you a big box of roses. Instead, I got you this."

He reached into his pocket and took out a heart-shaped pendant. Gold plate.

"Like it?" he asked.

It probably only cost a few dollars. It had "Charlie Loves Odyssey" engraved on it. It's the thought that counts. Martin never got me anything, unless it was a big holiday, and then I had to remind him ten times.

Charlie kissed me and I let him. He tasted of tomato sauce and red wine. He put his arms around me and he smelled strongly of musk.

"Tell me you love me, Genius."

"I hate your guts, Charlie Gore."

He kissed me again and I felt myself turning into a soft pile of lust.

It was past midnight. Charlie and I had made love for I don't know how long. I was pretty much spent and feeling relaxed and tingly all over. I helped him clean up his stuff in the driveway and bring it back in.

Now Charlie was sitting up and drinking beer and watching a Bogie flick on TV. I was wishing he'd get amorous again, but there wasn't much chance of that, so I got up and went into the kitchen and made some herb tea. A neighbor on the other side of the fence that runs along the property line must have been having a party; I could hear the chatter of voices and some music.

I was thinking of a dead cat and a beat-up whore, and what Mr. Frampton was going to do to me for not obeying orders. I didn't think he'd fire me. But then again he might. If he did, what would I do? Go into business for myself? Go to another agency? I didn't want to go to another agency. I didn't want to be in business for myself.

It had been a hell of a week so far. I messed up my job and my private life as well. I sure blew it with Martin. I wondered how it might have been if we had gotten married. Would we have had children? I wondered, too, why I had let Charlie make love to me when I should have known Martin might come back at any moment. Had I lost my mind? Was it for revenge because Martin hadn't come to me the night before? Was it because I didn't really love him and my making love with Charlie was my sub-conscious straightening things out for me?

Wondering wasn't getting me anywhere.

I read a little poetry written by a Berkeley poet, Septimus VII. He's in his sixties now. He has long white hair, a face that looks like it was chiseled in alabaster, and eyes that burn with the righteous indignation you usually find in a twenty-year-old. His lead poem in the collection called *Post Mortem Modern* is called "Ill Wind."

> *Winds, winds, winds, of no-thought*
> *is all it is*
> *no-thought, and no-thought, and more no-thought*
> *but what do you expect when you turn on your set?*
> *Plato?*

Not a very good poem, but I liked the sentiment. A commentary on the vacuousness of television. Septimus hates television, I know. I did a job for him once. His wife had run away with another poet and he hired me to find her. I found her and talked her into going back to Septimus and the next day she put a .32 bullet in him. Hit him in the left testicle.

> *Tessie puts the thing in her hand*
> *and looks at me, sad, resolute*
> *Bang!*
> *How could she love me more?*

I chuckled. Septimus tried so hard. He always cheers me up. He takes himself so seriously I could never tell him that, though.

Suddenly Charlie, wearing only his boxer shorts, burst into the kitchen: "They just flashed it on TV—Holmcroft's been gunned."

"Ha, ha, very funny."

"Not that funny. He's dead. I'm gonna go see what I can find out."

It wasn't possible. Couldn't be. I went into the bedroom. Charlie was hurriedly getting dressed.

"You aren't kidding," I said. "Who did it?"

"Didn't say. But let's take a guess. I'll bet she has red hair."

I lowered myself into a chair. Could I have been this wrong?

"You coming?" Charlie asked.

"Coming?"

"Come on, Genius, don't you see what this means? Morrison Holmcroft hired me to protect him and now he's dead. You got any idea what this is going to do to my reputation? And what about your reputation?"

"My reputation?" I didn't quite get what he said because I was replaying the interview I had with Rachel Collins. I was so sure she'd meant it when she said she was through with the whole affair. Or maybe I was a gullible fool.

On the TV Bogie was pressing Sidney Greenstreet to tell him where the Japanese were going to attack, but Sidney wasn't talking.

"Don't you get it?" Charlie said. "When you found her she probably figured Holmcroft was going to do something to her, so she just figured to get him first." He threw me a pair of jeans and a shirt. "Well, Genius?"

"If she did it," I said, "I'll track her down to the ends of the earth and bring her back and strap her into the gas chamber myself."

TWELVE

■

We got into Charlie's car. It was raining lightly. The streets were nearly deserted. The 300 ZX throbbed with power. I ached to drive it. He hot-rodded it. He shifted smoothly, but his clutch work was off. But you can never tell a man anything about his driving. They all think they're Mario Andretti.

We went down Lombard and turned up the hill on Gough, which is one-way, going south. We parked around the corner from the Marconi Club. Before we got out of the car, I said: "One thing, Charlie. Let's not say anything about Rachel."

"Ooooo, withholding evidence is naughty-naughty."

"I mean it, Charlie. Something isn't right here. I want to hear Rachel's side of it first."

"Okay, whatever you say."

He kissed me to seal the bargain. How gallant.

The Marconi Club is in what used to be a mansion on a street full of mansions. Most of them have been torn down to build apartment buildings. The club sits back from the street about seventy-five feet, but the apartment buildings on either side were built out to the street. A wide walk leads up to the club's front door, which has one of those canopies over it. There's a waist-high hedge on either side of the walk and a row of imitation gas lights line the walk.

A couple of cop cars sat in the street blinking red lights. A handful of gawkers stood around. No TV people around, so the excitement was over.

We started up the walkway to the front door. An outline of a man was painted on the walk about twenty feet from the street. The walk had a dark stain on it. Blood.

A cop approached. "Nothing to see, folks, just keep moving."

Charlie said, "We weren't doing nothing."

"I didn't say you were," the cop said. "Just move along."

"How'd this happen?" I asked.

He sighed. "Why don't you go home and watch it on TV like everyone else?"

"Our TV is broken" I said, giving him a friendly, sexy smile. "Did they catch the killer?"

"She got away."

"She?"

"A woman. She had a red Toyota. She parked over there." He pointed to a space across the street. "The victim came out of the club, walked up to here, saw her, turned to run, and she shot him twice in the back. Now will you move along? Why don't you just read all about it in the *Chronicle* tomorrow?"

I took Charlie's arm and we started back for the car. Somebody called my name: "Odyssey! Odyssey Gallagher!"

I knew the voice. Detective Sergeant Tomas. Pronounced like the Spanish, Toe-MAS.

I glanced around and there he was waving to me from the front door of the club. He was about fifty-five, pale, heavy, war-weary. He wore his black-framed glasses low on his nose.

Charlie and I walked toward him. As we got closer, I could see his narrowed eyes going from me to Charlie. Sergeant Tomas used to be friendly to me, but then when I got lucky and solved a case he was working on, he became hostile. It seems at the very moment I'd found the murder weapon—a belt that belonged to the killer—the good sergeant was booking the wrong man into city jail. The papers made a big deal about it.

"Well, if it isn't Odyssey-the-brain-Gallagher and Charles-no-brain-Gore. Not good company for a good little girl like you, Odyssey."

"I have an adventurous spirit, Sergeant. What can we do for you?"

"I'd like to talk to you for a couple of minutes. Come this way."

"We haven't done anything," Charlie said.

"I'll bet," Sergeant Tomas said. We went through a sort of lobby into the bar. A couple of other detectives were taking statements from a few employees and some customers. The sergeant offered us a seat.

"Now then, what's your connection to this?"

"What do you mean?" I asked. "We were out for our evening constitutional."

"That's right," Charlie said. "Evening constitutional."

Sergeant Tomas smiled. "What's your connection to Morrison Holmcroft?"

"Who's Morrison Holmcroft?" Charlie said.

"Oh, I see we're going to play games," Sergeant Tomas said. He turned to me. "Morrison Holmcroft a client of yours?"

"I'm a private detective, Sergeant, as you well know. I can't go around saying who is or is not a client, that's privileged information."

"That has not been so ruled by the California Supreme Court," he said. "You aren't a lawyer, you have no client privilege."

"No matter," I said. "You know no ethical private investigator would discuss who his or her clients are or are not."

"What about you?" he said to Charlie. "He one of yours?"

Charlie yawned. "I don't know nobody or nothing, and if I didn't *not* know nothing, I'd forget what it was I was supposed to know. You know how it is, right, Sergeant?"

Sergeant Tomas shook his head. He knew Charlie was fooling

around and he didn't like it. Sergeant Tomas said, "Either of you know what the penalty is for obstruction of justice in a murder case?"

"No," I said.

"Same as accessory after the fact," Charlie said. "Eight to ten, you do maybe a nickel with good deeds."

"You hear that?" Sergeant Tomas said to me.

"Yes," I said.

"You two fish don't seem to understand that I got an important man here who's been dumped on the sidewalk and I got a hot suspect and I want to find her fast."

Charlie yawned.

"Perhaps if you could tell us who it is you're looking for," I said. "Then maybe we could help you and tell you just exactly what you want to know."

"We've got eleven witnesses. Apparently it was a woman called Rachel Collins. A couple of witnesses saw her assault Holmcroft three weeks ago right here in the club."

"Did anyone get the license number of the getaway car?"

"The doorman got it. RACHEL C. We're looking for the car now."

"I don't know her," I said. "Do you, Charles?"

"Never heard of her. Can we go now, Sergeant?"

"No. First you give what you know."

"Why, Sergeant," I said, trying to sound as amazed as possible, "you mean you don't think we're being straight with you?"

"I never met a private eye that gave me the straight scoop if I asked him—or her—for the time of day."

"Come on, it's getting late," Charlie said. "Me and Odyssey got things to do, you know." He winked. "You must remember how it was." Charlie was trying to be funny. "Can we go, please?"

Sergeant Tomas bared his teeth. "I'd love to lock the two of you up and throw away the key," he said, pushing his glasses back up into position at the top of his nose. "Rachel Collins has been missing for three weeks—we've already been to her apartment. Where is she?"

105

"How would I know?" I said.

"Yeah, how would she know?" Charlie said.

Sergeant Tomas glared at Charlie, then at me. "I find out different, you two are going to do some down time, got my meaning?"

"Yes, sir," I said.

Charlie just nodded.

"Okay," Sergeant Tomas said. "Get out of here."

We walked out the front door and headed toward the street and there, standing in the middle of the sidewalk, was Mr. Frampton.

He was pacing back and forth with his hands behind his back. I could see he had his pajamas on under his coat. He gave Charlie a nasty look. He walked along with us.

"What are you doing with *him*?" he said to me.

I shrugged. He scowled. He didn't like Charlie much.

Mr. Frampton said, "We may be in serious difficulty. You better tell me everything that happened tonight. As your employer, I have the right to expect that you will carry out your assignments as you are instructed to. Did you make a full disclosure to Mrs. Holmcroft of everything you found—including Miss Collins's address?"

"No, I didn't. I still have a conscience, Mr. Frampton."

"She has a conscience," Charlie said, grinning. He had a loathing for bosses.

Mr. Frampton said, "I want a written report—a complete, detailed, written report on exactly what happened between you and our client. I want that report on my desk by noon tomorrow, is that clear?"

"All right, Mr. Frampton."

We walked another half a block in silence. Then I said, "How'd you know I'd be here, Mr. Frampton?"

"I called you when I heard the news. You weren't home. Where else would you be?" At the corner, he said, "Whatever happened between you and the client is over. There's been a murder. Please stay out of it, Odyssey. I wouldn't want to see you hurt."

106

Whenever he called me Odyssey, he was either drunk or being fatherly.

"I'll be careful," I said. He gave my arm a little pat.

Mr. Frampton crossed the street and got into his car. Charlie and I walked to the Z.

"You think she still might be at Pendergast's place?" Charlie said.

"One way to find out."

"If she shot Holmcroft, she may see us coming and start blasting away."

"Exciting occupation we're in, isn't it?"

He slammed the gear into low and we took off like a shot, then he slammed second and squeezed around the next corner and fishtailed up Sacramento Street. Poor Charlie sure could have used a driving lesson.

THIRTEEN

■

We drove over to Geary Boulevard and headed west. The fog had rolled in and the streetlights glowed eerily. The wet pavement shimmered in Charlie's headlights.

Charlie said, "You know something, Genius, I hate to point this out, but Rachel Collins is not a client."

"I know she isn't."

"Then might you please tell me why we're protecting her?"

"I think of her as a friend."

Charlie shook his head and made a gurgling sound in his throat.

I turned around and looked over my shoulder to see whether we were being followed. There was one car half a block behind. Charlie glanced in his mirror, then dropped down into third gear and punched the accelerator. We shot up a small hill and made a quick right, tires squealing. The car stayed with us.

"Hang on!" Charlie said, downshifting again. The car fish-tailed up the block, the engine roaring.

"Having fun?" I asked.

He made the next left, drifting across two lanes, and shot past the Kabuki Theater. At the next corner we made another left through an amber light. Whoever had been behind us was gone.

"Goddamn cops," Charlie spat.

We went over to Fell and through the park, then cut over to Fulton, made a left, and headed toward the ocean. The fog was thick and swirling. We found Hickock Drive and made a right, headed up over a little hill, and cruised past Pendergast's place. No lights on. Nobody around on the street. I had half expected the place to be surrounded with cops. Charlie drove around the corner and parked.

"We've got no strong reason for going in there," he said. His voice was low. ·

"Aren't you curious, Charlie?"

"Not in the least."

"Then wait here."

"You're pretty sure about her, aren't you?"

"She might have killed Holmcroft. She might have had a good reason. But I don't think she has any reason to harm me. I can't give you objective proof of that. Sometimes you just have to trust. Besides, if she did kill him, she wouldn't hang around here."

I got out of the car. A cold wind blew from the ocean a block away. I felt scared and excited at the same time. Pumped up. Alive. I started toward the house. Charlie caught up with me.

"Thanks for coming along, Charlie."

"I know it's dumb, but after all, it's a man's duty to protect his woman." He put his arm around me.

I shook him off. "You're more scared than I am."

"Who's scared?" He opened his jacket and took out a big handgun. "Meet Wilbur. Wilbur, Odyssey."

"Bringing that is not such a good idea," I said.

"You know, there's no substitute for a gun when you need to shoot somebody, that's what I always say." He stuck it in his belt.

"Just so long as you don't use it," I said.

109

"Not unless I have to."

Put a gun in a man's hand and he turns into Clint Eastwood.

A car came by, loud rock and roll playing on the radio. Its taillights disappeared in the fog.

"You got a permit for that cannon?" I asked.

"Sort of," he said.

"How can you 'sort of' have a permit?"

"I didn't get it through the usual channels."

"But it's good?"

"It's semi-good."

Whatever the hell that meant. Charlie had fog between the ears sometimes.

We went up the front stairs onto Pendergast's front porch. The house was dark. We crept to the door.

"You gonna knock?" Charlie whispered.

"No."

I tried the door. Locked. I motioned for him to follow me. We tiptoed back down the stairs and went around to the side of the house, to the driveway. We went up the driveway and I took out my lock-picking kit.

"This is gonna be good," Charlie whispered.

I worked the lock for about ten seconds, there was a clicking sound, and the garage door popped open. I had this lock down cold.

"Hey, Genius, I'm impressed."

"Shhhhhhh."

He lifted the door and we slipped under and closed the door behind us. The Jag was there, but no red Toyota. We checked the Jag; it was locked. He shined a flashlight in and around it. Nothing unusual about it.

"Where's her car?" Charlie whispered.

"I guess she's making a run for it."

"So she did it, huh? How about that?"

"I didn't say she did anything."

He shined a flashlight onto the pavement where her car had been and found a spot of oil. He bent down and touched it and sniffed it.

110

"What are you looking for?" I asked.

"I'm not looking *for* anything. I'm looking *at* what's here."

"And what's here?"

"Her car has a leaky crankcase."

"So?"

"So I'm just telling you. It has a leaky crankcase."

"Big deal. Let's go upstairs."

He looked toward the door. He didn't seem too enthused about the idea. I went over and tried the door. It was unlocked.

"Pssst," I said to Charlie.

He was still testing the oil with his fingers like he was really onto something. Whatever it was, I had no idea. I guessed he didn't want to go into the house and was stalling. I went back over to him.

"You want to wait here?" I said.

"What are you saying, I'm chicken?"

"If it clucks, has feathers, and lays eggs . . ."

He stood up and hiked up his pants. He took his gun out and gestured in the direction of the door. "Okay, let's go." I went in first.

It was dark inside. Charlie clicked on his flashlight. Nothing in the basement. The wine cellar cage was locked. We went upstairs. With just the flashlight the kitchen seemed even larger than when I'd been here earlier. There was a center counter, lots of small appliances, pots and pans and utensils hanging everywhere, and a large stove with a huge copper hood, everything shiny and sparkling.

I checked the cozy little room where Rachel and I had been drinking that afternoon. Our empty margarita glasses were still sitting on the bar. I went back into the kitchen. Charlie motioned for me to have a look at the pantry.

On the floor, just inside the door, was a smashed bottle. The liquid made a large, sticky puddle. Two small aperitif glasses sat on the counter. I picked up the broken pieces of the bottle and read the soggy label. Chartreuse. I doubted some obscure French liqueur would be Rachel's drink.

I looked at Charlie. He shrugged. He didn't seem interested in it in the least.

I followed him through the dining room and into the living room. No one there. Charlie admired the tapestry with the hunt scene. One of the ashtrays had a pipe in it. I couldn't remember if it had been there before or not.

The stairs to the bedrooms were off the foyer. We paused at the bottom to listen. No one snoring. We took off our shoes and kept to the sides of the stairs as we made our way up.

At the top of the stairs was a central hallway. The doors to the three bedrooms and the study were open. Nobody there. I checked the master bedroom. The place was a mess. Clothing scattered around, drawers thrown open, blankets and sheets on the floor.

"What do you make of this?" I whispered.

"Guess she packed in a hurry."

I clicked on the light. Charlie looked at me.

"Shining flashlights around tells the neighbors something's fishy. If a neighbor sees a light on, so what?"

"Got a point there."

I looked in the closet and found a couple of skirts, blouses, one blue blazer. In the bureau was a pair of panty hose, some costume jewelry, one brown shoe with a spiked heel, one running shoe with no tread worn off. Nothing in the wastepaper basket but a few tissues and a used-up eyebrow pencil.

I checked the vanity. Lots of beauty paraphernalia. Curlers and creams and combs and brushes. An arsenal in the love-as-war game. A couple of used towels. Lots of eye pencils, mascara, lipsticks, perfumes: Ode to Triumph, City Night, Born to be Wild. I couldn't resist a sniff of Born to be Wild. It was wild.

Charlie said, "Let's split."

"What do you make of this?" I asked. "Why did she just take her clothes?"

"What do you mean?"

"She left her cosmetics."

He shrugged. "Maybe she forgot them."

"Would you forget your he-man deodorant?"

112

He shrugged again. "If I was running, and that's what I think she was doing. She shot the guy, came back here, picked up everything she could jam into a suitcase or two, and took off."

"I don't know, Charlie."

"I'm going to see if there's any beer in the fridge."

I took a quick look in the study. The usual stuff. Pendergast's desk had a checkbook in it. Just ordinary entries. Clothing stores, charge accounts. I didn't know exactly what I was looking for. The bathroom seemed undisturbed. Everything was pretty much as it had been when I'd searched the place that afternoon.

I went back downstairs and found Charlie sitting on the counter drinking a beer. He'd turned on the pantry light.

"Guinness Stout, want one?"

"No thanks."

"There's Heineken, some domestic lights. Take your pick."

I slid up on the counter next to him. I said, "What do you make of that broken bottle in there?"

"Probably left it for the maid to clean up. You know how these rich sons-a-bitches are."

"Chartreuse isn't exactly your everyday drink. Perhaps Pendergast knew whoever was coming over and bought it special."

"Maybe," Charlie said. "But it looks to me like this guy has every kind of hooch imaginable."

"Whoever he was going to drink with, it wasn't Rachel. She said she only drank margaritas. They made music in her head."

"People sometimes switch drinks."

"I don't think an obscure French liqueur would catch her fancy. You sip a liqueur. Rachel doesn't sip, she gulps."

He shrugged. I said, "Why would they go in her little car when they had the Jag?"

"Don't know. Have you seen enough?"

"Yes."

"Let's get out of here."

We went back down through the garage. Charlie lifted the door for me and I scooted under it. There was somebody standing in the driveway. I froze. Then I looked up slowly.

It was Sergeant Tomas.

113

FOURTEEN

∎

After reading us our rights and relieving Charlie of his friend Wilbur, the police handcuffed us and put us in the back of a patrol car. A wire mesh screen separated the front from the back. The back seat smelled like someone had thrown up in it not too long ago. A uniformed officer sat in the front seat smoking a cigarette. Sergeant Tomas and half a dozen other cops went into Pendergast's place with the crime lab people.

Charlie said, "We didn't lose them when you said we did."

"I guess not."

"So it was your fault, us getting nabbed."

"How do you get that? You were driving."

"You were the lookout."

"You were the driver."

"But you were the lookout."

"What if I hadn't been in the car?"

"Then I would have been my own lookout."

"If I'd been driving, I'd have spotted the tail."

To that he said, "Humph."

We were quiet for a moment. He just sat there looking out the window. The cop just sat smoking.

I asked Charlie if he'd like to hear a poem.

"I'll bet I'm gonna hear it whether I like it or not."

I recited one of Septimus VII's favorites:

> *All is not despair*
> *All is not despair*
> *All is not despair*
> *All is not . . .*

"Well, Charlie, what do you think?"

Charlie grumbled. "Genius, if that's poetry, I'm the pope in Rome."

"Septimus had just passed through his Zen phase," I said. "You can clearly see the Zen notion of nothing, not as nihilism, but as negating despair. I know it's a dumb poem, but he was trying hard."

"Bah," Charlie said. "All is not despair. All is sex."

Charlie Gore, philosopher.

I said, "I guess they're going to know Rachel was staying here. We might as well say so."

"I'm not gonna say nothing about nothing, even if they use a rubber hose. I mean, I never give the cops nothing. My lawyer'll get me out. They're just wasting their time trying to get me to talk."

"Same here," I said.

"We'll see," he said.

I took that as a challenge.

Sergeant Tomas came out of the house and gave a signal to the cop sitting in the car with us. The cop started up the car and drove us downtown, where they booked us on a breaking and entering rap and accessory to murder after the fact. I knew they'd never make the second charge stick. They were just trying to scare us.

115

I told myself there was no reason to be scared. But still, my palms were sweaty.

The jail cops took my wallet, keys, handbag, belt, shoelaces, Swiss army knife, and lock-picking kit. I told them I used them for working my nails. The jail cops had a big laugh over that.

They let me have a phone call. I called Mr. Frampton and woke him up. He did not sound happy to hear from me. I explained what happened. He said he warned me. I asked him if he'd get me out. He said he'd think about it. The age of chivalry is as dead as a pickled oyster.

They took me to a cell. I got a single. It had a cot, a toilet, and lots of paper shredded up on the floor. Looked like the previous occupant had nothing else to do but shred paper. The woman in the next cell was moaning like hell. Down the hall a TV was on. Godzilla was eating Detroit.

I paced around and contemplated my sins. I kept my ki flowing out. I hated being in a cell when I could be tracking down a killer. But it did give me a chance to think some things through. I was still pacing when they came for me at five-fifteen in the morning and took me to a small interrogation room.

Sergeant Tomas paced up and down the interview room. A female officer in uniform stood by, I guess to bear witness that I wasn't being raped.

"Now then, young lady, let's hear it," Tomas said.

"I resent being called 'young lady,' " I said. "I find it demeaning and sexist."

The woman officer grinned. Tomas shot her a hard glance. He'd had a tough night. He had sacks under his eyes big enough to farm potatoes. I knew what was stressing him. Holmcroft was upper crust, and in San Francisco they don't like it when someone of the upper crust gets killed, and the big shots were going to want poor Sergeant Tomas to come up with the killer quickly.

He took a deep breath. He wheezed. I wasn't going to let him push me around, but I felt for the guy, I really did.

He put his hands on his hips. "Miss Gallagher—you don't mind if I call you 'Miss' do you?—Or do I have to call you 'Mizzzzzz'?"

116

"I think you have a problem with women, Sergeant. I really do. I'm a grown-up person, just like you. Why don't you call me Odyssey?"

He looked a little confused for the moment, appealing mutely to the woman in uniform, who shrugged and folded her arms across her chest and leaned back. She looked like she was enjoying the proceedings immensely. She had an impish look in her eye.

Sergeant Tomas turned a chair around and sat down, leaning his arms on the back. "All right, we're going to get along. First things first. You lied to me when we spoke earlier, didn't you?"

"Lied? *Moi?*" I tried to look appropriately shocked.

"You said you didn't know where Rachel Collins was. But you did know."

"Yes, sir, I did." I figured it best to play it straight.

"How long have you known her?"

"I interviewed her as part of a confidential investigation."

"When was that?"

"Yesterday. I got to know her pretty well. I can tell you absolutely she did not kill Holmcroft. She's not the type."

"She did time for assault with a deadly weapon." Sergeant Tomas said this with an exasperated look on his face.

"She assaulted that man in a fit of passion. Sure, she could get mad and hit, or shoot somebody, but she couldn't commit a crime like this. The flare-up with Holmcroft was three weeks ago. A woman like Rachel Collins lives from day to day, week to week. Three weeks is half a lifetime."

That was a result of thinking it through when I was in the cell. I think he bought it, at least a little bit.

"Hummmmm," he said.

He got up and paced, his hands in his pockets. His lower lip made funny little twitching movements. People with peptic ulcers do that with their lips.

After a moment he said, "Who were you working for?"

"Frampton Investigations—but you already know that."

"Who's your client?"

"Can't say—now maybe you can make me say who it is by keeping me on ice, but maybe you aren't that dumb."

"I'm not, am I?"

He quickly realized what he said and flushed red.

The woman officer chuckled, and he shot her a glance that would have sunk the *Bismarck*.

"How about we make a deal?" I said.

"What the hell you think this is, a TV quiz show?"

"Won't you at least hear what I have to say?"

"Okay, what's the deal?"

"Rachel Collins is probably dead," I said.

Sergeant Tomas wiped some sweat off his forehead. "What makes you say that?"

"Someone carefully set her up, so she had to be killed. Pendergast probably had to be killed too."

"Can't buy it."

"I know for a fact Rachel Collins did not pack her belongings. Somebody else did."

"How do you know?"

"Because she didn't take anything from her vanity. Rachel Collins would not leave her makeup behind when going anywhere."

"She'd just killed a guy! She was on the run, for Christ's sake."

"Nobody got a good look at her at the Marconi Club when she allegedly shot Holmcroft. If it was Rachel Collins, and she was planning all this, why didn't she pack before she shot him?"

"People who shoot people aren't always that logical."

"Sergeant, you are not only dumb, you're blind."

He kicked a chair. Gorillas do that when they don't get what they want.

"I know what's eating you, Sergeant," I said.

He glared at me.

"You don't think she did it, either."

"I'm not paid to think," he said. "I'm paid to get convictions. Who was having the drink of Chartreuse? Rachel? Rachel and Pendergast? A visitor?"

"I don't know, Sergeant, honest. I was wondering about that myself. Look, Sergeant, I've told you everything I know, which is damn little. What do you say you let me go home and get some sleep? In fact, you ought to get some sleep yourself."

He dropped back into his chair and rubbed his face. "If I do let you out of here, what are your plans?"

I knew he was thinking of the Billingham case, which I solved for him. I said, "What do you want me to do?"

"I want you to let me know if you find out anything. I want you to be straight with me."

"Okay."

"You find out anything, you give it to me."

"All right."

"You hold anything back, I put you back on ice forever."

"I understand perfectly."

He put his hand out and I shook it. We had a deal.

"You going to let Charlie go, too?"

"He spilled everything he knew five minutes after he was in here. How Holmcroft hired him, how Mrs. Holmcroft hired you, how you found out where Rachel was living—everything. We let him go two hours ago."

At my release, they gave me back my personal effects, all but my lock-picking kit.

When I got back to my place, Charlie They'll-Never-Get-Anything-Out-of-Me Gore was gone. He left a note saying he was flying to Seattle where he had a lead on Holmcroft's killer and he'd be back tomorrow. The note was hastily written in big bold letters and signed "C." He didn't say what time to expect him. He didn't say "Love, Charlie." What a creep.

I took a hot shower and put on a silk kimono and dropped into the sack and was asleep in five seconds.

When I woke up it was late in the afternoon. Somebody was knocking at the door. I managed to get up, none too sure on my feet, and, by steadying myself on some furniture, made it to the door. I pulled back the curtain and looked into the face of Mr. Frampton. He had a large document case tucked under his arm.

I opened the door and he came in and shook some droplets of rain off his hat. Outside a light spring rain was falling.

"Hello," I said. He didn't look angry. His eyes get large when he's angry. They were normal size. That was a good sign.

"Hello," he said.

Mr. Frampton took off his raincoat and put it over a chair, carefully laid his hat on top of his coat, and said:

"Are we alone, Miss Gallagher?"

"Yes."

"We have to talk."

"I'll get some clothes on," I said.

I went into the bedroom and got dressed. When I came out again he was making two cups of tea. We sat at the kitchen table. Small streams of rain ran down the window. Out on the street the rush-hour traffic crawled by.

He squeezed some lemon into his tea, then stirred in three heaping spoonfuls of sugar. His eyes were narrow, as they usually were when he was in a serious mood, and I figured he was trying to sort through his vast vocabulary and find just the right words to say what he had come to say. Finally he took a sip of tea, smacked his lips with satisfaction, and said:

"I don't suppose there's any way I can talk you out of pursuing this case, is there?"

"No."

"I didn't think there was. All right, you are part of the firm, the firm stands behind you. We'll find this killer, this Rachel Collins."

"The killer was not Rachel Collins."

"It wasn't?"

"No."

"You have some proof of that, I suppose."

"Not yet."

"But she is the chief suspect. We should at least find her so the police can interrogate her."

"She's dead, most likely."

"All right, we'll proceed on that assumption."

He opened his briefcase and pulled out a sheaf of papers.

120

"Here, Miss Gallagher, is what I've been able to find out about all the parties concerned. Mr. Fisk found out that one of Rachel Collins's suitors was Mr. Holmcroft's ex-partner, Mr. Preston Chang."

"I know."

"Here's something perhaps you don't know. Pendergast, despite his opulent lifestyle, was, alas, broke. He owed money all over town. I have Mr. Pendergast's bank records right here—you can see that he had a balance of two hundred ten dollars."

He did indeed have the record. Bank of San Francisco Thrift. Two hundred ten dollars, eleven cents.

"Anyway," Mr. Frampton went on, "there's a copy of Holmcroft's application for a property loan last year. He was worth eleven million dollars. A fair sum, by any standard."

"Who gets the money?"

"The will is still sealed. I presume Mrs. Holmcroft gets most of it."

He finished off his tea and stood up. "As far as Rachel Collins goes, it seems she had a checking account, but the police have confiscated it. My computer people can't get into the record." He slid the papers across the table at me. "You can have these, Miss Gallagher. And please, keep the illegalities to an absolute minimum." He put on his hat and coat. "Promise me you'll be careful. Please."

"Worry not."

He gave me a smile and a wave and went out.

I dragged my exercise bicycle out of the closet and rode it for a few dozen miles, then did some stretching exercises and practiced a few aikido throws using some ropes and springs fixed to the walls to simulate a human hulk, 225 pounds plus.

I had a stale bagel with cream cheese while I looked over the papers Mr. Frampton had left. Most of them were photocopies of deeds, credit reports, property transfers, and the like. I glanced through them, but didn't find anything that struck me as a lead.

So I put on my coat and went out. When you don't have a lead, you go back to the last place the subject was seen. Pendergast's.

121

FIFTEEN

■

I got to Pendergast's place a little after sundown and found the cops still there. Two blue and whites sat out in front and a lab truck and a couple of unmarked cars were parked in the driveway. As I pulled up, Sergeant Tomas, shoulders slumped, came down the steps. A ton of stress was mashing him slowly into the ground.

"What are you doing here, Miss Gallagher?" he asked. He sounded as if he really didn't want to know; it was more an expression that he wished I were elsewhere.

"Nothing nefarious," I said. "Just nosy. Find any clues I might have overlooked?"

He didn't answer. He just scowled and said: "Rachel's probably out of the state by now."

"You and I both know better."

"But I have superiors, and they think she's in flight to avoid prosecution."

I said, "In the meanwhile, have you canvassed the neighborhood around here?"

"We have."

"Anyone see them leave?"

"No."

"You don't mind if I talk to them?"

"Why not, we're on the same side, aren't we?" He said this as if he didn't quite believe it.

"Sure we're on the same side," I said.

"If you find out anything, call my office. I'm going home and get some sleep." He got into his car and drove off.

I went over to Pendergast's neighbor's house. The wrought-iron railing on the stairs was rusty and varnish was peeling off the awning over the door. I rang the bell, which sounded like a Chinese gong. An old man came to the door dressed in a lavender bathrobe. He had red veins in his face and his hands shook.

"Whatever you're selling, I ain't buying."

"My name's Odyssey," I said, cheery as hell. "I'm a friend of poor Mr. Pendergast and I was wondering if you could tell me if you've seen him lately. Has he had any visitors?"

He looked at me blankly. "Why are you bothering me with this?"

He shut the door. I rang the bell about ten times. Finally he opened the door again.

"Persistent, aren't you?"

"You never get anywhere in this world by being a sheep. You were right not to buy my story. I'm not a friend of Pendergast's. I'm a private eye and I'm looking into his disappearance."

"He's disappeared?"

"Yes, didn't you know?"

"I've been in bed."

"Didn't the cops talk to you?"

"I guess they did. I didn't really get what they were asking or why."

"It's been on the news."

"I have no interest whatever in the news. Nor in my neighbors. I have the gout, that's all I care about. I mind my own business and expect other people to mind theirs."

He slammed the door shut.

123

So much for him.

I tried the house on the other side. This one had well-trimmed shrubs and the edge of the lawn was cut as straight as a surveyor's line. I went up the stairs and knocked. A woman's small voice answered from within:

"Yes."

"My name's Odyssey Gallagher, I'd like to speak to you for just a moment."

"No English goot."

"I just have a couple of questions—about Mr. Pendergast."

"No English goot."

I heard footsteps move away from the door. I knocked and rang and kicked the door, but she didn't come back.

So much for her.

I tried the house across the street. The man who answered the door was wearing a loud plaid smoking jacket and a scarf at his neck. He had razor-cut hair, a deep tan, and looked fit. I guessed he was about fifty, fifty-five. He opened the door and said, "Come in."

I did.

He looked me over top to toe. "Can't say as I go much for the packaging, but I sure like the product. What'll you have?"

I didn't know what he meant. I just looked at him.

"I'm having scotch-rocks," he said.

"Nothing for me, thanks."

"Another first," he said. "You sure? Might help you get into the mood."

"My name's Odyssey Gallagher," I said.

"Odyssey is nice. The connotation is right. Nice sound to it. Perfect. This is going to be a night to remember."

"I don't think I'm who you think I am," I said.

"You're not?"

"I'm a private investigator. I'm looking into the disappearance of Mr. Pendergast, your neighbor."

He flushed. Then he smiled slowly, showing nice even white teeth. "You're right. You're not who I thought you were. I think I better have a double scotch-rocks."

124

He went over to a small serving bar and poured himself a drink. The place was furnished nicely—modern stuff, lacquered black with white cushions. A lot of oriental brushwork paintings on the walls.

"Sure you won't have one?" he said.

"Maybe just one." I figured if I were sociable, he might be more helpful.

"I'm very sorry about the mix-up," he said. "A friend of mine fixed me up with a blind date tonight . . ."

"No need to apologize," I said. He handed me a cut-crystal glass filled with enough scotch to make a race horse tipsy.

"Cheers," he said. He downed his in two quick gulps. I took a ladylike little sip. Not cheap scotch. Smooth. No bite. No medicine taste. I took a couple more sips.

"So how can I help you?" he said.

"How well did you know Mr. Pendergast?"

"From what I hear, he mooched off women. I don't think much of a man like that."

"You know the woman who was staying with him? A redhead?"

"Sorry. The cops were here a while ago asking all kinds of questions about Pendergast. I'll tell you what I told them. Every time I see the guy he's polishing his car. It's a passion with him. Women go for a man with a fancy car. A fancy car and his fancy house, and he doesn't have a nickel. I know. I had my credit people check him out just for the hell of it—I'm in the used car business. Horsetrader Henry. I've got four lots."

"How about the other car?"

"I saw it in his garage—the little red Toyota with a bashed-up right quarter panel. I saw a woman drive it, but not him."

"A redhead?"

He shrugged.

"Did you see them leave yesterday?"

"Just like I told the cops—no."

"Did you see anyone else around the place?"

He got a strange, faraway look in his eyes, like he was remembering something. "As a matter of fact, I did see someone yesterday about eight, nine o'clock—she had on a trench coat. She went up to the door . . .''

"What'd she look like?"

"Nice ones."

"Pardon?"

"Legs. She had nice legs. I liked the way she walked. Sort of important—know what I mean? Like a queen or a movie star."

"What color hair?"

"Couldn't tell you. Hair doesn't get me, know what I mean?"

"What was she driving?"

"Nothing. She was walking. I didn't think anything of it at the time, but now that you mention it, it is sort of strange that a woman like that would be walking."

The doorbell rang. He looked startled. He glanced at the door, then at me, then at the door again.

"I better be going," I said.

"Ah, you wouldn't mind going out the back way would you, Odyssey? That way, through the kitchen. Take the drink with you."

"Thanks for your help, Mr. Henry."

"Look, if you're ever in a mood to party, Odyssey, don't forget the old Horsetrader."

I said I just might take him up on that.

I went out the back and circled the house. I crossed the street to my car and found a uniformed officer waiting for me. He couldn't have been more than twenty-one, a tall, brown-eyed hunk, sugarcoated with earnestness and innocence.

"Miss Gallagher?"

"Yes?"

"Sergeant Tomas phoned and said you're to come with me."

"Where we going?"

"Number one Redwood Alley."

"That happens to be my address," I said.

"That's where he said I was to take you."

"I have my car. Can I follow you?"

"No, ma'am, he said I was to drive you." Gad, I hate it when

126

a hunk calls me "ma'am." Even if he is more than ten years younger.

"Okay," I said.

So I got into a patrol car with him and we drove down Geary. It was the tail end of the commute traffic, when those still left on the street really get ugly. But when you ride in a patrol car everyone is so polite, they get out of your way as soon as they see you coming.

"You mind telling me what this is all about?" I asked.

"I can't say, ma'am, he just told me to find you and bring you to number one Redwood Alley."

Ma'am. Ugh.

I wondered what it could possibly be. Were they going to arrest me? I figured they maybe had searched the apartment and found the unregistered gun. If Fisk got me into trouble over that stupid gun, I was going to make him eat it.

As we neared the apartment I could see the cop cars and a coroner's meat wagon and a lump formed in my throat and a wave of nausea washed over me.

"What's happened, officer, tell me."

"I can't say, ma'am," he said. "I really don't know."

"Who's dead?"

"They didn't tell me."

He pulled up on the curb and turned on the red lights. I got out and started down the driveway alongside the liquor store. A half dozen reporters and a TV news crew were herded into the parking space beneath my deck. Uniformed cops lined the stairway.

My throat tightened up and my knees felt shaky under me. *Be a professional*, I told myself. Keep up your demeanor. And then it hit me that maybe Martin had come for his things, and Charlie had come back, and they had a fight and Charlie might have killed Martin.

A feeling of horror came over me.

I made my way up the stairs. The young cop accompanied me, holding my elbow. I felt like I was somehow detached from the whole thing, as if I were watching all this through a thick piece

127

of cellophane. There were my blooming azaleas. I could hear the traffic in the street, it was all so strangely clear.

Then at the top of the stairs I met Sergeant Tomas, whose sad, tired face looked pained. He nodded to the young officer, who retreated down the stairs.

Sergeant Tomas led me into the kitchen without saying anything. Martin was sitting at the table with handcuffs on, looking bewildered and terrified, and then he saw me and he shook his head as if to say no—no to what? Then he pointed to himself and nodded yes. Yes to what?

He was flanked by two huge uniformed cops, their hands on their hips.

"There's been a murder," Sergeant Tomas said. "We caught Mr. Martin Roberts trying to wipe out the evidence."

"Martin Roberts? *My* Martin Roberts?" Which was a dumb thing to say, but somehow it just spilled out. Damn. I wasn't being professional.

"I'd like to see the package," I said. Cop talk for the corpse.

Sergeant Tomas nodded and showed me into the bedroom. Right there in the middle of my floor at the foot of the bed was the white outline of where they'd found him. And a small river of dark red dried blood that ran toward the open sliding door by the deck.

I fought back the sickening feeling in my stomach.

The coroner's men had the corpse in a body bag on a stretcher. Lab people were vacuuming up fibers and dusting for fingerprints.

I went over to the body bag and unzipped it. The first thing I saw was Charlie's checkered sport coat. My whole body turned to ice. Then the coroner's man pulled the bag open some more and I could see it wasn't Charlie. It was his gofer, his stooge, Mickey Fingers. His eyes were open and glassy and he had a snarling expression on his face. The bullet hole was about the diameter of a pencil—a .32, I figured—just to the right of his nose. The exit hole was larger and on the top of his head.

I looked back to the outline on the floor. From the flow of the blood out the top of his head, I figured he must have fallen

128

straight back. The gun was fired from an upward angle. Either the gunman had fired from the hip or he was sitting on the bed and took aim. The bed hadn't been made, so it was impossible to tell.

Sergeant Tomas said, "We figured it happened about six P.M. We got a call from a neighbor—a Mrs. Eversole—that she heard gunshots, and a patrol car was dispatched. When the officers arrived on the scene, they saw Mr. Roberts standing over the body with a gun in his hand.

He held up a plastic bag. It contained the automatic Fisk had given me. So Martin must have seen Mickey Fingers, thought it was Charlie, and shot him. But what was Fingers doing with Charlie's coat on?

They wheeled the body out.

Sergeant Tomas and I went back out into the kitchen. Martin was where we'd left him. One of his guards had gone, but the other was hanging in there close. You've got to keep your eyes on desperados like Martin. Martin looked up at me and smiled wanly.

"I'd like to talk to Martin—alone, Sergeant, if you don't mind."

"I can't do that."

"Sure you can. We're on the same side, remember?"

He made a sour face, then gestured to the cop standing guard to step outside. The cop shrugged and went out through the kitchen door. Sergeant Tomas followed him. A moment later the three lab people left and Martin and I were alone. Out the window I could see them loading poor Mickey's body into the back of the black station wagon.

I sat down at the table across from Martin. His face looked brighter. "Well," he said, "I guess after thirty-eight years on this planet I finally did one decent and honorable thing."

"You want to tell me about it?" I said.

"Tell you about it—what's there to tell you?"

"Tell me what happened."

"What the hell do you mean, Od? You know what happened. Why don't *you* tell *me* what happened?"

129

"If you're trying to confuse me, Martin, you're doing a pretty good job. Just start from the beginning."

He stared at me blankly for a moment, then said: "Do you know a good attorney? That's what I need. And making bail. What's past is past. I did what I did for you, and I'm proud I did it, and if I have to go up the river—that's what you call it, isn't it—then I'll gladly go."

"You killed him for me?"

"Is that what you want me to say?"

"What the hell do you mean is that what I want you to say? I want you to tell me what the hell happened."

"Why don't you tell me what happened first, you shot him, I didn't."

"I shot him?" I ran my hands over my hair. I couldn't believe this.

He nodded. "Pretty stupid to run off and leave the gun lying right there on the floor. Even I know that. I was cleaning your fingerprints off the gun when the cops showed up. I could have been killed."

I felt lightheaded. Perspiration formed on my forehead. I said, "I didn't kill him, Martin."

"You didn't?" He blinked at me.

"No, Martin, I didn't."

"But—but, he was lying on the floor and the bed was all messed up. I didn't look at him real close. I just saw the blood. I thought—"

I leaned across the table and kissed him. "You're wonderful, Martin." I fought back tears. It was both wonderful and terrible.

He looked confused for a moment, his sharp eyes darting around. Then he said, "But if you didn't kill him, and I didn't kill him, who did kill him?"

"That's a really good question, Martin. I guess I better find out before they send you up the river."

SIXTEEN

■

I told Martin to tell his lawyer everything and tell the cops nothing. I watched him being put into the back of a patrol car, hands
cuffed behind his back. He looked terrified.

I watched the patrol car pull out of the driveway and turn
toward Divisadero. Sergeant Tomas left. The lab people left.
Then I sat down and cried. My whole body shook as I wept, and
all the time I was telling myself I was being an unprofessional
jerk.

In an hour I was cried out. I took a shower and changed into
some slacks and a pullover and tried to avoid looking at the white
outline and the bloodstain on the floor.

The phone rang: It was Mr. Frampton. He asked me if I could
come down to the office. He said he'd heard what happened and
he really needed to speak with me. I knew why he didn't want
to come to my place. Mr. Frampton did not like the nearness of
death and avoided it whenever possible.

I told him I'd be in as soon as I could.

I called a cab and took it over to Pendergast's place, where I'd left my car. As I headed east on Geary Boulevard toward downtown I was thinking about Mr. Frampton calling me in. The firm was getting a bad name out of this, and that would be uppermost in his mind, I thought, and that made me indecently angry. This was no time to be worried about bad publicity, not when Mickey Fingers lay dead and Martin was in custody.

When I arrived at the office, I found Mr. Frampton pacing back and forth in his office, his necktie down, his vest unbuttoned, his eyes narrow with worry.

He stopped pacing and looked at me. "Come in and sit down, Miss Gallagher."

"No need to sit, I'm not staying. I'm know why you've called me in. You no doubt want my resignation. I'm prepared to give it to you."

He cleared his throat. "You are?" His eyes narrowed even more. I thought he'd be pleased.

I said, "I know what you're thinking—you're thinking I've gotten the firm a lot of bad publicity, and I know how much you hate bad publicity. But you know something, I'm in a hell of a lot of trouble, and Martin is in even more trouble, and he didn't kill Mickey Fingers and I think that his troubles and my troubles are so terrible that they make the bad publicity meaningless—"

"That's enough!" he snapped.

He clenched his teeth and the veins on his neck bulged out. His face suddenly looked like a piece of carved black marble, hard and cold. "Sit," he said. "Sit down and listen and shut the hell up!" His eyes opened large and angry.

I'd seen him angry before, but never this angry. He looked as if he might have a coronary occlusion. I made a wide circle around him and sat in the chair.

He said, "I don't know what the hell you must think of me if you think I got you over here to talk about publicity! Yes, I care about this firm, I built it from nothing and we do a good job for our clients and I'm proud of it. It provides me and you and Mr. Fisk and Mrs. Kentfield with a living. And we do have a fine reputation—but that doesn't mean I'd count its worth so great

132

that I'd turn away from you in a time of dire need! What must you think of me, Miss Gallagher, to believe I could do such a thing?"

I felt strangely chilled all over. "I-I don't know what to say, Mr. Frampton—I just knew how much this place means to you, and I felt . . ." Damn, I was tearing up.

"Stop it, I won't have any bawling in my office!"

I got up and hugged him and he hugged me back, a firm, fatherly hug, and then he eased me back into the chair. I felt warm now, and strangely happy. He passed me a box of Kleenex, taking a few for himself, then went around the desk and sat down.

"There now," he said, "let's get down to business. I plan to instruct Mrs. Kentfield to tell anyone calling in that we can take no new business. Mr. Fisk will be handling everything except this case, so you and I can devote all our energies to it. Now then, what happened today at your place?"

He took notes on a big yellow pad as I told him about Charlie leaving me the note about going to Seattle, how Martin showed up and found the body, and what he did. When I was through with the briefing, Mr. Frampton pondered silently for a while, then turned to his computer without saying anything. He punched away at the keys for five minutes, then said:

"Charlie Gore did not have reservations on any scheduled airline."

"Then why did he leave me that note?"

He shrugged. He punched some more keys. "He made no credit card transactions today or yesterday."

"He might have used another name."

"Do you know any of his aliases?"

"Afraid not."

He clicked off his computer and put away his yellow tablet. "Let's get something to eat."

"I'm too upset to eat."

"You don't want to lose your strength. Come on. A good meal will do us both good."

Mr. Frampton took me to dinner at Pier Five, a tourist trap

133

that specializes in Creole food. I had the Heart of Dixie dinner; he had a spicy chicken dish. They should have served our dinner with fire extinguishers. During dessert Mr. Frampton said: ''I know how troubled you must feel at this moment, but you should remember that you and I are two of the best investigative brains in the country. We're going to prove Martin's innocence.''

''I know we will, Mr. Frampton.''

''There's something else,'' he said, stabbing his fork repeatedly into his raspberry cheesecake. ''It's about Charlie Gore.''

''What about him?''

''I don't know how to say it, Miss Gallagher, but I don't think you ought to associate with him.''

''Bad for the company's image?''

''Bad for Odyssey Gallagher. The man has criminal tendencies. And he's no gentleman.''

''I've noticed,'' I said.

''He might have been the true target of the murderer.''

''I guess it's possible.''

''He might even have been the murderer.''

''I refuse to believe that.''

''Nevertheless, it's a possibility.''

Mr. Frampton finished the last of his cheesecake and pushed the plate to the edge of the table. ''It might be wise for us to check out his office. Perhaps we could find a clue as to his whereabouts.''

''When?''

''Tonight. Now.''

''Okay,'' I said.

Charlie's office was in what they call the South-of-Market section of town, on Fifth Street. We drove down there in Mr. Frampton's Cadillac. It was ten after ten when we arrived at the address in the phone book. Turned out it was a freight hauling outfit called King Karrier. How cute, fixing up the spelling that way. The office was in a concrete block building with a lot full of battered vans along the side.

We got out of the car and Mr. Frampton looked the place over.

134

Trash in the alley. I looked up to the third floor and saw a sign, Gore Security Services. I nudged Mr. Frampton.

He put his hands in his pockets and looked up and down the street. "Well, Miss Gallagher, do we go in surreptitiously or not?"

"Elbert Hubbard once said, 'All progress begins with a crime.' "

"And Emerson said, 'Nature delights in punishing stupid people.' "

I chuckled. "Why don't you go back to the office, Mr. Frampton?"

"I'm afraid we cannot take the time to observe the usual amenities on this case, Miss Gallagher." With a wave of his hand indicating that I should follow him, he headed down the alley between King Karrier and an auto body repair shop next door. At the end of the alley was a fire escape about ten feet off the pavement.

"How about I give you a boost, Miss Gallagher?" he said, forming a little foothold with his hand. I stepped into his hand and he raised me up to the ladder and I pulled it down.

We went up the fire escape to the third floor, where we found a painted-over window.

"No alarm, is there?" Mr. Frampton asked.

"I don't see one."

He wiped his hands with a handkerchief and straightened out the wrinkles in his trousers. "I'm afraid I haven't done anything like this in years," he said. "Last time I had the presence of mind to bring a few tools."

I took out my Swiss army knife. "Does everything but tell your fortune." I opened the biggest blade and slid it all around the window frame, looking for a catch. It hit some obstruction. I wiggled the knife around and tried to open it, but it wouldn't open.

"Now what?" he asked.

"When finesse fails . . ."

I took off my jacket and wrapped it around my fist. "Turn away," I told Mr. Frampton as I took a swing at the window, smashing it in. I cleaned the remaining loose bits of glass from the frame and stepped inside, using my feeble little penlight to see where we were going.

"I believe we have so far committed a misdemeanor breaking and entering," Mr. Frampton said, following me in. "Be sure we don't take anything, I'd hate to boost it up to first-degree burglary."

"I'll keep my hands in my pockets," I said. We stepped inside.

We were in a large empty room with a few scattered pieces of paper on the floor. The place had a cold, musty smell and huge water stains on the floor and walls.

We crossed the room and opened the door on the other side and found a hallway leading toward the front of the building.

Mr. Frampton breathed heavily and followed close behind me. The yellow light from my penlight made eerie shadows on the wall. Along the hallway were doorways with office names on them: Cosmo Importing, Sung Toy Company, Tasty Party Favors. Gore Security Services was at the end of the hall. I tried the door. Locked.

A hiss escaped Mr. Frampton's lips.

I took out my Swiss army knife and tried running it down between the strip of board along the edge of the door jamb and the jamb itself. I found the lock and tried to pry it back, but it wouldn't give.

"Let's get out of here," Mr. Frampton whispered.

"Faint heart never won fair maid," I said.

"The expression does not apply in this case," he said.

I tried jamming the leather punch on the Swiss army knife into the lock. That sometimes works, but it didn't work this time.

"Okay, we tried," Mr. Frampton said, and started back up the hall.

"Wait a second," I said. I raised my foot and gave the door a kick. It sprang open with a bang.

Mr. Frampton froze. He moved back into a shadow and stood there as if he expected the cops to come storming in.

"Nothing to it," I said in a loud whisper. I stepped into the office. Some light from the street lights below filled the room with yellowish shadows. I shined my penlight around. An open suitcase full of clothes in a corner. Milk cartons and old fast-food restaurant wrappers in the wastepaper basket. A half dozen styrofoam coffee cups littered the desk. An army cot stood in the corner. Obviously, this was Charlie's home sweet home.

The light from my penlight fell on the filing cabinet and on the other side there was someone standing in the shadows.

"Come out of there!" I said. "And put your hands up. I've got a gun and I know how to use it!"

The lights clicked on. Behind us was a uniformed cop, and on the other side of the filing cabinet was my old pal Sergeant Tomas. He took off his hat and scratched his head.

"Okay, Miss Gallagher," he said. "Let's see the gun."

"I don't have a gun," I said. "A bluff."

The uniformed cop, a cold-eyed fatso, patted down Mr. Frampton, then me. He grinned as he ran his hands along my thighs.

"Okay, Hennessy," Sergeant Tomas said to the uniformed cop, "go get a cup of coffee."

"Want I should get you one, Sergeant?"

Sergeant Tomas shook his head. The uniformed cop went out.

"If we are being placed under arrest," Mr. Frampton said, "I will wish to have an attorney present during questioning."

"Who is this guy?" Sergeant Tomas said to me.

"My boss, Mr. Hampton Frampton."

He stared at Mr. Frampton for a long minute. "I remember you," he said to Mr. Frampton. " 'The Black Shamus' they used to call you."

"An epithet in which I took no shame," Mr. Frampton said.

"Are we under arrest?" I asked.

"How'd you get in?" he asked. "The fire escape up to the third floor?"

I nodded.

"I had to have that ladder oiled so it would slide down. You come through the window in the big storeroom?"

I nodded. "I broke the glass, I'm afraid. Might I ask what you're doing here, Sergeant?"

"Why is it whenever we get together for a little chat, Miss Gallagher, it is always you who does most of the asking of questions and me who does most of the answering?"

Mr. Frampton gave me a little wink. He liked it when his operatives were on top of things.

"I've cooperated with you all along, Sergeant," I said. "If there's anything you want to know, ask away—I'm sure you want to know why we broke in, right?"

"Among other things."

"We wanted to get a peek into Charlie's files. Find out where he went. You must also be pretty curious. In fact, you must think he killed Mickey Fingers."

"Naw. Martin Roberts killed Fingers. We've got it pretty much figured out. He saw him wearing Charlie's coat, thought it was Charlie. It was dark in the bedroom so he didn't get a good look at his face. He knew about the gun Eddie Fisk had given you— that's right, he told us where you got it. He hasn't admitted killing him, but we know he did. Motive: Jealous rage and mistaken identity."

"He found the body and the gun and thought I did it. So he was covering up for me when you caught him."

Sergeant Tomas smiled faintly. "And you might have done it at that. Now then, all we have to settle is where you were at the time of the murder."

"Talking to you, and to Pendergast's neighbors."

"But you could have killed him just before that. The neighbor heard the shot sometime between five-fifty-five and six-twenty-five. You and I talked at six-ten, which means you could have killed him and then come directly to Pendergast's place."

"You don't believe that, do you, Sergeant?"

He scratched his head. "I *could* believe it. When you've been doing this as long as I have, you could believe anything."

"So what are you doing here?" I asked.

"Charlie Gore maybe ducked out of sight because he knows too much and somebody's trying to nail him. I figured they'd come here trying to find a lead. But the only company I've had is you two. Somehow I don't think he's hiding from you."

"So what have you found here?" I asked, pulling the drawer to the file open. The drawer was stuffed with file folders, most of which had very little in them. I pulled out the one that said Holmcroft on it and opened it up. Inside was a single slip of paper from a notebook. On the paper was a bunch of scribbles and some words: "Dead Cat" "Check on P.C." "H.H. not x." "P and R?" And lots of dollar signs, arrows, and scribbles, none of which made the least sense.

"What's it mean?" I asked.

"I have no idea whatever. Don't you?"

"It looks like a bunch of doodles."

"You figure any of it out, you remember, we're on the same side." Sergeant Tomas went to the door. "You two lock up here when you're through, would you? I'm going to have a few beers at my favorite bar, then go home and sleep for three days."

"You mean you're not arresting us?" Mr. Frampton asked.

"Some other time."

After he was gone, I said, "P.C. must be Preston Chang."

"Holmcroft's ex-partner?"

"And R must be Rachel Collins. Rachel Collins thought he and Mrs. Holmcroft were teammates. It must be that Preston Chang is behind all this. Charlie is after him up in Seattle."

He nodded. We went downstairs and got into his car and drove back to the office.

"We'll meet tomorrow morning at Holmcroft's office, nine o'clock," Mr. Frampton said. "Maybe we can get some leads on this Preston Chang. I have the feeling he holds the key to this whole thing."

"I'll be there, Mr. Frampton."

And then he said, "You'll be okay for tonight, won't you?"

"Yes. And thank you for asking."

SEVENTEEN

■

That night I couldn't sleep. I worried half the night about poor Martin stuck in a jail cell, and the other half the night about Charlie, whose disappearance alternately worried me and made me mad. He could have at least called, damn his hide.

Mr. Frampton must have spent the night worrying too, because when I saw him the next morning sitting in his car in a loading zone in front of the Transamerica Pyramid he looked like a poker player after a three-day game of Texas Hold 'Em. His eyes were red and puffy and it looked like the fire had gone out of them. His tie was crooked. The first time in the five years I'd known him that he had a crooked tie.

He got out of his car and met me on the sidewalk.

A clown on roller skates in a red and blue costume came by handing out leaflets. I got one. Monroe Donut Shop was having a special. Two dozen glazed for the price of one. A gust of wind blew. Mr. Frampton put his hands in his pockets. The sky was overcast. The air smelled as if it might rain again.

"I've already been up to Holmcroft's office," Mr. Frampton said. "The police are swarming all over the place, interrogating everyone."

"Is Sergeant Tomas up there?"

"Yes, but Lieutenant Horne is in charge now. I've had dealings with him before. A man who does not appreciate practitioners of our profession."

"He kicked you out?"

"Indeed."

"Let me handle him," I said.

"No trouble, Odyssey. Remember, we wish to maintain good relations with the police."

"Worry not."

The wind gusted and he turned his collar up. "I'm going back to the office," he said. He fiddled with his tie, cinching the knot tighter. "Keep me posted."

I took the elevator to the tenth floor. I crossed the hall and went into Holmcroft Financial Services. The desks were all empty, the computer monitors blank. Cops, some in uniform, some in suits and ties, stood around talking to the employees. Some were looking through files. A few employees sat in a lounge at the far end of the office. The place had the quiet and solemn feel of a funeral home.

Everyone seemed tense as hell. Perhaps Holmcroft had been into something dirty and everyone was a little afraid that the cops would arrest them when it came out. Sergeant Tomas came over and asked me what I wanted. I told him I wanted to talk to some of the employees. He called Lieutenant Horne over. Lieutenant Horne had white hair and heavy jowls, and wore the expression of a man who liked to kick dogs.

"You from Frampton Investigations?" he asked before I had a chance to get a word out. "Wasn't there someone else here from Frampton Investigations not long ago?" Sergeant Tomas nodded.

"That would be my boss, Captain," I said to the lieutenant. They always like it when you give them a promotion. I gave him my card. The real one.

"Lieutenant," he corrected.

I smiled. "Lieutenant."

"What do you want here?" he asked.

"Charles Gore and I were working for Mr. and Mrs. Holmcroft," I said, "and now Mr. Gore has turned up missing, and I'd be most pleased if you'd let me ask a few questions of the staff, sir. I won't be in the way, I promise. I have been cooperating fully with Sergeant Tomas, haven't I, Sergeant?" I sugarcoated all that as much as I could.

Horne glanced at Sergeant Tomas. The good sergeant gave a nod. The lieutenant turned back to me: "What specifically do you want to know?"

"I usually just let people talk."

"She has given us an assist now and then, sir," Sergeant Tomas said. "On this and other cases as well."

Lieutenant Horne thought about it for a minute while he studied my card, drumming his fingers on the counter. I caught a glimpse of Hillary Hoyle coming out of an office, a sheaf of papers in her arms. She looked pale and drawn, her business suit slightly disheveled. She was taking Holmcroft's death pretty hard. She wiped her eyes and stiffened up before going into a conference room.

Lieutenant Horne said: "Can't see any reason for you to be here," and walked off.

"Don't I get an appeal?" I called after him. He just kept on walking.

"Sorry," Sergeant Tomas said. "The lieutenant is a very difficult man."

Hillary Hoyle came out of the conference room she had just gone into. She looked as if she might collapse. She steadied herself on a chair, straightened herself up, and went down a hallway.

"I'd like to speak to Ms. Hoyle for just a moment, Sergeant."

"Sorry, the king has given his decree. You'll have to leave now, Odyssey."

"Can't you just tell her I'd like to speak to her in the hall?"

"Nope. Just scat."

142

I took the elevator down. I had a hunch about Hillary Hoyle. Most of my hunches aren't worth a dead cat, but this one was pretty strong. Hillary Hoyle was far more shook up over her boss's death than a secretary ought to be. I called Holmcroft Financial Services from the lobby and asked for Hillary Hoyle.

"I'm sorry, but she's in a meeting," the receptionist said.

"This is Janet Clavelle," I said. "I'm with Patient Services here at Mount Sinai Hospital. Could you tell her, please, there's a family emergency?"

"Just a moment, please."

I waited. Muzak played. A Beatles tune, "The Yellow Submarine." Hillary Hoyle came on the phone: "This is Hillary Hoyle."

"Odyssey Gallagher. I'm sorry I had to tell a little fib, but I had to speak to you."

"Well, I don't have to speak to you."

"Don't hang up! Look, Ms. Hoyle, I know what you've been up to. Now unless you want the cops to know, you better meet me at Maxine's Coffee Shop in five minutes."

"What do you think I've been up to?" Her voice crackled with fear.

"Just be at Maxine's in five minutes."

I hung up.

I was sitting in the back booth at Maxine's when she came in. She walked directly over to me and stood next to me. Her face was drawn, her eyes puffy behind her large round glasses.

"Please have a seat," I said.

"I don't much like being bullied, Miss Gallagher."

"I'm sorry," I said. "I don't mean to be a bully. Honestly I don't. Please . . . sit down. I have to talk to you."

She sat down, folding her hands on the table in front of her. "Just what is it you think I've done?" Her voice sounded as if it were coming out of a straw.

"I spoke with Rachel Collins and she told me something very interesting."

"Oh, what was that?"

"That Morrison Holmcroft wasn't in love with her."

"Oh, is that so?"

"What's more, he was in love with someone else."

Her eyes teared up. Her lower lip trembled. "Why would that be of the least interest to me?"

"I also spoke to a whore by the name of Molly Tens. Preston Chang beat her up to get to Rachel, because Morrison Holmcroft was selling off his assets and was going away with someone. That someone was you, wasn't it?"

She burst into tears now, and put her head down on the table. She sobbed for a few minutes, then managed to get control of herself. She sat up. Her face was bathed in tears.

"He was a great man," she said in a shaky voice. "The others, they didn't know him the way I knew him. Sure, he could be gruff. But he could be tender, too. And sweet. As nice as anyone."

I said nothing.

She said, "Are you going to tell the police I was the other woman?"

"What would be the point?"

"Thank you, Odyssey." She blew her nose on a napkin. The waitress came by; I told her we'd order in a few moments. When she was gone, Hillary Hoyle said, "I hope they kill that Rachel Collins when they find her."

"She didn't murder Mr. Holmcroft."

She glared at me.

"She's been framed," I said. "She was ready to forget Mr. Holmcroft."

"You can't believe that."

"I think whoever framed her probably killed her, too."

"Who would want to frame her?"

"At this point, I don't know. It wasn't you, was it?"

She sniffed. "I wouldn't kill Mo, I *loved* him."

"Have you any of Mr. Holmcroft's personal papers in the office—his checkbook, personal bills, anything like that?"

"No. He kept his personal business completely separate from the company's."

144

"How about personal correspondence, anything like that?"

"No."

"How about Mr. Gore? Did he have a record of hiring him?"

"We did have a file on him, but the police have taken it away. The only thing in the file was a simple personal services agreement."

"Then you don't know why he went to Seattle?"

"No. Why would he go there?"

"I don't know. The police are checking into the possibility that Mr. Preston Chang might have been involved in this case. Do you think that's possible?"

"I can tell you that Mo was scared of him. And very angry that he disappeared like he did. It cost Mo a great deal of money."

"I'd really like to talk to that man."

"Nobody knows where he is."

"Do you know any of his friends, associates, girlfriends?"

She thought for a long moment, then nodded. "He has a daughter. Her name is Samantha."

"Have the police talked to her?"

"No. They don't have her address."

"Do you know it?"

"I'm sorry, I don't."

"Do you know anyone that knows her? A friend, a relative?"

She pressed her knuckles to her lips for a moment while she thought about it. Then she said, "I saw her one day in a restaurant, the Fire Dragon East, and she introduced me to her fiancé. He was one of the waiters."

"You wouldn't happen to remember his name, would you?"

"I remember. His name was Fong Wu."

EIGHTEEN

∎

The Fire Dragon East was a tourist trap on Grant Avenue, right in the heart of Chinatown. I'd eaten there once; the prices were high and the mu shu pork was tasteless. It was situated next to a curio shop selling everything from painted fans and brass dragons to T-shirts that said "I did it in San Francisco."

The front door of the Fire Dragon East was leather covered, fitted with brass tacks. Inside, the tables were packed tightly together, covered with white tablecloths, which were in turn covered with clear plastic. A model of a Buddhist temple was pushed up against the back wall.

The head waiter was a balding little man in a dark suit. I asked for Fong Wu and he looked me over as though he thought I was trouble. Folks in Chinatown don't trust outsiders much.

"Look, I know he works here," I said. "I just want to talk to him." I gave him one of my cards, the one that says: Odyssey Gallagher, dealer in fine art. Anybody'll talk to an art dealer.

"He may not be in today," the head waiter said. He kept his inscrutable Asian eyes on my card.

146

"You tell him I'm here about Samantha."

His expression showed nothing. "Sit, please," he said, pointing to a table by the kitchen. I went over and sat down and a few minutes later a waiter brought me a pot of tea and asked me if I wanted something. I ordered some sweet and sour prawns, brown rice, and a half order of pot stickers—dough filled with pork and vegetables.

A few tourists drifted in. Most of them wanted to sit in front by the windows and look at other tourists going by on Grant. I preferred to look at the paintings on the walls. They were Taoist prints, the kind that show forests and mountains as important objects and people as little more than specks. There's something about those proportions that seem right to me.

The food came. The sweet and sour sauce on the sweet and sour prawns was too thick and too sweet, and the prawns were more like baby shrimp. The pot stickers were flavorless and the dough hard. But the tourists seemed pleased enough. Tourists have a tendency to like anything in a brightly colored package.

After the plates were cleared away the head waiter came over to my table and asked if I had enjoyed the lunch.

"Very delicious," I said. "Where's Fong Wu?"

"Mr. Wu is wanting to know what it is you wish to speak to him about."

"I want to speak to him about Samantha's father. He is in a great deal of trouble and I want to help."

"I will pass on the message." He went back to his station near the door and picked up the phone. I took the leatherbound notebook out of my shoulder bag and made a few notes in a shorthand that can be read only by me.

The head waiter returned once again and said, "The boy will speak to you."

"Where is he?"

"You are to go down the street to Stockton and turn right. Walk one half block and stop in front of the herbalist."

"Why can't he come here?"

"He did not say."

I paid the check and left the waiter a tip and went into the

147

street. The wind had calmed down and the overcast was gone. It was a nice and sunny California day. The sidewalks and ticky-tacky tourist shops were packed with tourists. I threaded my way down to the corner of Stockton, feeling uneasy.

I started down Stockton, walking slowly behind a couple of ancient tourists who I thought must own Kodak from the way they were snapping pictures. They stopped in front of the herbalist, who had all kinds of dried herbs in his window and everything from ground-up rhino horns to pickled spider eggs. Everything for what ails ya.

I looked around and didn't see anybody looking for me or spying on me, or drawing a bead on me with a sniper's rifle. Then I saw a note, crudely hand-painted and tacked onto the window: Lady Art Dealer, this way, with an arrow pointing to the right. I looked to the right, and there was another arrow pointing down an alley.

I took a look down the alley. A lot of trash cans. Some doors. No way out at the other end.

I took a deep breath and told myself that I was just going to meet a kid who was scared that I might be a cop. Perhaps he was an illegal alien. Lots of illegal Chinese in Chinatown. But I still didn't move into the alley. Then I told myself that I was a professional detective, and damn it, sometimes you had to do things that might be a bit dangerous. So I started down the alley, all my senses on alert.

Funny, but just a few feet into that alley and it seemed as if I were in another world. It was dark and cool, and smelled of garbage and decay. The traffic noise from the street grew quiet. A tingle spread from my back all over my body. I could hear someone laughing. A coarse, hard laugh, coming from above me somewhere. Then the sound of a lot of sewing machines. Someplace pretty close was a sweatshop, where probably hundreds of Chinese women were working their asses off for a buck or two an hour.

To my right, a door opened. An elderly Chinese man in a dark suit came out, looked at me, smiled, and sauntered off toward the street. The sweatshop owner, maybe. I just hoped somebody didn't think I was from the Department of Labor. Halfway down the alley was a door with faded gold letters on it: Sung and Tong, Caskets. Another note for me. Lady Art Dealer, come in, it said.

I took another deep breath and concentrated on keeping my ki flowing out.

I stepped through the door and found myself at the bottom of a flight of creaky stairs illuminated by a single, low-wattage bulb at the top. I started up slowly. The door slammed shut behind me of its own volition. My ki kept flowing, but there was a knot in my stomach the size of a basketball. I kept thinking about Molly Tens and how her face looked. At the top of the stairs there were two doors. One right, one left. The one on the left was closed and locked with a padlock. The other one was open. I knocked on it. A man's voice called from another room: "Come in." The voice sounded raspy.

I went in and found myself in a narrow hallway. A bubbling sound, like something cooking, came from one of the rooms. At the end of the hallway was a living room. Clean and small, with simple wooden furniture. An old man sat in a rocker by a window. Three young men sat at a small table. All four of them silently kept their eyes trained on me.

"I'm Odyssey Gallagher," I said. "I'm a private eye. I'm working on the murder of Mr. Morrison Holmcroft. I'd like to get in contact with Mr. Preston Chang."

"I am Curtis Chang," the old man said. "My son is Preston Chang. These three men work for me. I'm in the fruit business."

They did not look like they were in the fruit business. I nodded to them. They merely stared.

"Where can I find Preston Chang?" I said.

"What do you expect to learn from him?"

"I don't know."

The old man smiled a little.

"I think your son and I may be able to help each other. It isn't going to take the police long to figure out that Rachel Collins didn't kill Morrison Holmcroft. When they do, they'll start looking for other suspects. It could have been a man dressed as a

149

woman. They will suspect your son. If he didn't do it, I might be able to help him prove it."

The old man turned to the three young men and nodded. "I think we should let her see him."

One of the young men got up. About my height, he had tattoos on his arms and was muscled as if he knew his way around a weight room. His eyes were cold and black, and he sneered as he looked me over. Then he took my arm as though I were a sack of soiled linen.

"Come—"

He didn't get a chance to finish what he was going to say because I twisted his arm and kicked his leg and sent him flying upside down into a wall.

The two young men at the table burst out laughing. The old man nodded his appreciation. "Japanese technique," he said. "Very nicely done."

The one I dumped got to his feet. He glared at me with clenched teeth, his fist doubled tight. A slight growl escaped his lips and I braced for an attack, but the old man waved him away.

"Perhaps," the old man said, "I should take you myself."

The old man and I took a cab over to the Sutter-Stockton Garage, where I'd parked the Banana Slug. We got in and he told me to drive out Geary Boulevard toward the beach. He sat sunken into himself in the passenger seat. He was very old and his breathing came hard. He held his walking stick in front of him, clasping it with a knotted hand.

We made the curve by the Cliff House restaurant and drove along the beach. The afternoon fog was rolling in. The sea was gray. We passed Fleishacker Pool and the old windmills that used to pump water out of deep wells to water Golden Gate Park. We kept going along the beach for a mile or so to a parking lot. He told me to turn in and park. I did.

I looked around. A VW van painted with yellow daffodils sat nearby. The flower children who came twenty years ago are still coming, though in much smaller numbers. They bring with them a sort of charming innocence. It takes a while for the city to turn them into cynics.

Further down I could make out a large recreational vehicle, one of those thirty-footers, and a couple of cars next to it. No one around.

We sat for a long moment, then I said: "Well?"

The old man turned to me and said, "Patience." Then he turned back toward the ocean and looked at it with a solemn look of pleasure on his face. We just sat there for twenty or thirty minutes. He said nothing. I said nothing. The fog covered us, rushing past the windows.

Another ten minutes passed. Finally the old man took a deep breath and opened the door. "Wait here please," he said. He got out and closed the door. I watched him disappear into the fog like a ghost. The knot of iron clamped my stomach. For a moment I thought about getting out of there. *Courage,* said Mark Twain, *is mastery of fear—not absence of fear.* Knowing that didn't help.

I turned on the radio and listened to a talk show. Everyone seemed hot about the Giants moving down to Santa Clara. I wondered if they loved the Giants so much, how come they didn't go out to the ballpark and support them. They wouldn't be moving if they were drawing the crowds.

Then: A tapping on the window. Startled, I turned. The old man stood beside my car, motioning me to come. I got out.

"This way. My son will see you."

I got out. The wind was strong, but not cold. I followed the old man to the large R.V. He opened the door for me. "I will wait in your car," he said.

I stepped inside and up the three steps to the driver's compartment and kitchen. A man stood there, mid-fifties, compactly built, Chinese, wearing a silk shirt, open at the collar. He didn't look like the kind of man to beat up women. He had steel-gray hair and deep black eyes, and he looked nervous. About as nervous as I felt. He didn't seem to be armed. He didn't have fangs. I breathed a little easier.

"Welcome to my humble home on wheels," he said with a forced smile.

"I'm Odyssey Gallagher," I said. "Are you Preston Chang?"

"Yes." He shook my hand and walked toward the back of the vehicle. At the end was a couch in a U-shape. The curtains were drawn. He clicked on an overhead light. A heater fan blew warm air in my direction. We both sat on the couch, turning to face each other. This was no cheap R.V. The paneling looked rich, the couch looked custom made. Cellular phone built in.

"You've been living in this?" I asked.

"Only for a few days. Would you like a drink?" he asked.

"A little early for me."

"You wouldn't mind if I had one?"

"Not at all."

He was certainly polite, I thought. My grandmother always said that manners, not clothes, made the man.

He pressed a button and a small serving bar rotated out of the wall, ice cube server and all. He poured himself a tall scotch on the rocks. He drank half of it and sat back on the couch.

"I suppose you have many questions for me," he said. "I have many questions for you. Would you mind if I started?"

"Not at all."

"First, do the police think I was at all involved with the killing of my former partner?"

"Not at this time. Not as far as I know."

"But they have been at the office."

"Yes."

He got up and paced nervously back and forth in the narrow space. I sometimes have that effect on men. This wasn't one of those times. "I am a careful man," he said. "You may look into my business dealings and you will never find even a hint of impropriety."

"Morrison Holmcroft wasn't that careful, was he?"

He looked surprised that I knew. Then he said, "No."

"Do you think he was killed over his business dealings?"

"It was Rachel Collins who killed him. There were witnesses."

"No one got that close a look. Besides, she might have had accomplices."

"Me perhaps?"

152

"Perhaps. Mr. Holmcroft thought you might have sent the dead cat."

"Dead cat? I don't know anything about a dead cat."

"Rachel Collins thought you might have taken a shot at her."

"I did not. I have never held a gun in my hand in my life."

He wiped some sweat off his forehead and sat back down.

"Are they going over the books?" he said suddenly. "Have they brought in accountants?"

"What would they be looking for?"

"I don't know."

"Why would Charlie Gore go to Seattle?"

"I don't know any Charlie Gore."

"He was looking for you."

"Not in Seattle. I have never in my life been to Seattle." He got up and made himself another drink.

"Rachel Collins said she thought you and Mrs. Holmcroft were plotting something."

"Not true, *totally* not true. I did go to her when I knew he was selling his assets. I told her I thought he was going to run away with Rachel Collins. That's all. She thanked me and I left, that is all."

"When was that?"

"One month ago."

"How did you know this?"

"I have my ways. Believe me, I knew exactly what was going on in that office. Forty percent of that company is mine."

"Why, after your falling out, did you disappear?"

"I just wanted time to think things over. We had a lot of good years. I needed a plan to quit the business graciously."

I didn't believe that. "Do you mind if I ask you where you were at the time of the murder?"

He let out a long breath. "That's just it. I was driving down from the mountains. I'd stopped at the rest stop just outside of Vallejo at sunset, made some dinner for myself, and ate. There was a Giants game on, so I watched it. The reception at that particular place was very good. Then I drove on into an R.V. park in Daly City. Got there about ten, ten-fifteen."

153

He was looking me straight in the eye. Either this man was as innocent as a rock, or he was the greatest living liar since Joe Isuzu.

"What you're saying is you have no alibi?"

"That's right. I don't."

"What was your relationship to Rachel Collins?"

"I never met the woman. All I know about her is what others have told me."

"I happen to know differently," I said.

His jaw drew tight. "I never met the woman in my life."

He'd just given himself away. I had him now.

"You never met her in Lemming's Lounge?"

"I did not."

"She said you did. Others back her up."

"I refuse to answer any more questions."

"Charlie Gore was looking for you, you must have found that out. His friend is dead and he's gone away. Where is he? What have you done with him?"

"I never heard of him, I told you."

He folded his arms across his chest. It suddenly occurred to me that Charlie might be in more trouble than I'd imagined. If Charlie went after Preston Chang, and Preston Chang got onto him, he might have done something terrible to Charlie. The iron ball of fear in my gut was back. I couldn't let this man leave. I had to take him in somehow and let the police investigate him.

I stood up. "I think you'd better talk to Sergeant Tomas," I said. I reached for the cellular phone.

"Put that down."

I said, "I have a brown belt in aikido, Mr. Chang. I happen to know for certain you did know Rachel Collins, in fact you met her on several occasions at Lemming's. The way I heard it, you were in heat for her."

"Put down that phone!"

"I won't be lied to."

"Very well. I did meet with her once or twice. She was an evil woman. I wanted to date her, she wouldn't go out with an Asian."

154

"That's not the way I heard it."

I started to dial and he grabbed my wrist. I put a move on him, swinging him around and pushing him into the wall with a bang. He got his balance and retreated toward the front of the van and went into a karate stance.

"You put down that phone," he said, "or I will break your bones."

I took my aikido defensive stance. We stared at each other for a long moment. Then I saw a blur as he made a move, and I felt a foot hit me in the midsection, taking the wind out of me.

I tried to grab him, but I felt a whack on the head and it seemed as if the floor turned into a large black blanket that rose up and wrapped around me. And then the world went away.

NINETEEN

■

Somewhere in the dark netherworld of my unconscious, I could hear my sensei saying, "Never challenge a superior warrior."

I opened an eye. Darkness.

My senses came alert. I could smell the stink of seaweed and salt air. I heard the sound of a bird. There was sand in my mouth. I spit. I rolled over and sat up, cold and stiff. I was surrounded by fog and high reeds. A ship's horn sounded. Waves crashed against the shore. I patted myself all over to make sure I wasn't bleeding. I wasn't. My head hurt. My eye hurt. My side hurt. My pride hurt.

I got to my feet and found myself a little unsteady. An image of my college professor father passed through my mind, a vivid image of him telling me I was an idiot for giving up my tenure-track job in the English Department at the University of Kansas. His voice rang in my ears. *You'll rue the day you became a detective.*

Boy do I hate it when you're right, Dad. I'm ruing it. I'm ruing it big.

I staggered up the beach and up a path that led to the parking area. The fog was thick and I couldn't see more than a few feet. *Make the most of your regrets . . . to regret deeply is to live afresh.*

Thoreau said that. Funny, I regretted deeply, but did not feel like I was living afresh.

I stumbled around the parking lot for a few minutes and found the Banana Slug, pretty much as I'd left her. Loyal and trusting beast that she is. I opened the door. My purse sat on the seat. Mr. Chang must have left it for me. I got in and found my keys and started the engine. I rolled down the window and spit some more sand.

Switching on the interior light, I took a look at myself in the mirror. I had a shiner over my right eye the size of a golf ball. It would have looked good on Mike Tyson.

I drove home slowly and carefully, and took a shower. My side was black and blue. It felt as if I had a cracked rib. Breathing deeply made it ache. I put on clean slacks and a pullover. I fixed my eye with some makeup and dug up a pair of sunglasses.

There were two messages on my tape machine. One from Martin's lawyer asking me whether I knew anyone who had property to put up to guarantee Martin's bond, and one from Mr. Frampton, who wanted me to call the office.

I called Martin's lawyer and got his machine. It was already after seven. I left a message that I'd try to find someone with some property. I called my parents. No answer. I guessed they hadn't come back from Greece.

Next, I called Mr. Frampton and he said he had some news. He wanted me to come into the office. I said I'd be there in half an hour.

I made one of those instant noodle things and scarfed it down, then took a couple of Tylenol, blow-dried my hair, and drove over to the office through the last of the rush-hour madness. An accident on Geary Boulevard had everything snarled up. It was eight o'clock by the time I got to the office. I came up the back stairs hoping to miss Fisk, just in case he was in the office we shared with Mrs. Kentfield. Mr. Frampton's door was open and

157

I went on in. Fisk was there, sitting in one of the chairs facing Mr. Frampton's desk.

"Hello, Gorgeous," Fisk said. "Nice touch."

He meant the dark glasses.

Mr. Frampton smiled. "I do believe I see a little swelling there above the eye. Someone has given you a present?"

I took off the glasses and sat down. "Okay, have a laugh and get it over with."

"That's bea-u-ti-ful!" said Fisk.

"Who got in the lucky punch?" Mr. Frampton asked.

"Preston Chang. I caught him lying about knowing Rachel Collins. We had words."

Fisk chuckled deep in his throat. I so wanted to throw him out the window.

Mr. Frampton reached for a file folder on his desk and opened it. He scribbled something. "I guess we can put Preston Chang at the top of our list of suspects. It all fits. Preston Chang and Rachel were in on it together, and Pendergast was their helper."

"Not a chance," I said. "Chang and Rachel? Never."

"Then why did Chang attack you?"

"I was using his telephone without permission."

"What's his connection with Rachel Collins?"

"He went over to Lemming's Lounge to see if he could get a date with her. He wanted information from her, but she wouldn't give him a wink."

Fisk said, "So Rachel Collins wouldn't give him a wink, eh? That ain't the way I heard it." He tugged at the ends of his bow tie and took a package of gum out of his pocket. Doublemint.

Mr. Frampton said, "We will need more facts to make a determination one way or the other. But I have found some evidence of shady dealings at Holmcroft Financial Services. They were buying up bad loans from shaky savings and loans, spiffing them up a little, and selling them off to banks. So far, though, I can find them in no clear violation of the law. During the last two months Holmcroft had been very quietly liquidating his assets."

I said, "He'd fallen in love and was going away with his beloved."

"There you go," Mr. Frampton said. "Holmcroft got Rachel all pumped up about going off together, then he had a change of heart and so she popped him."

"I told you before, she didn't kill him. She was set up to take the fall."

"By whom?"

"Don't know yet."

"You want my theory," Fisk said, shoving a stick of Doublemint into his mouth, "what you got here is a classic triangle situation. Preston Chang loved Rachel, Holmcroft loved Rachel, Rachel and Chang dump Holmcroft."

"So who killed Mickey Fingers at my place? And what happened to Charlie Gore?"

Fisk shrugged. "I figure Gore caught Fingers stealing something, maybe, so let him have it. It's as good a theory as any."

I didn't believe that for a second. Charlie would not have killed Fingers. Not with a gun anyway.

Fisk turned to Mr. Frampton. "Should I tell her?" Mr. Frampton gave a solemn nod.

"Did you find him?" I asked.

"I've found his *wife*," Fisk said.

I felt a little jolt of electricity to the front of my brain. "Wife? As in *married* wife?"

Fisk handed me a slip of paper. "Here's her address. Her name's Stephanie."

My mouth was suddenly dry. I said, "Ah, perhaps I should talk to her. She might know what happened to Charlie." Funny, but I suddenly felt cold all over.

Mr. Frampton said, "Why don't I go along with you?"

"I can handle it."

"You're sure you're all right?"

"I'm all right."

Fisk said, "If I run into Gore, what should I tell him?"

"Tell him he hasn't long to live."

He laughed real hard at that, so did Mr. Frampton. When the laughter died down, I asked Fisk if he had another entry assistor, which is a euphemism for a lock-picking kit.

He gave me a wink. "There's some hope for you yet."

"I don't want to know what you two are talking about," Mr. Frampton said.

Fisk gave me another lock-picking kit, this one in a little gray sack. I went back downstairs telling myself to keep my ki flowing out, to be professional, and all that stuff I say to calm myself down, but this time it wasn't working. I got into the Banana Slug, slammed some gears, and tore out of the parking lot.

Stephanie Gore lived on Golden Gate near Hyde in the Tenderloin. Her apartment was up over a porno movie house. It was eight-thirty when I got there.

I parked a half block away in front of a liquor store. A young black hooker, about fourteen, stood on the corner, wearing long leather boots and a skirt the size of a cocktail napkin.

When I walked by her, she said:

"Honey, you in the wrong neighborhood."

"So are you, sweetheart."

The front door of the apartment building had been smashed in so I walked right on in and up the stairs. The place smelled like a stable, pungent and raw. I knocked on the door. A huge guy with a potbelly, wearing a pair of dungarees and a T-shirt, opened the door. A faded tattoo on his upper arm said BORN TO RAISE HELL. He looked me over and a slow, lecherous smile came to his pale lips.

"Wellll, hellooooo there," he said, rubbing the stubble on his cheek. His breath smelled like rancid cooking oil. "Somebody sock you?"

"Fell in the shower. I'm here to see Stephanie Gore."

"Too bad," he said. He opened the door wide and invited me in with a sweep of his hand. "My name's Frank, what's yours?"

"Odyssey."

The place had an old tattered carpet on the floor that had a map of America on it, faded and worn through to the threads. For furniture: one green stuffed chair, one coffee table, one end table that didn't match, and a long, low, yellow couch. The curtains over the two windows were tattered. One was pink, the other burgundy. Beer cans were scattered around, at least a

160

dozen or two. Ash trays were full. A plate of what had once been spaghetti sat on the heater by the window.

A woman was sitting on the couch with her feet up on the coffee table. She wore a plain print dress and had a beer can in her hand. Her face was round and puffy and she might have been pretty about thirty pounds ago. She had her glasses down low on her nose and her eyes were closed.

"Somebody to see you, Steph," the man said.

She opened her eyes. "Who are you?"

"A friend of Charlie's."

"My Charlie's?"

"Yes."

She sat up and rubbed her eyes with the tips of her fingers without bothering to remove her glasses. "Something happen to him?"

"He's missing."

"So what? I don't give a damn."

"Makes sense," Frank said. "You ask me, it was him that shot Mickey Fingers."

"Nobody asked you," Stephanie said.

Frank shrugged. "You want a beer?" he asked me.

"Thanks, but I'll pass."

"That's real funny," Stephanie Gore said. "Charlie's missing." She laughed suddenly. Then she said it again, "Charlie's missing," as if it had some private meaning, and she laughed until her eyes watered and she finally started coughing. She coughed furiously for perhaps a full minute, her face bloated red, then she got up and hurried out of the room.

"You gotta excuse Stephanie," Frank said. "She ain't in the best of health. She's been in the hospital trying to dry out. Charlie put her there. Paid the whole thing, but it didn't take. It's over between them, but he still feels he ought to do something."

No wonder Charlie was sleeping in his office. Paying off a hospital is like paying off a loan shark.

"You think he might have killed Fingers?" Frank asked.

"No."

161

"I guess you're right. This guy Martin Roberts that the cops got must have done it."

"No he didn't."

"Well, somebody did it. You?" He laughed. I laughed with him.

Stephanie came back in the room guzzling one of those huge Australian beers. "You sure you won't have a beer, Miss . . ."

"Call me Odyssey."

"You one of his gal friends?" It hurt her to say it, I could detect the pain in her voice.

"We were working on the same case," I said. "I'm a private investigator."

"A shamus, eh?" Frank said. He laughed. He sat down by Stephanie on the edge of the couch. I didn't want to sit, I didn't plan to stay long. "Did you talk to him lately?" I asked.

"He phoned yesterday," she said slowly, as if she wasn't sure she should be telling.

"Did he say anything about where he was going or who he was meeting with?"

She looked at Frank, who just smiled a greedy little smile.

"How much is it worth to you?" Stephanie Gore said. Nothing subtle about this woman.

"Twenty bucks," I said.

"Make it fifty," she said. "Fifty bucks, I tell you everything he told me, right down to the last syllable."

I counted out two twenties and two fives and put them on the coffee table. Frank picked them up and put them in his pocket.

"Okay," she said. "Here's what he said, exactly. That he'd bagged the big one and he was going to get me back in the sanitarium. It's my lungs, you know. Bad lungs. That's why I drink, to put out the fire in my chest. Now that's exactly what he said. Exact."

"What did he mean, that he'd bagged the big one?"

"He was gonna hit a bank, something like that," Frank said. "A guy like Charlie, you never can tell."

"I think he solved a big case for his client, something like that," Stephanie said. "He was like getting a big reward or something. Why don't you ask his client?"

"His client's dead."

She grunted. "Then you've got a real mystery on your hands, haven't you?"

TWENTY

■

I drove around for a while, stewing. So Charlie Gore was married. And he never bothered to tell me. So what if they didn't live together. Married is married. My stomach was burning. Images of punching him in the nose filled my head. How could I have been such an idiot to get mixed up with him?

Make the most of your regrets . . . to regret deeply is to live afresh. I was sure getting a lot of practice at regretting deeply.

I stopped at a coffee shop on Nineteenth Avenue and had a cup of coffee and a bran muffin. I couldn't think about Charlie Gore and the physical abuse I was going to heap upon him at the moment. I had to be professional. I had to find a killer first. If, in the course of my investigations, I also found Charlie, that would be a bonus.

I started going through my notebook. I made some notes about my interview with Stephanie Gore and tried to imagine what Charlie could have meant by "bag the big one." Was it possible that his disappearance had nothing whatever to do with the Holmcroft case?

And maybe Mickey Fingers's murder didn't either.

I had another muffin and more coffee. I had taken my dark glasses off, but the waitress didn't seem to notice my shiner. At least she pretended she didn't.

I went back to reading my notebook.

Since I had no clues to point me elsewhere, I decided for now at least to proceed on the theory that everything was somehow tied together. A good detective never trusts coincidence. Emerson said, *shallow men believe in luck . . . strong men believe in cause and effect.* He would have made a great detective.

Charlie said he tried to sell Rachel's whereabouts to Mrs. Holmcroft, but that she wasn't home. Could that have been a lie? Then he told Mr. Holmcroft where Rachel was hiding, and he didn't seem to care, he said.

So then Holmcroft was murdered and Pendergast and Rachel Collins turned up missing. When Charlie and I searched the house, he didn't seem as much interested in looking around as he was in having a beer. The cops came and we were taken in for questioning. Charlie was released first and went to my place and left a note saying he was going to Seattle.

But Mr. Frampton found out he probably didn't go to Seattle. At least he didn't fly there using his own name.

So where did he go, and what does it have to do with Mickey Fingers getting killed?

I had no idea. I couldn't even think of any way the facts might fit a possible scenario. But it was possible that when Charlie said he'd "bagged the big one" he'd found out something that somebody was willing to pay a lot of money for. And Holmcroft might have left some clue to what trail Charlie was on. I had no choice but to ask Mrs. Holmcroft if I could have a look around.

So I drove over to her house. On the way I thought about poor Martin. Now that I'd found out Charlie was married, I felt more guilty than ever about Martin. He really was a nice person. Nice, and smart, and educated, and had a good future. My grandmother would have approved. And he actually put himself at risk by covering up a murder he thought I had committed. If that didn't prove a man's love, what did?

165

I had misjudged poor Martin. He was a better man than I'd ever imagined.

And how did I repay his love? By going to bed with a liar like Charlie Gore. Somehow I had to put it right.

Mrs. Holmcroft's maid answered the door in a bathrobe and slippers. It was just after ten in the evening and she opened the door only as far as the thick metal chain would allow.

"Mrs. Holmcroft, please," I said. "I'm here about Mr. Holmcroft's murder. It's extremely important that I see her."

"Wait a moment."

She closed the door and I stood on the doorstep under the porch light. A thin mist was in the air and it was cold. I was wearing an unlined fake-leather jacket and it cut the wind, but it wasn't warm enough. I heard the door chain rattle, then the door opened. The maid said I was to follow her.

She took me into the library. "Mrs. Holmcroft will be down in a moment. Can I bring you some refreshment?"

"A cup of tea would be nice."

She glided out of the room as Mrs. Holmcroft came in. Mrs. Holmcroft was wearing a pink flowered lounging robe and had on small wire-rimmed reading glasses that didn't seem to suit her face. She was wearing no makeup, and her face was pale and drawn.

"I'm quite surprised to see you, Miss Gallagher," she said tonelessly. "I thought at our last meeting all that we had to say to each other had been said." She stared at my black eye, but said nothing about it.

"May I offer my condolences on the death of your husband? I know it must be a great shock and I'm sorry to have to intrude on your bereavement."

She made no acknowledgment of my condolences. She said, "What do you want?"

"Do you know Charlie Gore?"

"We've met. My husband asked him to look into the same matter for which I engaged Frampton Investigations. I was frankly not much impressed by Mr. Gore's qualifications."

"Charlie told me he was going to Seattle," I said. "As far as

166

we can find out, he had no intention of going to Seattle. But he was onto something, and I think your husband may have given him some kind of lead."

"What is it you want from me?"

"I've checked Charlie's records and I've checked with your husband's office and no one seems to have the least idea where Charlie might have gone or who he was going to contact. I thought there might be an odd chance that your husband might have said something or that Charlie might have told him what lines of investigation he was following."

"I'm sorry, my husband said nothing about him at all."

The maid came in with my tea. Mrs. Holmcroft turned to her and said, "Miss Gallagher isn't having anything, thank you."

The maid backed out of the room with her tray.

Mrs. Holmcroft turned to me. "I believe I've answered all your questions."

"Did your husband have an office at home?"

"No, he did not. His secretary at the office took care of the household bills. He signed the checks, of course. Will that be all, Miss Gallagher? I'm quite tired and my son has been quite upset by the death of his stepfather and I should be with him."

"Preston Chang gave me this black eye."

Her eyebrows went up slightly. "Did he now?" She obviously approved.

"He told me that you and he were working together to try to find out what your husband was up to." This was a stab in the dark, of course, but I felt it was a good stab.

"He told you *what*?"

"You might as well tell me about it, Mrs. Holmcroft. You're going to have to tell it all to the police eventually. Preston Chang might have murdered your husband, and you might have helped inadvertently."

"Never come here again, Miss Gallagher, do you understand me?"

She walked with me to the door and showed me out without saying good night.

* * *

167

I parked around the corner and sat in the car and wondered for a while if it might be true that she and Preston Chang somehow conspired to kill her husband. And I wondered, too, just what it was her kid was so upset about. Holmcroft obviously hadn't liked the boy much. I remembered he'd called Conrad his wife's idiot son. Then, too, I wondered why Mrs. Holmcroft lied about her husband taking care of the bills at the office. Or was it his secretary who had lied? I didn't believe that. She wouldn't have told me the truth about her relationship with Holmcroft, then lied to me about his records.

I was curious about what might be in that desk in the library that she didn't want me to see. What kind of a security system did they have? I wondered. Could I get through it? My heart started beating fast. There's nothing quite so exciting as illegal entry. But then I thought that if I got caught, Aletha Holmcroft would see to it that I didn't get probation and I'd end up in denim at the county work farm wishing I'd stayed in academia.

Eventually the lights on the first floor of the house went out, then on the upper floor front. That would be Mrs. Holmcroft's room. The light downstairs in back stayed on for another half hour before it went out. That would be the maid.

My plan was simple. I'd drop over the back fence and go in through a rear window. I had my trusty Swiss army knife, my penlight, and my new lock-picking kit. Everything a girl needs for an exciting night on the town.

And I was just about to do it when a big Lincoln came around the corner and pulled into the short driveway at the back of the house. The garage door opened and the car went in. The chauffeur, I figured. Must be he had an automatic garage door opener. I got out of the Banana Slug and crossed the street. He was just coming out of the garage when I was coming past it on the sidewalk.

"Hello," I said. Real friendly.

He stopped and looked at me in the dim light of a street light. He was fiftyish, white-haired, had a potbelly.

"Hello," he said. Real friendly in return.

"Through for the day?" I asked.

"Matter of fact, I am."

"How about I buy you a drink?"

"You a reporter?"

"I'm Odyssey Gallagher."

"Oh, Mrs. Holmcroft said I should be on the lookout for you."
Then he whispered: "I'm not supposed to be speaking to you."

"I'm not deadly. All I want is to ask you a few questions." He
looked me over through one eye. "Promise I won't bite," I said.
"Just a few drinks and a little talk. Honest."

He rubbed his chin and said, "Know Fifer's on Van Ness?"

"Sure."

"Be there in twenty minutes."

I drove over to Fifer's. The mist had turned to rain. I parked
in the lot in back and went inside. Fifer's is a piano bar, catering
mostly to tourists staying at the Holiday Inn up the street, from
what I could tell. A cozy, dimly lit little cave behind a gourmet
hamburger place. The piano player was slightly hunchbacked
and had a crooked smile. He could tinkle out any tune you
wanted.

I ordered a vodka martini and waited for the chauffeur. Two
drinks and ten songs later, including two sentimental renditions
of "I Left My Heart in San Francisco," he showed up. He slid
into the booth opposite, tilting his chauffeur's cap on the back of
his head. There were tiny beads of rain on the brim. He had a
square Irish face that showed drinker's veins.

The chubby little waitress knew his name and his drink. "Here
ya go, Freddy," she said, putting down a glass in front of him.
It looked like a bourbon on the rocks. "Thank you, darlin'," he
said, giving her bottom a pat as she headed for another table.

He smiled at me, one of those superior male smiles they give
you after they've gotten away with the petty humiliation of a
woman.

"Well now, Miss, what is it I can do for you, and how much
will ya be willing to pay?"

"I thought we were going to be friends," I said

"After we do a little business we can be friends."

I fished a twenty out of my pocket and handed it to him. He

looked at it as though it might have fleas. I gave him another. "You give me something worth more, you'll get more," I said.

"I guess I'll have to trust ya." He took a few quick gulps of his drink and brought out a pack of cigarettes, jammed one into his mouth and lit it with a gold Zippo. "That's a pretty nice-looking eye you got there." He chuckled.

"Do you know Charlie Gore?" I asked.

"I don't know him exactly, but I know who he is. He rode a couple of times with Mr. H."

"He told me he was going to Seattle yesterday morning. I haven't seen him since."

His face exploded with a smile. "Is that what he told you? Oh, my dear woman. He was at the house, I saw him with Angelica yesterday afternoon."

"Angelica?"

"The maid—I saw them going into her bedroom."

"Like they were having an assignation?" I couldn't believe it.

"Is that what you call it? Looked to me like she was gonna give him a good time. Had that guilty look, ya know."

I gave him another twenty.

"Now we're getting someplace," he said, snapping the bill between his fingers. "Was your parents from Ireland?"

"My father's grandfather."

He nodded as if that told him something meaningful about me. He gulped down his drink; I signaled the waitress for another.

"So how are things at the house? I saw Mrs. Holmcroft tonight and she looked a little pale. Grief, I guess."

"And ain't it a bit of a puzzle, too? She and Mr. H. didn't seem to get along all that well. They had a terrible fight the afternoon he was killed, which was a bit strange in itself, since they hardly ever spoke to each other. He had an eye for the girls, you know. She used to work off her anger down in her target range, I guess."

"She has a target range in the house?"

"Sure does. It's supposed to be a secret, but I got a key to the basement she don't know about." He winked. "Guess whose picture she used as a target?"

170

"Her husband's?"

"Pretty good guess. Ain't that something worth knowing?"

I gave him another twenty. Mr. Frampton was going to flip at my expenses. "Where is this target range?" I said.

"For another twenty I might even show you." He held up a set of keys. "This one's to the back door. I can even turn off the alarm."

"Would you take a check?"

He grinned. "Sure, you being a Gallagher and all, we're practically cousins." He gulped down the remainder of his drink. Was it possible, I thought, that the woman in the trench coat who pulled the gun on Holmcroft and me outside the Transamerica Pyramid was Mrs. Holmcroft wearing a red wig? And that she did the same thing the night her husband was killed?

Suddenly, I felt like the hunter who's had a glimpse of his prey.

We drove back to the Holmcroft house and I parked around the corner. The fog, agreeably, had moved in. Nothing like a little fog when you're sneaking around. The chauffeur was taking labored alcoholic breaths as we went through the back gate. He quietly hummed an Irish lullaby, "toor-a-loora, loora." My grandmother used to sing it to me when I was a kid. I gave him a couple of *shhhhh*'s, but he ignored me.

We crept along the back of the house. No lights on above us. No lights on in the house behind the Holmcrofts' either. At the rear, an outside stairway led up to a deck with a couple of planters that had some leafy bushes growing in them. Underneath was another stairway leading down to the basement. The chauffeur headed down and I followed him. He knocked a sprinkler can over.

"Shhhhhhh," he said, holding his finger to his lips. He chuckled. We both stood quietly for a moment and listened. We couldn't hear anything inside. I flicked on my penlight and we went on down the stairs. At the bottom was a door. Next to the door was a small box for the alarm. He put a key into a slot in the box and turned it with a click. A green light came on.

171

"I tole you," he whispered.

"Shhhhhhh."

He inserted another key in the lock and the door opened with a groan. We went in. He clicked on the light. We were in a dusty basement full of the usual clutter—gardening tools, old trunks, boxes of junk. It smelled vaguely of natural gas, dust, and old leather.

"Come this way," he said.

I followed him through a sort of storeroom, past a furnace, past some more storage rooms, and down a hallway that ended at a makeshift wall made of old, unpainted, mismatched wood. There was a small door in it, which the chauffeur shoved open. We went in. I flashed my penlight around and found the light switch and switched it on.

We were in a long, narrow room. The walls were covered from top to bottom with old ceiling tiles and newspapers. On the far wall pictures of Morrison Holmcroft had been pasted. They were peppered with bullet holes.

"Now ain't this something?" the chauffeur said. "A shooting gallery right here in Pacific Heights."

I checked the bullet holes. Bigger than a .22, but not a .38. A .32 or a 7.65 millimeter. Just like the ones used on Holmcroft. Behind the targets were stacks of bundled newspaper. I pried a couple of the bullets out and stuck them in my pocket.

"Didn't I tell you this was worth seeing?" he said. He pulled a half-pint bottle of hootch from his pocket and took a swig. It ran down his chin. "Want some?" he asked.

"No."

"Okay, we kin go?"

"I'd like to get a look in the desk upstairs in the library," I said.

He knitted his brows. "Goin' upstairs is just a mite risky. Mrs. H. ain't no heavy sleeper."

"How about I kick in another fifty dollars? I promise I'll be quiet as a mouse."

"Have to be twice that."

"A hundred dollars?"

"A hundred is cheap. Not a penny less."

"All right," I said.

"Could I have the check now?"

I made out another check, using his back for a writing stand, and handed it to him. We stepped back into the storage room and closed the door. I followed him outside and up the back stairs. He took out his keys and unlocked the door to the house. It creaked open. He said, "Shhhhh," just a little too loudly. A dim night light in the kitchen made heavy shadows.

The chauffeur waited for me there while I went down the hall to the library. The door was open. I went in and gently closed it behind me.

I switched on my penlight and checked the desk, opening each drawer silently in turn. Nothing in it. It was absolutely empty. Not even an old postage stamp or a paper clip.

I heard something moving in the hall. Suddenly, Mrs. Holmcroft burst into the library, switching on the light. She had the chauffeur in tow. Her jaw was set hard, like a chunk of rock, and her eyes glared, her face red with rage.

"Did you let her in here?" she asked the chauffeur through clenched teeth.

"I-I-I" he stammered.

"You're fired!"

He nodded and looked downcast. The man was a born servant. I figured the best thing to do was go on the offensive: "How do you explain the desk being cleaned out, Mrs. Holmcroft? You know, it's funny that your husband's secretary says she never saw a bill or a personal check—yet you say she took care of all the bills at the office."

"You broke into my house! I'm going to have you arrested!" She turned to the chauffeur. "Call the police!"

"Yes ma'am," he muttered, and headed for the phone.

"Better hold it a minute," I said. "I've broken no law coming in here. I'm a guest, invited in by someone who has a key."

The chauffeur looked at Mrs. Holmcroft, then at me, then at her. She was still shaking with rage, but she didn't tell him again to call the cops.

"So what is it you're hiding?" I said. "What was in the desk? It has something to do with hiring Charlie Gore, doesn't it? What he'd found out?"

"I don't have to explain anything to you. Get out of here! Out!" She turned to the chauffeur: "Pack your things! Give me the keys to this house."

The chauffeur dutifully obeyed. He took the set of keys out of his pocket and dropped it into her hand. She marched out into the foyer and held the front door open. The chauffeur and I left.

Outside the fog had thickened. In the dull porch light, the chauffeur looked like a ghost standing next to me.

"Well, I guess I be heading north for the summer, do some fishing," he said. His shoulders sagged.

"I don't know what else to say—except I'm sorry."

"I don't mind so much. Mr. Holmcroft, he was a real sport. His wife, never did like her much." He sniffed the air. "What do ya say we go over to the Abby Tavern and toast the Irish in each of us?"

"Not tonight. I've got a couple of little chunks of lead here I've got to get to the cops. It just might be we'll have our murderer."

TWENTY-ONE

■

I drove down to the Hall of Justice and gave the slugs to a desk sergeant and told him to get them to Sergeant Tomas. The desk sergeant made me fill out a form and show him some ID before he'd take them.

Then I went home. I went directly to the bathroom and took a shower. I ached all over. I put on a light cotton nightgown and climbed into bed. I opened my mail. Bills, a postcard from my parents from Athens, and a letter from Septimus VII, wanting to know what I thought of his latest poem:

> *Evil to the left*
> *Evil to the right*
> *Into the Valley of Death*
> *we ride*
> *Why, why, why?*
> *the forever question*
> *asked and asked and asked*

> *but no one has an answer*
> *and so*
> *into the Valley of Death*
> *we ride*
> *Evil to the right*
> *Evil to the left*

He could have been writing about me. Surrounded by evil. Like all poets, great and small, he was telling how he sees the world. He always wanted me to tell him he was a great poet because I'd read a lot of poetry at one time and he thought that made me a good critic, but I'm not. I don't want to judge poetry, I want it to hit me. This one hit me a little. I *felt* it. Septimus sees the world as a rough place where no one can keep his sanity without drugs, booze, or poetry to help him through the night and at the moment I was feeling the same way.

I clicked off the light. Noise from the street and music from the other side of the fence that ran along the property line filtered in. The red neon light from the liquor store flickered on my wall. Evil to the left. Evil to the right. Sleep overcame me suddenly.

A couple of hours later I woke with a start.

At first I thought someone was in the room, but when I looked around, no one was there. It was raining outside; I could hear the water beating against the window. I glanced at the clock. Ten after four. The neon sign of the liquor store was off. No one was playing music on the other side of the fence.

I reached for the light by my bedside, but then thought better of it. Had I dreamt something? Was I cracking under the stress?

No, damn it, something woke me.

I reminded myself to keep my ki flowing out. I slid out of bed, leaving the blankets piled so that it looked as if somebody was still there. I crawled across the living room to the sliding glass door on the deck, my senses fully alert. I could hear my own breaths.

I saw nothing and heard nothing to indicate there was anyone else around. The rain was coming down hard against the deck outside. I pulled the drape back slightly. The glass door was open about an inch. It had come up against a safety stopper that Martin had installed—so someone had tried to get in.

I froze.

Could I have left it like that by mistake? I tried to remember whether I had bolted the kitchen door. I must have. I always did.

I turned and made my way across the floor to the door leading to the kitchen. I paused and listened. No one there. Of course I'd thrown the bolt. What the hell was wrong with me? I was being silly. I stood up. I must be stressed out, I thought. Mental fatigue. Too much evil to the left and right.

Just for the hell of it I said: "I know you're there. I've got a gun and I know how to use it."

A crashing sound came from the kitchen and I caught a glimpse of someone in the light of a passing car—the frizzy hairdo, the trench coat.

I dropped down as a gun went off, the muzzle flash lighting the kitchen, the bullet smashing the sliding door behind me. I rolled to my right as two more shots rang out.

I came up on my feet and threw myself at the drape, crashing through the glass door onto the wet deck. Another shot; I felt a sting on my earlobe.

I vaulted over the deck's railing and dropped into the mud below and made a dash for the scrub brush that had grown thick along the fence at the edge of the property. I came around the trunk of a tree and looked back toward my place. I could hear footsteps come down the stairs, then more footsteps racing up the driveway.

I waited. Nothing more. After a few minutes there were sirens wailing in the distance. The neighbors must have called the cops. Mrs. Eversole, no doubt. Always on the lookout, bless her soul.

I waited where I was until I saw the cop cars come up the driveway. I came out of the bushes with my hands up. A cop approached me. His eyes went over me in my wet and clinging nightgown, the lech.

"Where's the intruder?" he said.

"He's gone," I said. His partner put a slicker over my shoulders and walked me into the house. My knees were shaking.

"Could you identify your assailant?" the cop asked me. The cop was young and dark. High cheekbones.

"No." I told him what I'd seen. He used my phone to call in a description, but it wasn't much. A trench coat. Frizzy hair, perhaps a wig. Two more cops showed up. A man and a woman. They looked around. They found where my door had been jimmied. I hadn't set the deadbolt. They scolded me about that. "I was tired, okay?" I said. That's all I said. I wasn't in the mood to be scolded.

One of the cops found a slug in a door frame, so maybe they'd be able to match it. I asked if there were any footprints and he said no, the assailant must have run down the driveway.

I put on a big pot of coffee for the cops and called a glass company's twenty-four-hour hotline for somebody to come and board up the place before my floors got ruined. Then I went into the bathroom to get cleaned up. I put a bandage on my ear and washed the spots of blood off my neck.

I went into the bedroom and sat on the floor with my legs crossed and meditated for a few moments to ease the tension out of my body. Then I got dressed and went back out into the kitchen and found Sergeant Tomas sitting at my kitchen table dunking a doughnut into a mug of coffee.

"What are you doing here, Sergeant?"

"I got it in the computer that they should call me if something happens to you. You get a good look at the shooter?"

"No."

"You okay?"

"No bullet holes, if that's what you mean."

"How'd you get the black eye?"

"Slipped in the shower."

"Yeah, those showers can be real slippery."

I poured myself a cup of coffee. Not that I really needed it, I was feeling pretty wired already. I took a bite of a plain doughnut and I found I was hungry. Fear makes you hungry. Funny thing.

"Didn't they tell you it's a dangerous life, being a shamus?" he chuckled. I think he was trying to cheer me up. It wasn't working.

"I made a friend last night," I said. "Holmcroft's chauffeur. We had a few drinks down at Fifer's."

"I know the place. They got a pretty good piano player. A hunchback."

"After we had a few drinks, the chauffeur took me back to Holmcroft's place. He took me into the basement and showed me a little target range down there."

"Whose target range?"

"Must be Mrs. Holmcroft's because it sure wasn't her husband's. Pictures of him were being used as targets. That's where I obtained those two slugs I left for you."

"Yeah, the lab called me. No match, I'm sorry to say. They were not fired from the gun that killed Morrison Holmcroft. We ran it through our old crimes computer. No matches there either. A virgin gun, far as we know."

"That's strange. I figured the intruder was looking for those slugs. But why would somebody come over here looking for the slugs, if the slugs didn't mean anything?"

"Perhaps you picked up the wrong slugs. A shooting gallery could have been used for any number of guns. You think Mrs. Holmcroft had something to do with her husband's killer?"

"I think she got dressed up in a red wig and a trench coat and went down there and blew him away herself."

He stared at me for a long moment, holding a doughnut halfway to his mouth. Then he said, "That doesn't make sense. Why would she kill him? Not for his money. She has enough money in her own right to buy half of this city."

"Her husband was having an affair."

He chuckled again, shaking his head. He bit into his doughnut and said, "Rich people don't kill each other over affairs. To them, it's like tennis."

"He was going to leave her."

"Who said so?"

"Confidential sources. She must have somehow found out that I was in her basement and got those slugs and that's why she came here—to get them back."

"You think Mrs. Holmcroft assaulted you tonight?"

179

"Yes, I do."

He shook his head. "Very doubtful. The assault took place, oh, thirty to forty minutes ago?"

"Yes."

"Then it couldn't have been Mrs. Holmcroft. At that time she was filing a complaint against you for illegal entry. I took the complaint myself. Personally."

"Why'd she wait over two hours?"

"Had to confer with her attorney."

I went into the living room and poured myself a stiff shot of brandy. Sergeant Tomas came with me. I poured some brandy into his coffee. I clinked my cup against his.

"Just lock me up and throw away the key," I said. "I've had it."

The good sergeant did not arrest me, since I had committed no crime. Just as I'd told Mrs. Holmcroft, the chauffeur, as a resident of the household, had let me into Mrs. Holmcroft's place; that qualified me as a "guest." At least as far as the law was concerned. I didn't steal anything, except the two slugs, and she didn't know about them and Sergeant Tomas wasn't going to tell her, so I was in the clear.

Then the sergeant explained that the reason Mrs. Holmcroft made a police report was she was probably setting me up for a harassment suit and I'd probably better stay the hell away from her.

I swore a blood oath I'd do just that.

Sergeant Tomas started to leave. I said, "I'd like to see Martin."

"Now? It's a quarter to five in the morning."

"Can you arrange it?"

He nodded. I guess he understood how I was feeling. He made a call.

I drove down to the Hall of Justice and went in through the metal detector. The officer on duty must have been told I was coming, because he told me to go up to Homicide on the fifth floor.

180

I got off the elevator and crossed the hall and went into the squad room. A couple of detectives were doing paperwork. One looked up. He had a round face with a cigarette dangling from his mouth.

"You Gallagher?"

I nodded.

He jerked his thumb toward an office. The sign on the door said LT. HUXLEY. I went in.

Martin, wearing prison denim, was standing by the window looking at the rain. I closed the door behind me. He looked back over his shoulder and his eyes lit up. We ran to each other and held each other in a long embrace. It felt good to hold him and be held.

Then he pulled away from me and looked me up and down. His eyes watered.

"I'm so happy to see you, I don't know what to say," he said. He tried to smile. "How'd you get the eye?"

"Slipped in the shower."

"You've got to get out of this business."

"Are you going to be able to make bail, Martin? Your lawyer called. I've been so busy . . . my parents are in Greece. When they get back they might be able to help."

"We're filing a writ of something to get the bail reduced. I think that's what he said. Oh, Od, I've missed you. I've missed you more than anything."

He took hold of my hands and kissed them. "You don't know how frightening it can be in here. The stories you hear, it's too terrible to believe. I saw a man stabbed with a home-made knife. He only needed a couple of stitches, but the blood was terrible. Odyssey, you've got to get me out of here."

"I'm trying."

"I love you, Odyssey, you've got to believe that. If there's anything I've learned in here it's what you mean to me. I forgive you for being untrue to me, I mean, I know how inattentive I can be. I don't blame you for wanting the attentions of another man. Anyone can get carried away in the heat of the moment, especially since I was such a ninny the night before. I swear to you,

181

it'll be different when I get out of here. I know now that you mean more to me than anything. My career is nothing. Odyssey, please don't ever leave me. We'll get married just as soon as all this is cleared up, what do you say?''

"Martin, I . . .'' Damn it, I couldn't get the words out.

"You can't want that oafish cretin, Odyssey, don't tell me that.''

"No, Martin, I don't. He's already married, anyway.''

"A married man?''

"I didn't know he was married.''

"I should hope not. So it's over between you two?''

"It's over.''

"Then we can get married?''

"We'll talk about it as soon as you're out of here.''

"I want it settled, Odyssey. I want you to say you'll marry me. It's terrible in here, but I can stand it as long as I have something to hope for, something to look forward to when I get out of this hellhole. Please, Odyssey, holding onto that hope is all I have. Promise me we'll be married as soon as I get out of here.''

There was such desperation in his eyes, in his voice. All I could think of was that he was in there on account of me, that he loved me so much, that I owed him. I found myself nodding; his face exploded with happiness, he hugged me and kissed me, tears of joy streaming down his face.

And all the time I kept telling myself that I could love him, that we could be happy, but at the same time a picture of Charlie Gore looking his Sundance Kid best kept popping into my mind, and no matter how hard I tried to make it go away, it wouldn't.

A jail cop showed up to take Martin back to his cell. Martin kept throwing kisses back to me all the way across the squad room. He looked as happy as I'd ever seen him. As he went through the door he cried, "I love youuuuuuuuuuu.''

"I love you too!'' I called after him. It echoed off the walls of the empty squad room.

One time I was late for work and was driving too fast down Geary Boulevard and ran over a puppy. The little boy who owned it was waiting for the school bus on the corner and the

182

puppy had gotten loose and had run to the kid, right in front of me. I hit the brakes, but skidded over the animal. The kid cradled the dead puppy in his arms and looked up at me through his tears and said, "Why did you kill Flubby?"

That's about as bad as I'd ever felt in my life until this.

TWENTY-TWO

■

I stopped by my place only to pick up a few things. The window people had already boarded up the sliding glass door.

I drove over to the Barbary Coast Motel on Lombard and checked in under the name of Daisy Smith and got a few hours sleep on a water bed. I got up at nine, feeling dull, put on some running togs, and went for a run on the Marina Green.

It was rainy and cold, but I ran anyway, letting the rain beat against my face and clear my head. I was sick about Martin. I'd promised to marry him, and part of me said that was a good idea, at least things would be settled. But another part of me kept saying no, that it was Charlie Gore I really loved. But I didn't love Charlie Gore. I couldn't love Charlie Gore, the man was an ill-mannered lout.

Thinking about this was making me dizzy. Since Martin was in jail and Charlie was off doing whatever it was he was doing, I really didn't have to decide anything at the moment anyway. I had a case to worry about.

Things would work out, I told myself.

I put my mind on Aletha Holmcroft and how I was going to trap the snake. Even if she was talking to Sergeant Tomas at the time I was attacked, it didn't matter; she was behind it. She'd hired whoever it was and had him or her wear the same disguise she'd worn when she'd killed her husband. And somehow I was going to prove it.

I stopped by my place to pick up some more clothes. The workmen were putting in the new glass door. After a hot shower back at the motel I was feeling pretty good. I had a cup of coffee and a stack of blueberry pancakes at the International House of Pancakes, then drove on over to the office.

The always-cheerful Mrs. Kentfield sang good morning as I came in. She said Mr. Frampton was in his office and wanted to see me. I noticed Fisk wasn't in yet. Good. Maybe I'd be in and out before the scum showed up.

In Mr. Frampton's office, the computer printer in the corner buzzed away, flipping out sheets of paper like a Reno blackjack dealer handling cards. Mr. Frampton was sitting behind his desk wearing what looked like a new vested suit, a new shirt, and a new tie. Whenever he was down and needed a boost he always bought a new outfit. I didn't even have to look to know that he had new shoes as well.

"Good morning, Miss Gallagher," he said brightly. "I have much to report," he said, indicating a large stack of computer paper. He gestured for me to have a seat. He leaned forward over his desk and clasped his hands in front of him. He was wearing two large rings, one on the ring finger of each hand. A green stone in one, a red stone in the other.

"Did you know," he said, "that your friend Charles Gore once lost his professional license because of conflict of interest?"

"No, but I'm not surprised to hear it."

"Did you know he was arrested twice for assault?"

"Any convictions?"

"No."

"Then we must assume they were unfounded allegations—

185

why are you telling me all this, I know what kind of a man Charlie Gore is."

"Such a man makes a lot of enemies. I think we should start working on the theory that he might have been the victim of foul play. This might be another Jimmy Hoffa kind of deal. It might be just a coincidence that he disappeared while he was looking into the Holmcroft case."

"He left me a note, remember. I think he's working leads. He was very upset that he lost a client. Whatever else he might be, he's a damn good detective and he never quits."

He sat and looked at me for a long moment like he was letting it sink in, but I don't think it was sinking in. Then he said, "May I tell you another theory?"

"Love to hear it."

"His wife's new boyfriend, according to Fisk, is Frank Jackson. I did a little research on him. He's been in Attica, Sing-Sing, Quentin. Armed robbery twice, bad checks, moonshining. Once he nearly beat a man to death in a barroom fight. I think Charlie's wife might have told Frank to make Charlie go away."

"Not when Charlie's been paying her medical bills."

He frowned. "I didn't say it was a good theory, I only said it was a theory. Have some coffee." He pushed his pot in my direction. It not only looked like mud, it smelled like it.

"No thanks."

He leaned back in his seat and folded his arms. "You're a very good operative, Miss Gallagher. Smart. Imaginative. Daring. You handle people well. But you do have certain—shall we say— blind spots."

"I do?"

"You think Mrs. Holmcroft killed her husband, don't you?"

"Yes."

"Not a chance in a million."

"You want to hear what I found in her basement?"

"I've already spoken to Sergeant Tomas, so I know all about it. Miss Gallagher, I think you ought to take a few days off. Go someplace. Rest. Mr. Fisk and I will wrap this up for you."

"Wrap what up?"

186

"We have some leads on Rachel Collins. A woman answering her description and driving a red Japanese car—possibly a Toyota—was seen not one half block from your house within fifteen minutes of Mickey Fingers's murder. Mr. Fisk found the witness. I think it might do you good to thank him. Help the peace around here." A small smile on his lips.

"You're saying that Rachel Collins killed Fingers?"

He nodded. "It's possible."

"Mr. Frampton, Rachel Collins did not kill Mickey Fingers."

"At this point in our investigations we should keep an open mind."

"I really think there's no point in even discussing it."

He smiled one of those male-superior-talking-to-a-poor-dumb-female smiles which have been known to set me off like a rocket to Mars. But I kept my aikido cool and just smiled back. Then I said, "What have your computers come up with on Mrs. Holmcroft?" I was being professional.

"She's on the board of directors of the opera and the ballet, she's active in the League of Women Voters, and serves tirelessly on a committee that raises a ton of money for St. Jude's Hospital for Children. I think it's in Memphis."

"Rich people are always on boards and committees. What else?"

"She is devoted to her son, who has had some learning disabilities. She's sent him to educational specialists all over the country."

"So she's a good citizen and a good mother. I'd still like to keep an eye on her for a few days. Can I borrow the van?" We use the van for stakeout work.

He sighed heavily. "For what purpose?"

"If you talked to Sergeant Tomas, then you must know someone wearing a trench coat and a frizzy hairdo broke into my place last night looking for some slugs I'd taken out of Mrs. Holmcroft's basement. At least I think that's what he or she was looking for."

"Did you apprehend them?"

187

"No. Whoever it was fired several shots at me. One nicked my earlobe."

He looked at me with his mouth open. "I think we ought to back away from this one."

"I'm not backing away from anything. I want the van. Can I have it?"

"You'll have to swear you won't make a move without adequate backup, either from Mr. Fisk, myself, or the police. Please, Odyssey, I don't want to see you hurt."

"Don't worry, I'm not going to take any risks. I'm just going to keep an eye on Mrs. Holmcroft until she slips up, and then we're going to bag her."

"Somehow I think I'm going to deeply regret this." He handed me the keys.

On the outside the van looks like a rather beat-up window van with "Supreme Furnace and Air-Conditioning Service" written in large orange letters on the sides, now rather nicely faded. I parked it across the street from the Holmcrofts' place, down the block about fifty yards, where I could see the side of the house.

Inside, the van was pretty classy. It had four swivel chairs, some nice cabinets, a plush rug, a pretty good stereo system, a couple of good 7x binoculars on tripods, a TV video camera. There's a small refrigerator, a small stove, and a cupboard filled with canned goods. All the comforts of home. And if Mother Nature calls, there's a Port-a-Potty.

I played some jazz and blues on the stereo and listened through headphones so passers-by wouldn't hear it. Mr. Frampton has a very nice collection.

First, I did my nails. I buffed and filed them and worked the cuticles, polished them with clear polish. Toenails were next. I could do them and keep an eye on the Holmcroft place at the same time. When you do surveillance work, you get good at things like that. Nobody came in or out. The mail carrier came by. A few letters, no packages.

I leafed through the *Chronicle*. They'd executed some killer down in Florida and they included every last detail of the execu-

188

tion right down to the color of the socks the condemned man wore. I don't know what's more disgusting, the man's crime—he killed a liquor store owner—or the crowds that gathered outside the prison to celebrate and buy pins with a replica of the electric chair they call "Old Sparky." Or the lurid newspaper account. Or my reading every last grisly word of it.

I found myself fantasizing about putting Mrs. Holmcroft in the chair and pulling the switch. Gad, what stakeout can do to you.

I made myself some instant coffee. I did the crossword puzzle. Couldn't figure out a six-letter word for "fetter" that started with *m*.

At one-fifteen the drapes in the living room were drawn closed. I tried to see who closed them, but all I could make out was a shadow.

An emergency rescue vehicle roared by at two-thirty, then roared by again in the opposite direction a half hour later.

I did some push-ups and sit-ups and rested a while, then did some more. No one in or out of the Holmcrofts'. I was beginning to feel like an idiot.

Then the front door opened and the maid came out. She hurried off down the street. I got out of the van and followed her on foot. I wanted to talk to her. I'd have to take the chance of missing Mrs. Holmcroft, but I thought perhaps the maid could tell me something about Charlie's disappearance. After all, he'd been balling her.

She walked north for four blocks to Union, a commercial street. She browsed for a while in a boutique. I could see her through the window picking at things on the rack as though she really wasn't interested. Then she came out, crossed the street, and went into a little coffee shop. She used the phone in back, spoke for a few minutes, then went to the counter and ordered a cup of coffee. When she turned around she saw me standing behind her.

"Oh," she said. "It's you. Who told you I come here?"

I ignored the question. "Can I just ask you a few questions?"

She nodded. She was wearing a scarf around her head. Her dark eyes looked terrified. Coffee slopped onto the saucer.

"You'd better sit down," I said.

We took a booth along the wall. The place wasn't doing much business. She stirred sugar into her coffee and kept her eyes down.

"Charlie Gore has disappeared," I said.

She glanced at me, but didn't say anything. I had a feeling there was a lot of brain activity going on behind those eyes. "The coffee here is very good," she said. She stirred it slowly.

"Where is he?" I asked.

"How should I know?"

"He visited you at the house, I know."

"What do you mean?"

"You know what I mean."

"Who you been talking to? Freddy?"

Freddy was the chauffeur. I nodded.

She said, "You can believe nothing that man says."

I grabbed her hand. She tried to pull it away, but I held it tightly. "You may be in danger. She killed her husband, you know."

"Who killed her husband? Mrs. Holmcroft? You must be crazy! She killed nobody! Let go of me."

"If she gets the idea you're a threat to her, she'll kill you, too."

She just glared at me. I let her go. She slid out of the booth and walked out of the place.

I went outside and headed back up the hill. When I reached the van I got in, boiled some water for a cup of tea, and was trying to decide whether to have chili con carne or corned beef hash when suddenly Mrs. Holmcroft came out and headed for the garage.

190

TWENTY-THREE

■

A gray Mercedes backed out of the garage and swung a wide arc in the street and, with a squeal of rubber, shot down the hill.

I leapt into the driver's seat of the van and cranked over the engine, put it in drive, and hit the gas. It stalled. I cranked it up again and it started. I took off after the Mercedes.

At the bottom of the hill on Union, a bread truck was making a left and blocked the intersection. I pulled around it to the right and caught a glimpse of the Mercedes heading west on Union. I accelerated and took off after it, keeping my distance. The way to tail is to stay back and watch the lights. It's tricky, especially when you're in a truck.

The Mercedes turned south onto Divisadero and went up the hill and made a left on California. Mrs. Holmcroft was circling, obviously worried about being followed. I couldn't tell if she had spotted me, so I stayed back a block. She took a right on Van Ness. I followed about a half a block behind, but then I caught a red light at the next intersection and the cross traffic was so heavy I couldn't take a chance on going through it. When the light changed I hit the gas and took the next block at forty miles an hour. At the next intersection I couldn't see her. I guessed she must have gone left, so I waited for the cross traffic, then hung a left and shot up over the hill. There was a moving van in the next block and traffic was backed up behind it. No gray Mercedes.

She must have made a right back at the last intersection, I thought. I swung around, cutting off a guy in a little Isuzu pickup. He honked his wimpy little horn.

I came back over the hill. I could see five or six blocks in front of me. When I stopped at the light at Franklin, I took out my binoculars and took a look ahead of me. No gray Mercedes.

The driver of the Isuzu pickup beeped because I hadn't moved when the light changed. I started slowly forward, still not knowing what to do. Then I spotted a public parking lot up ahead on the right and thought she might have gone in there. It was worth a look.

I started into the lot and there was Mrs. Holmcroft walking straight at me, not twenty feet away. She had a shoulder bag on her right shoulder, hanging as though it was pretty light. I hit the brake and ducked down behind the dash. I waited for a moment, then lifted my head. She'd walked past me and was heading for the street. I pulled over into a space marked for the handicapped and got out.

I dashed out onto the sidewalk and caught a glimpse of Mrs. Holmcroft crossing the street. She was hurrying and glancing around, I guess to see whether she was being followed. I ducked back when she glanced my way. She walked past a branch of Bank of America. It was Friday, they were still open. She stopped, looked both ways, then retraced her steps and went into the bank.

I went back to the van, feeling excited. She was up to something and I was going to find out what it was. I took out the homing device Mr. Frampton keeps under the seat, switched on the cigarette-pack-size sending unit, and turned on the receiver. It beeped away.

192

I took the sending unit and found the gray Mercedes in the parking lot. I put the magnetized sending unit under the car, then went back to the van and waited, feeling pretty lucky and clever. I deduced she was in the bank getting some money in order to skip. I figured she'd come back to her car, get in, and drive to the airport. I planned to follow her and confront her and get a confession out of her.

I put in one of Mr. Frampton's jazz tapes, Billie Holiday with a big band behind her, and waited. Five minutes later Mrs. Holmcroft was back. I had maneuvered the van so it was facing away from the Mercedes, so I could watch her through the mirror. She had the bag under her arm, securely tucked under her elbow. Now it looked stuffed. With cash, no doubt. She got into the Mercedes and started up and pulled out of the lot. I waited until the Mercedes got into the street and turned right before I went after it, the homing device beeping confidently away.

She made a left on Gough Street. She was going to the freeway, I was certain now. The freeway would get her to the airport. But going down the hill before the on ramp, she maneuvered into the right lane.

I stayed with her. She continued driving down Gough until she got to Fell Street, then she made a right. I was six cars behind her going up over the hill, past the DMV and the Golden Gate Park panhandle and into the park itself.

She went up John F. Kennedy Drive, made a left, and parked by the Music Concourse. I stopped in a white passenger zone in front of the De Young Museum across the street. I took my binoculars and scanned the area. It was still daylight. I could see her moving along with the tourists heading for the Academy of Sciences, a large, white, Greco-Roman building. Between us was the Music Concourse, a grassy area with park benches set theater-style facing a stage. There was a small crowd of people listening to a classical music concert. Romantic stuff. Most of them were old folks.

I got out of the van and ran through the crowds and into an underground walkway that comes up on the other side of the

193

Music Concourse, in front of the Academy of Sciences building. When I came out of the tunnel I took a look around. Mrs. Holmcroft was walking back toward the parking lot. She was empty-handed.

I jumped up on a nearby bench and scanned the area with my binoculars. I caught a glimpse of a man in a checkered sport coat and brimmed hat with what looked like Mrs. Holmcroft's shoulder bag under his arm. He was heading around the side of the building toward a wooded area. I took off after him, threading my way through the tourists coming out of the show at the planetarium. When I got to the woods I could see the man ahead of me, hurrying along a paved path. He had shoulder-length brown hair and when he glanced back I could see he had on dark glasses and wore a beard.

Charlie? Not possible. No way. Couldn't be. He had to be a confederate of Mrs. Holmcroft's, I thought. Somebody who had helped Mrs. Holmcroft set up the crime and now she'd paid him off. I planned to follow him and make a citizen's arrest.

I could see ahead that the trail curved to the right. I cut through the woods, fighting my way through a thicket, and headed him off. I came out of the thicket and hit the trail. He was nowhere to be seen. I jogged back up a small rise and he was gone.

He must have cut through the woods some way. I asked a bicyclist if he'd seen a man in a checked coat. The cyclist just shrugged. There were only two ways the guy could have gone. One led to the tennis courts and the other way to Martin Luther King, Jr., Drive. I guessed he'd be headed that way. I took off through the woods. After a quarter of a mile, I found another trail, turned to my right, came around a bend, and collided head-on with the man I was chasing, knocking him to the ground.

I got to my feet and turned to catch a foot in the face that sent a flash of stars through my consciousness. I fell over backward and rolled to my feet. I shook my head to clear out the stars and saw my man hobbling off down the trail. He must have hurt his foot, either when we collided or when he kicked me. Served the bastard right.

I took off after him. He bumped into a jogger coming the other way and that slowed him down even more. I caught up with him at the crest of a small hill and made a diving tackle. He skidded along on his stomach.

"You are under citizen's arrest," I said, scrambling to my feet. I had hold of his arm, and was twisting it behind his back. "I'm holding you for the police."

He panted hard and I could smell his sweat and his cologne and aftershave, and suddenly I knew I'd been right the first time—

"Charlie!"

He stopped struggling. I let go of his arm. He turned and took off his hat and shoulder-length wig and stupid-looking false beard and dark glasses.

"Hello, Odyssey, how are you?"

"Kicking me like that, you could have killed me!"

"I didn't know it was you."

"Who in hell did you think it was?"

"Hey, you attacked me! I'm the victim. I was only defending myself."

I noticed that we were in a clearing and had attracted a small crowd of onlookers. I turned to them and said, "Excitement's over, folks, just move along."

I'd heard cops say that and for them it always seemed to work. For me, it didn't. These folks didn't move. I turned to Charlie. "Give me the bag."

"No."

"Charlie, give me the bag."

"It's mine."

"I know what's in there."

"You do?"

"Yes. I saw where she got it. I was tailing her."

"I told her to make sure she wasn't followed. Never trust an amateur."

"Give me that bag."

195

I reached for it. He pulled back.

"Give me that bag, Charlie. I mean it."

"What do you plan to do with it?"

"It's evidence."

"Evidence of what?"

"Evidence that she killed her husband."

An old lady who was listening said: "Who killed her husband?"

"Butt out!" Charlie said to her.

She slinked away.

"Come on, Genius," he said, "let me buy you a drink."

"You aren't talking me into anything."

"Okay, I'm not talking you into anything. But we can at least be civilized, can't we?"

We walked down a trail and turned onto another path that led to a small parking area near a kids' playground. We were both hobbling. I'd skinned my knee and it smarted. We got into his car and he started driving.

"How much did you get?" I asked.

"Two hundred thousand."

"Is that all? Or is it just a down payment?"

"Hey, what do you take me for? I gave the woman my word, this is it."

"Until you blow it. Then you'll want more. Isn't that the way blackmailers work?"

"Odyssey, Odyssey, what you must think of me. This is not blackmail. I was working for her husband, this is payment for services—plus a bonus."

"Two hundred thousand? What's your hourly rate? Ten grand? What a sleaze you are, Charlie. The scum of the entire planet."

"Gee, Odyssey, you make it sound like we aren't in love."

"In love! Is that what you call it?"

"What do you call it?"

"Hormones. Chemical imbalance. Temporary insanity."

"All words for the same thing. We're nuts about each other."

196

He smiled at me, his glittery smile. I wasn't going to let it work on me.

"How come you didn't tell me you were married?" I said.

"I'm not married. I mean, not *really* married. I just haven't gone through the paperwork."

"You've been missing for almost three days. This may surprise you, you lunkhead, but I was worried about you."

He hung his head a little. "Yeah, well, when I heard Fingers got it, I figured the bullet was meant for me and I didn't want to take any chances, so I just didn't come back."

"And you couldn't let me in on it? No, you just let me imagine all sorts of terrors. Your note said you'd be back in a day. That you went to Seattle."

"Okay, so I'm a knothead. Forgive me?" He smiled again and looked at me with those deep blue eyes, eyes that would melt the polar icecaps. We were out of the park, heading downtown. I had no idea where we were going. Charlie didn't seem to know either.

"You've committed a major felony, Charlie," I said.

"I have?"

"Damn right you have. Blackmail is serious."

He shrugged. "You can't prove it's blackmail, no one could. This is what Holmcroft owed me. I often get a bonus when I do a good job."

"A good job! Your client got offed!"

"I wasn't hired to protect him. I'm being paid for—for other services, confidential services."

"In cash? In the park? From the murderer herself?"

"Mrs. Holmcroft's no murderer. Rachel Collins is the murderer, as far as I know."

I asked him to pull over. He did. We were on Oak Street along the park panhandle.

"Okay, what?" he said.

"Listen, Charlie. You and I are going to have to go downtown right now and you're going to have to tell the police exactly what happened—we'll pretend that we were trying to get her to show her hand or something."

He gave me a queer look and shook his head. "What are you saying, Genius? Are you out of your mind? If I told the cops this, I couldn't keep the two hundred thou." He zipped open the bag and grabbed a bunch of hundred-dollar bills. The car filled with their aroma. Money does have a nice aroma.

"Run your fingers through it, Odyssey. I tell you what, I'll give you a helper's fee, say ten percent."

I shook my head.

He said, "You know what I hate about you, Genius?" His voice rang with anger. "You really do think you're smarter than everyone else. Want to know something? You're not. Mrs. Holmcroft didn't kill Fingers and she didn't kill her husband. If I thought she killed Fingers, she'd be shark food right now. I don't know what happened to Pendergast and Rachel Collins. As far as I know, they took off together."

"How do you know she's not a murderer?"

"I'm not saying. You're such a great goddamn detective, you find out for yourself."

"Why'd she give you all this money if she didn't kill anyone?"

"I told you, this is payment for services, plus a bonus."

"You talk about love. If you love me, drive to the police department right now."

"I won't be coerced."

"If you won't go, I'll report what I saw."

"I won't be threatened either, it's your word against mine. I need this money—I can't tell you why. I have to have it."

"For your wife, I know."

"She's got bad lungs and a bad liver, if she doesn't get off the booze, she'll be dead soon. It's over between us, but I feel I owe her. She started drinking because of me, because I didn't treat her right."

"This isn't the way to help her."

"It's the only way I know."

"I mean what I said, Charlie. I have to report what I saw."

He reached across me and opened the door. "Get out," he said.

"You're not even going to take me back to my car?"

198

"Sorry, I'm not going that way."

I glared at him. He glared back. The muscles of his face twitched.

"Very well," I said. "I guess we won't be seeing each other anymore."

"I guess not."

"You may come and get your things tomorrow morning any time before noon. After that, I burn them."

"There's nothing there I want to keep."

I got out of the car. "Then I guess this is good-bye," I said.

"If that's the way you want it."

"You're making a mistake," I said.

"Just close the door."

I closed the door.

TWENTY-FOUR

■

I took a cab back to the van and then drove over to my apartment, all the time imagining that I had my hands wrapped around Charlie Gore's throat and was squeezing until he turned a lovely shade of chartreuse.

I had a peanut butter and jelly sandwich made with stale bread and kept looking at the phone, but I just couldn't use it. I just couldn't blow the whistle on him no matter how much I was sure it was the right thing. Blackmail is blackmail. But could I really prove it? He had the money well hidden by now. I didn't have any witnesses, except Mrs. Holmcroft, who wouldn't back me up because if she admitted to paying blackmail, she'd have to admit to having a reason for paying it.

I wondered what that reason could be. Charlie said Mrs. Holmcroft didn't kill her husband or Fingers. If she hadn't, why did she pay Charlie all that money?

She must have done it. She must have been planning it from the very day she hired me to find Rachel Collins. What a nice plan. Make it look like Rachel Collins was harassing her husband, then kill her husband while she was disguised in a red wig on a foggy night in front of some drunks coming out of a club. Drunks who had seen or heard about Rachel's attack on Holmcroft at the very same place. Really cute.

The phone rang. It was Mr. Frampton.

"Sergeant Tomas called and said he thinks they've found Rachel Collins's car in ten feet of water just off the breakwater at Candlestick Park."

"I'm on my way," I said.

I drove out to Candlestick Park. It was, as usual, windy and cold out there. The top of the louvered stadium glowed red in the rays of the setting sun. There wasn't a game or a concert that night, so it was easy to spot the cop cars and the emergency vehicles at the edge of a small estuary down the road from the entrance to the ball park, right at the edge of the bay.

As I drove up, Sergeant Tomas spotted me and walked over to my van. He looked as if he still hadn't had a hell of a lot of sleep. His tiny pupils told me he had ingested some chemical to keep going. Amphetamines, probably.

"How you doing, Miss Gallagher?" Sergeant Tomas said. He smiled an I-told-you-so smile. I knew what he was thinking. He was thinking that they'd just blown my theory that Rachel was innocent. It looked as if she'd probably ditched her car here so it'd never be found.

A tow truck on a small strip of beach had a winch and cable leading into the dark water. In the deepening twilight, the police cars had their patrol car headlights pointed out over the water. In the surf were a couple of divers; a couple more were in a small boat.

"How did they find it?" I asked Sergeant Tomas.

"A fluke. A kid doing some fishing got his anchor stuck. It isn't all that deep, when he was working it loose he looked down and saw what he thought were a couple of taillights."

The winch on the tow truck started up. Lieutenant Horne stood at the water's edge, his shoulders hunched, his hands jammed into his overcoat pockets. We were thirty yards from the truck when suddenly the water broke and the top of a red car appeared and seemed to hang up for a moment, then slid up onto the beach, water gushing out from under its doors. It was covered with kelp and seaweed and brown silt. None of the glass was broken. The license plate was missing on the back. I walked around the front. The front plate was gone, too. I couldn't see in; there was too much silt on the windows.

Lieutenant Horne was the first to approach the car; he cleaned a spot off the window and looked in. Then he waved to Sergeant Tomas, who went over and spoke to him and looked in. I stepped closer, but one of the cops gestured for me to back up. The lieutenant opened the driver's door, let the water gush out, and stuck his head in. Sergeant Tomas did the same, then withdrew quickly. He said something to the lieutenant, then came over to me.

"Two bodies. A man and a woman. Rachel and Pendergast, must be. Looks like a murder and a suicide. The gun in the woman's hand."

My stomach got tight. I said, "I'd like to have a look."

"I'll have to get an okay from the lieutenant."

He walked over to the lieutenant, who listened, looked at me, then nodded. Sergeant Tomas motioned for me to come over. Everyone was so quiet. The only sound was the surf and the crackle of the tow truck's two-way radio.

I went over to the car. The sea smell was strong and rank. I looked in. The stench of rotting flesh made me gag.

The woman's face was turned to the left, away from me. Her body was flopped up against the wheel, bloated and hideous, her hair a twisted mess over her head, but I could see the bullet hole in her right temple. Her left arm was limp at her side. She was wearing a green skirt and a blouse. Rachel's skirt and blouse, I was pretty sure.

I backed off. Sergeant Tomas took my arm. "You okay?" he said.

"Let's take a look in the other side," I said.

We went around to the other side of the car. A trickle of water was still coming out from under the door.

Sergeant Tomas opened the door. I reached down and picked up a gardening glove with big green stripes and gold stars. Sergeant Tomas opened a small clear plastic bag and dropped the glove in. I knew where I'd seen a glove like that before. I'd seen it on Mrs. Holmcroft's kid, Conrad Winter, the first time I'd met him.

I said nothing.

I looked in the car now, holding my breath against the stench. Rachel's face was turned toward me; it was puffy and slick, like soap. The man was slumped forward, held by a seat belt. He had silver hair and there was a bullet hole behind his right ear.

"I've seen enough," I said.

I walked back to my van with Sergeant Tomas. He said, "The one thing about working homicide that isn't all that glamorous."

"I need a drink," I said. Sergeant Tomas told the lieutenant he was going to give me a ride back to my place because I was too shaky to drive.

We went to a sports bar in Daly City. Sergeant Tomas babbled on for a while about the Giants and how great they were going to be this year, and if only the pitching would hold up. I told him he was nuts, the Dodgers were the class team in the National League West, and the Reds were right up there, too, which started a nice long argument that kept my mind off that car and the two corpses. Sergeant Tomas had a couple of beers and I had a couple of martinis. After an hour or so I was feeling stabilized.

Then I said: "The murder-suicide theory is all wet."

"What do you mean?"

"If Rachel shot Pendergast, then herself, how did her car get into the water?"

"Easy. She shot him, then drove the car into the water. It takes a few moments to sink. Plenty of time to do it to herself." He gulped some beer.

I said: "I saw that glove before."

He looked at me.

"The glove that was on the floor of the car."

"Where'd you see it?"

"At Holmcroft's place."

He shook his head. His eyes showed disbelief.

I finished off my olive and said, "I followed Mrs. Holmcroft this afternoon. She picked up a lot of cash at her bank. She put it in a shoulder bag and took it to Golden Gate Park and gave it to a man, a blackmailer, I think."

"Could you identify the man?"

"No."

I gulped some martini. Damn that Charlie Gore. Here I was again giving false testimony in a murder investigation.

"You're not sure it was blackmail money."

"No. But what else would it be?"

He shook his head; he wasn't buying it. "It just doesn't make sense," he said. "Why would Mrs. Holmcroft kill her husband? Not for having an affair, that's for sure. She would have killed him a dozen times."

I said, "This time it was different. This time he had fallen in love."

"I still can't see her killing him," Sergeant Tomas said. "Really, I can't."

"He was going to leave her. I think that's what really got her."

I didn't want to mention Hillary Hoyle. No reason to drag her into this mess unless I had to.

"You can corroborate all this?"

I nodded. "If I had to, but I don't think I will."

He took a swig of beer. "Oh, and why's that?"

"I think when I tell Mrs. Holmcroft what I know, she won't be able to deny any of it. I'll have a transmitter on; you'll be waiting outside."

"Why'd you want to do a crazy thing like that? What if you're right and she is a murderer and she blows your head off?"

"I'm pretty good at jumping out of windows."

He stared into his beer for a long moment. "I've got to talk to Horne, see what he thinks. She's not just any citizen, you know. Her father was governor of this state. Her grandfather was on the Supreme Court."

"And she's killed four people."

* *` *

204

Sergeant Tomas called Lieutenant Horne while I ordered us some strong coffee and a couple of Reuben sandwiches. Sergeant Tomas came back into the bar and sat down in the booth looking none too happy.

"He wants us to come to the station. We're going to have a big powwow about it."

"He'll go for it, don't you think?"

He shrugged. "It's not my place to pass judgment on my superiors, now, is it?"

"Just between friends."

"He hasn't the courage of a skitter fish."

The Reuben sandwiches were good. Mostly because the sauerkraut was crisp and the Russian dressing had a nice tang. The coffee was strong. I had three cups.

It took us fifteen minutes to get to the Hall of Justice.

Lieutenant Horne's office was right next to the captain's. He had a plain metal desk, and half a dozen straight-back chairs. Ashtrays. On the walls were pictures of the mayor and President Bush with his dog. The desk was neat. A little American flag stuck in a seashell served for a paperweight.

The lieutenant sat behind his desk glaring first at Sergeant Tomas and then at me. He told us to sit.

"Now then, what is this so-called theory of yours, Miss Gallagher?"

I told him what I'd told Sergeant Tomas. About how I had followed Mrs. Holmcroft to her bank and then to the park to make the payoff. And about the glove in Rachel's car. And that Mrs. Holmcroft's husband was intending to leave her.

He leaned back in his chair, but he kept glaring at me. He folded his arms across his chest. "Miss Gallagher, there are probably thousands, if not millions, of those gloves around. And as for giving money to someone in the park, I admit it's certainly suspicious—and we'll definitely look into it—but it's not enough even to suspect the woman of murder. Do you know who she is?"

"She's a murderer."

205

"If she's a murderer, tell me this: Just why in hell would she bring you in on the case?"

"She needed to find Rachel Collins. Her disappearance had foiled her plan. So she killed the cat to make it look like she was in a real panic. If you'll just get me wired up, I'll confront her with it, let's hear what she says."

He shook his head. "No way, lady. The department wants no part of playing games with her. You have not shown that the woman had an ounce of ill will toward her husband."

"You're forgetting about the target range in the basement, her husband's pictures for targets."

"Are you forgetting the slugs didn't match with any slugs in any body whatever? Get out of here, Miss Gallagher. Go home and sleep it off. And from now on, leave the police work to the police."

TWENTY-FIVE

■

Mr. Frampton looked at me over the top of his glasses. He turned toward the window and pulled back the drape and gazed down into the street, pondering, pondering. I looked over his phony African art collection. I liked it, even though it was fake and made by a white kid. He had the heart of a primitive.

Finally, Mr. Frampton turned to me and said, "You're asking me to go against the police. If this backfires we could both be prosecuted."

"I know," I said.

He shook his head slowly, puckering his lips. "We owe no obligation to Rachel Collins. We no longer have a client in this case. We've done as much as we could be expected to do. We've told the police all we know. I'm afraid, Miss Gallagher, that's about all we can do. I won't jeopardize the firm's license by delving into illegal bugging. I'm sorry, really. Go home and get a good night's sleep. We took on a new client today, a very interesting case involving defective hot water heaters, ought to keep us busy for a month."

I groaned. "Good night, Mr. Frampton."

Fisk left a number with our answering service that turned out to be Compton's Pool Hall on Howard. It was ten after ten when I got there. The air inside was layered blue from the cigarette smoke. Guys with their shirts unbuttoned hung around the walls watching the dramas unfold on the dozen or so green-topped tables.

The only other woman in the place was a waitress wearing tight jeans and a frilly blouse. She looked about sixty. She had milk-white skin and a nasty look on her face.

Fisk was leaning over the table taking aim with a cue ball on an eight ball, a cigarette dangling from his mouth. The eight ball was hanging on the lip of the pocket and looked easy enough for an eight-year-old, but Fisk took his time, wringing as much drama from the moment as he possibly could. Then he stroked the cue ball and it crossed the green felt and collided perfectly with the eight ball, dropping it into the pocket.

Fisk's opponent, a young black man, fished into his jeans and handed him some bills. Fisk bowed and signaled the waitress to buy the lad a beer. How gallant.

I headed for Fisk. A large curly-haired lug with tattooed snakes coiled around both arms blocked my way. He smiled. His left upper incisor was missing.

"Care to play, honey?" he said.

"I don't think you're my type. I go for human beings."

He chuckled. I maneuvered around him.

Fisk was trying to coax someone else to play when he spotted me. His eyes lit up.

"Hello, Gorgeous, what the hell are you doing here?"

"You're my last hope, Fisk. Where can we talk?"

We went outside. We were in an industrial district, with a few warehouses converted to nightclubs up the block. I could hear a hard rock beat coming from one of them. Half a dozen motorcycles were parked along the street. I told Fisk what I wanted and why. When I was through explaining, he said, "Why don't you ask Mr. Frampton?"

"I have asked him. He said no. Look, Fisk. I'm going over there. You can back me up, or you can stay here and play pool."

"What about Charlie Gore?"

"I have no idea where he is at the moment. Will you do it or won't you?"

He thought it over. I knew how he was adding it up. He loved notoriety, and he hated rich bitches. He would love to nail a rich-bitch murderer, he could brag about it to his scum friends the rest of his life. If it backfired, he could put the blame on me. He'd love to do that, too. Finally he spit out his gum. "For you, Gorgeous, anything. One thing. If we do bag her, I want at least half the credit."

"I'm not doing this for the glory, Fisk. You can have *all* the credit."

Fisk had the bugging device in the trunk of his car. He had a lot of little gadgets in his trunk. The one he gave me was about the size of a credit card, only thicker. He told me to slip it into my bra. I put it in my jacket pocket. He chuckled. Such a scum.

We parked around the corner from Mrs. Holmcroft's place. He pulled a gun from under his dash. Looked like a .38. Chrome-plated.

"I've only got one. We could go home, I've got more there."

Fisk lived in Oakland. I didn't want to take the time.

"You'll be right outside. If she looks like she's going for a gun, I'll stop her."

"Whatever you say, Gorgeous."

I put my hand on the door handle. "Well, I guess this is it."

"No need to talk loud. That thing will pick up a whisper. I'll get everything on tape." He showed me the tape recorder and receiver in a sling under his arm. "You need me, you just yell my name and I'll come bustin' in with my pardner here, so don't you worry."

"Do I look worried?"

He just chuckled.

209

I got out of the car reciting nursery rhymes so he could check the device. He signaled that it was working. Okay, it was time to go into action. I walked up to Mrs. Holmcroft's door. The night air was clean and fresh. The calming effect of the two martinis had left me long ago. I was wired now. My mouth felt dry as talcum powder.

I glanced around. Fisk had been behind me, but now he was gone. He was a sneaky little worm. That was good for me at the moment.

There were lights on all over the house. I rang the bell and waited. A moment later the door opened.

"Come in, Miss Gallagher. I've been expecting you." She didn't say why; I guess she had heard about Rachel's car being found on the news.

Mrs. Holmcroft had a vague, distant look in her eyes. She was wearing a plain charcoal gray dress, no jewelry. She showed me into the living room. The same room where I had met her on Monday morning. Here it was Friday night and everything had turned upside down.

"You said I should call you Odyssey," she said. Her voice sounded hollow. "Odyssey. A nice name."

She gestured for me to sit on the couch. In the soft light of the lamps, she looked ghostly white. Her hair was tousled. For just a second, a madwoman looked flashed in her eyes.

Upstairs, I could hear someone moving around. The maid perhaps, or Conrad.

"I know what you've done," I said.

"You do, do you?" she said. "My, how smart you are. You told me you were smart as a whip. I ought to have believed you."

"You killed your husband."

She said nothing.

I said, "I saw Rachel Collins's car when they pulled it out of the bay. I saw the glove you left behind. One of the gloves your son was wearing when I met him downstairs in the workroom."

"Conrad loves to work in the garden." She began to walk in a circle in front of me, her head down, her fist pressed against her mouth.

210

"I'm not armed," I said. I wanted her to know, just in case she felt I was a threat to her.

She gave me a hard look and I thought I saw some more of the craziness, but then her eyes softened.

"I know you paid blackmail. Two hundred thousand."

"Do you think they'll let me out on bail?"

"I wouldn't know about that."

"What will happen to Conrad? I've devoted much of my life to Conrad," she said. "He was always a special child. He needed a lot of care. Morrison resented him. I think he was a little embarrassed to have a special stepson. Conrad senses things. He knew Morrison hated him, but I don't think he ever hated in return."

"Did your husband abuse the boy?"

"Not physically. But he was hard on him—that's a kind of abuse. Conrad is a sensitive boy. Special. I knew that even before he was born. When he was growing in me."

"Is that why you killed your husband? Because he abused the boy?"

"Who knows why any of us really does anything? We tell ourselves we're doing things for the best of motives. Then things get all tangled up. Life is very complex. My father was fond of saying that. I never knew my father well. He was a cold man, silent. 'Silent Sam,' my brother and I used to call him." She laughed suddenly, but then her mouth twisted in an anguished scowl. "I can't believe this is happening. The very person I hired—you're recording everything I say, aren't you?"

"Yes."

She laughed again. "Are there police outside, ready to come in . . ."

"Not the police, but there are people out there."

She burst into tears, her whole body shaking. She stood with her face buried in her hands for a full minute or more before she just as suddenly stopped sobbing and stiffened and sat down in a chair. She took a shaky breath and wiped her face with a handkerchief.

After a moment, she said: "I knew if that damn car was found it was over." Her face changed again and she smiled a friendly smile. "Aren't you going to read me my rights?"

"The police do that, I'm not with the police."

"Well then, if you don't mind, I don't think I'll say anything more until I speak with my lawyer."

"All right," I said. I had heard enough. I was feeling a great sense of relief. This was going very nicely.

"I'm going to call the police now," I said. I said it calmly. The last thing I wanted to do was disturb her. I knew there was a phone in the entryway. I started to leave the room.

Mrs. Holmcroft said, "Do you think I'll get the gas chamber?"

"Not with the kind of lawyers you can buy."

She nodded appreciatively. You'd think I'd just told her she'd been chosen patron of the year at the opera. I opened the sliding door and found I was looking down the barrel of a gun. I froze.

Conrad was holding the gun about six inches from my nose. He was wearing the frizzed-out wig and a trench coat and had a look in his eyes a hundred times crazier than his mother's.

His mother said, "Oh, no, Conrad!"

"Nice to see you again, Conrad," I said. I know it was stupid, I just didn't know what else to say to a crazy person who was pointing a gun at me.

Conrad gestured with the gun for me to back up. I complied. I have a policy of complying with people who point guns at me.

"Do you want me to put my hands up, Conrad? Since you have that gun pointed at me."

"She's wearing a transmitter," Mrs. Holmcroft said. "She said that's for the people she has outside listening."

Conrad's eyes got even crazier. "I'll kill them, too," he said. "Like I killed stepdaddy and his girlfriend, and that Pendergast. And that pig in the checkered coat."

"Conrad!" his mother snapped. "No! Don't say anything!"

"I did it, me. Conrad Winter."

Mrs. Holmcroft was standing by me now, tears streaming down her face. She tried to speak, but she choked and couldn't get the words out. I felt sorry for her now. And I felt stupid. She had a crazy son who did her killing for her. And she loved him. That's why she paid off Charlie Gore.

"Don't cry, Mom," Conrad said. "It's going to be all right."

She sobbed: "It's never going to be all right, Conrad."

"I'm going to kill her," he said. "I should have killed her in her bedroom when she was asleep. But I'll kill her now, then we'll go to South America, way out in the jungle. They'll never find us. Please, Mom."

"Killing her won't do any good, Conrad."

"But she's spoiled everything."

Mrs. Holmcroft turned to me and said, "You see what your meddling has brought you? It doesn't really matter a damn to me if he kills you or not."

"It matters to me," I said.

"Right in the heart," Conrad said, aiming the gun at my chest.

At that moment a rock came sailing through the window. Fisk to the rescue! Conrad turned and fired toward the window. I kicked him in the side, then grabbed his gun arm and squeezed a pressure point. The gun went sailing through the air.

Conrad grabbed me and shook me with an insane frenzy, screaming, "Die, bitch!"

He kicked me and gave me a push that sent me flying over the couch. I rolled onto my feet. He dove for the gun, scooped it up, and ran out of the room. I took off after him.

He was already at the top of the stairs when I entered the foyer. I ran up the stairs and turned right. I heard the maid scream and a door slam. I headed in that direction. At the end of the hall was a closed door. Another scream. I kicked at the door and it sprang open.

Conrad was standing in the middle of the master bedroom, holding the gun at the maid's head, his other arm locked around her neck. His wig was now crooked and covering one eye. He looked frightened and confused; the gun was shaking and his eyes darted around as if he expected attack from all sides.

The maid seemed frozen; her eyes were begging me to do something, but I was ten or twelve feet away and there was nothing I could do. Then Mrs. Holmcroft came up behind me.

"Let her go," she said to Conrad. "I mean it, Conrad. Let Angelica go."

He let the maid go; she ran past us and down the stairs, sobbing as she went.

"I love you, Mother," Conrad said, putting the gun to his head. Then he said to me, "I killed them all. Me. No one else."

"I love you, Conrad," his mother said.

He pulled the trigger.

TWENTY-SIX

■

Conrad lay on the floor, a small black hole in the right side of his head. Blood ran out on the floor. The smell of the gunshot hung in the air.

I'd closed my eyes the moment the gun went off, and as I looked again he fell backward, still holding onto the gun. For a moment it felt unreal, but then I saw the blood running and it was very real. I fought back an urge to vomit.

Mrs. Holmcroft went over to him and touched Conrad's hand, gently stroking it. I heard what sounded like a sob coming from her, but she choked it back; then she turned around and her face was pale yellow and her eyes distant, yet cool.

"There now," she said. "You must be well pleased."

She walked out of the room, leaving me feeling as if I had killed an innocent child. I went into the bathroom and doused my face with cold water, my hands shaking. The medicine chest was half opened. Aspirin, Band-Aids, Amytal. Amytal is a barbiturate. A prescription for Mrs. Holmcroft. This is where Conrad got the barbiturate to drug the cat.

I came out and sat on the stairs, taking deep breaths. I could hear sirens.

Dozens of cops showed up, wearing flak jackets and carrying assault rifles, and I took a sergeant and a lieutenant into the bedroom. They took the gun from Conrad's hand and put it in a plastic bag. They went out and a couple of detectives came in, then police lab people, taking pictures. I went outside for some air. One of the cops told me not to wander off, they would want to get my statement.

Fisk was standing on the sidewalk, shoulders hunched, waiting for me to tell him off for not shooting his way in and rescuing me. But I didn't. I walked over and said, "Thanks for the rock. You saved my life."

He smiled, pleased.

"I figured to get the cops in on it."

"You did the right thing," I said.

"Yeah, I got pretty good judgment under fire." He nudged me on the shoulder just like I was one of the guys.

Sergeant Tomas and Lieutenant Horne showed up and took a statement from the remarkably composed Mrs. Holmcroft, then one from me, then one from the maid. Mrs. Holmcroft said she had had her suspicions about the boy, but after all he was her son, and she didn't want to admit to herself that he might have been a killer. She said it calmly, evenly, nothing showing in her eyes.

The cops couldn't have been kinder. You'd think she was the mother of a high school superstar who'd just won the Olympic decathlon.

Then they took my statement, which was short and to the point. They had Fisk's recording, they could listen for themselves to most of it. They seemed relieved to have it all wrapped up.

Sergeant Tomas told me they'd no doubt get the D.A. to drop all charges against Martin. The man I said I'd marry, just to be nice. Now what was I going to do? I hadn't the faintest idea. I just wanted to get stinking drunk.

The cops let Fisk and me go at two in the morning. I went

home and sat at the kitchen table and drank some lemon-lime soda.

Why wasn't I happy? The case had come to such a nice, happy conclusion. The bad guy got caught and put a bullet in his own head. He confessed to everything. The newspapers would make Fisk and me heroes. Martin would be let go. Mr. Frampton would be delirious with joy, even though I had once again disobeyed orders.

I went to bed and slept badly. The next day I got up and saw the front-page story; the headline read, LOCAL P.I.'S IN PACIFIC HEIGHTS SHOOTOUT. They compared it to TV. I didn't read the article. Instead, I went for a long walk along the Marina and watched the sea gulls and the sailboats heading out into the bay, and tried to analyze why I was not happy, why things didn't seem right to me.

I went back home and read through my notes on the case a half dozen times. If it was the kid I chased down the street in front of the Transamerica Pyramid, how was it he had Rachel's car with the dented fender? If it wasn't Rachel's car, whose was it?

I paced around and tried to think it through, but I wasn't getting anywhere. Then I went into the bedroom and took a nap.

At four-thirty in the afternoon Mr. Frampton called and said it was party time. I went down to the office. Lieutenant Horne and Sergeant Tomas were there and already half drunk. There were some other cops, Mr. Frampton's new lady friend, Miss Johns, some creeps from the Shipley Agency across the hall, and some tootsie pops—cop groupies—who hung around at Andy's bar down the block where a lot of cops went when they got off their shifts. Mrs. Kentfield put out some cold cuts and Mr. Frampton kept the booze coming.

I put on a cheery face and listened to them all congratulating themselves. Fisk was showing the cops how to pick pockets, and one of the tootsie pops got drunk and started doing a striptease on Fisk's desk. She got down to black lace bra and panties before Mr. Frampton got hold of his senses and stopped her. At nine-fifteen they all went over to Andy's, all except Mrs. Kentfield and

217

me. Mrs. Kentfield cleaned up the place and packed up the leftover food. I wanted to pore over my notes some more, hoping something would go click.

A little after ten-thirty Mr. Frampton came back and sat at my desk and put his feet up. I guessed that his date had gone home. His tie was undone and by the dopey look in his eyes, I guessed he had a pretty good buzz on.

"Miss Gallagher, may I say something of an uncomplimentary nature about your party behavior?"

"Sorry, Mr. Frampton, I guess I'm not in the mood."

"You may speak freely if there's something bothering you. I am here to listen. Has someone treated you ill?"

I made myself a small sandwich I didn't really want from a box Mrs. Kentfield had packed up, and sat down at Fisk's desk, which faced mine, where Mr. Frampton was sitting.

"No one has treated me ill," I said. "There's just something still bothering me about the case. I don't think the kid did all the killings. The car thing isn't right. I mean, I saw the dented right rear fender on a car that couldn't have been Rachel's."

"Odyssey, Odyssey." He called me Odyssey only after having a few belts. "You think it was Mrs. Holmcroft, don't you?"

"Yes, I do. She hired us to find Rachel so she could pin the murder of her husband on her, and then kill her."

"Odyssey, Odyssey, this is all a castle built in the air. You never did tell her where Rachel was, so there goes your theory."

"But somebody else did. Charlie, I'll bet. He denied it, but I'll bet he did."

"You're really guessing, guessing, guessing."

"I found Amytal in Mrs. Holmcroft's medicine chest. She had a prescription for it. That's a barbiturate. A barbiturate was used to put the cat to sleep."

"Conrad could have gotten into the medicine chest."

"But I doubt he did. Charlie had a little thing going with the maid. I think he found out something he shouldn't have—like maybe about the wig and the trench coat. Mrs. Holmcroft went to my place and killed Fingers by mistake because he was wearing Charlie's jacket."

218

He shook his head low. "Nooooo, noooooo, noooooo. You're daydreaming all this. This is not how a detective should think. Tomorrow we'll get to work on the hot water heater case and you can forget all this nonsense. Be happy, you flushed a murderer who confessed, then blew his brains out."

"He was completely devoted to his mother. I saw the way he was around her. He confessed and killed himself for her. The perfect mama's boy."

Mrs. Kentfield, who had been standing in the doorway the entire time I was talking, shook her head. "That's the most horrible thing I ever heard."

Mr. Frampton said, "Odyssey, you've got to stop doing this."

"Doing what?"

"Confusing reality with the way you want things to be. For some strange reason you've got it in for Mrs. Holmcroft. The poor woman has suffered enough over this. Now come on, let's go over to Andy's and party."

"I'm sorry, I just don't feel like partying. Good night, Mr. Frampton."

As I started to leave, he said: "You know, it's a little late, but I wanted you to know that the mass mailing I did to veterinarians with the picture you took of the cat did yield something."

"You found the cat's owner?"

"Mrs. Keller, her name is. She lives way out in the Richmond."

"I want to talk to that lady."

I phoned first. She said it was all right to come, even though it was late. I drove out to her house. It was an apartment on the second floor of an older, stucco apartment building. Mrs. Keller was about eighty, blue hair, thin as an inmate of the gulag, dentures that clacked.

Her tiny apartment was crammed with pictures of her in her glory days as a WAC in W.W. II. She sat in a wicker rocker and put me on the couch, which was covered with crocheted doilies.

"You said you wanted to ask me about Elroy."

"Elroy?"

219

"Mr. Elroy, his real name was."

I hadn't known cats had real names.

She said, "As soon as he turned up missing a week ago Friday, I knew he was dead. He never went farther than the Hongs' tree next door. Liked to sit under that tree when it was hot. Course out here with all the fog, it don't get hot all that often."

"Would you mind taking a look at a picture? I just want to make sure it's Mr. Elroy."

"I wouldn't mind."

I showed her one of the pictures I'd taken on Uncle Irving's kitchen table. It didn't show the wound in the neck. The cat looked asleep.

She nodded her head slowly and wiped a tear from her eye. "He was a good little boy," she said. "He was a comfy lapful. I guess I overfed him, but he so loved to eat."

"I'm sorry, Mrs. Keller, but what exactly happened to him? Did he just wander off?"

"No, he wouldn't. He was twelve years old. When he was three he wandered off and got hit by a car—that's when he had his leg pinned. He never went anywhere after that. He was fixed, you know. After they've been fixed they want to stay home."

"Have you been watching the news, Mrs. Keller?"

"No, it depresses me so. I watch a few shows. I like 'Golden Girls' quite a lot."

"It was on the news. A young boy killed himself."

"My, my."

"His name was Conrad Winter, the son of Mrs. Aletha Holmcroft. Did you know her? Ever see her? About fifty, dresses well, carries herself very erect. Shoulder-length gray hair?"

"What'd you say her name was?" She leaned over toward me to help her hearing.

"Aletha Holmcroft."

She shook her head. "No. Never heard the name. Never knew a Holmcroft. A Colonel *Holmsteed*, during the war. An awful man. Used to strut so. Winter? Never knew a Winter."

"How about Rachel Collins or a man named Raymond Pendergast who drove a Jaguar?"

"No, don't ring no bells at all."

"Well thank you." I got up to leave.

She walked me to the door. "Mr. Elroy never had much contact with anybody except me. Once in a while one of the kids who go to the school up the block pets him on the way by. One of the boys really liked him. Mr. Elroy even let him pick him up. He didn't let just anybody, you know. He was very particular that way."

I turned to her. "He wasn't a tall, lanky kid with pimples, was he? Had sort of sharp eyes?"

"Why, yes, he was, now that you mention it."

Driving home I fell into a dark, dark, deep, deep funk. I kept telling myself the boy loved that cat. He wouldn't have slit its throat. It had to be the mother. And there had to be some way to prove it.

I was sitting up in bed drinking a tall gin and orange juice about midnight when there was a knock on the door. A small knock.

I went into the living room: "Who is it?"

A man's voice: "It's me."

Martin.

I threw on a bathrobe and opened the door.

He was wearing a sport coat and wide blue-striped tie and was standing almost at attention, his arms at his sides.

"Hello," he said.

"Hello," I said.

He cleared his throat. "May I step in for a moment?"

"Of course."

He came in. I closed the door. I clicked on another light. He walked to the middle of the living room and looked around as if he hadn't seen the place for a long time. It had actually been only three days.

"Would you like a cup of tea, Martin? A drink?"

"I could use a drink."

"Scotch and a splash?"

"Fine."

While I made us a couple of drinks he wandered around the

221

living room. I noticed he stayed away from the part of the living room we'd partitioned off for his study. He ran his hands over the books on the bookshelves. It was like he was reacquainting himself with the place.

I handed him his glass. "Thank you," he said.

"You're welcome."

"Cheers."

"Cheers."

We drank. He smiled at me. I smiled at him.

"Well," he said. "To us."

"Us."

We drank again. "Thanks," he said.

"For what?"

"For getting me out. You're the one who got the boy to confess, after all. I've still got a misdemeanor thing hanging over me—tampering with evidence—but my lawyer says he should be able to bargain it down to a fine. A thousand-dollar fine ought to cover it."

"That doesn't sound too bad."

He smiled again. Shyly. He studied me.

"What are you looking at?"

"You. You look beautiful."

"Thank you."

"I missed you."

"I missed you, too."

He took a couple of gulps of his drink. "I guess I was sort of out of it at the jail."

"You had good reason to be."

"I did a lot of thinking while I was in there. About why you . . . why you were attracted to a man like Mr. Gore."

"If you figured it out, I wish you'd explain it to me. I can't tell you how sorry I am about your finding us like that, Martin. I lost my head. Temporary insanity. I mean it."

He lowered his eyes and turned away from me. "Do you still want to marry me?"

"I said I would, didn't I?"

"That doesn't sound too positive."

"We've been through a lot lately. Why don't we just go out, have a few laughs. Pay some attention to each other."

"I could use a few laughs," he said.

"Martin, I'm sorry I caused you pain."

"No, it was my fault for paying more attention to that machine in there than to you."

"But still, I had no right . . ."

"Enough, Od. Let's not talk about it anymore. The past is past."

He kissed me, not passionately, but long and lovingly, and although there were no rockets going off in my brain, I at least felt wanted. I held him tight for a minute, then I let him go. "Let me fix myself up a little, Martin," I said. "Just be a minute."

I went into the bathroom to give my teeth a quick brushing and to spray on a little Madness at Midnight, which I knew was his favorite. Then I put on a revealing black teddy, gave my hair a quick brush, and headed back into the living room. Martin was in the study; he had the light on over his computer and I could see him running his hand over it, caressing it.

I felt a pang of jealousy. For what? A computer? I could feel anger rising up in me. I wanted to punch something.

That's when I heard a car coming up the driveway. I took a look out the front window. It was Charlie's black Z. He got out and came bounding up the front steps. I went back into the bedroom and put my robe back on.

He knocked.

Martin said, "Get that, would you, Od?"

As I walked back through the living room, I could see Martin at his machine, his one true love, his face green in the illumination of the monitor. He was punching keys with relish. I guess in jail he'd had plenty of time to work out solutions to all his problems.

I opened the door. Charlie was wearing a suit and tie and had gotten a haircut.

"If you need a place to sleep tonight," I said, "the garbage cans are out in back."

He didn't laugh at my little joke. He said: "It wasn't the kid that did all those murders. It was his old lady."

"I thought so, too, but I found the lady who owned the cat. Conrad snatched it."

"He must have done it for his mother," he said. "I found the car," he said. "Took me almost twenty hours and two inches of shoe leather."

"What car?"

"The one Mrs. Holmcroft used. The red Toyota with the dent in exactly the same place as the dent on Rachel Collins's car. It's parked on the corner of Parker and Clement. How about you get Frampton's stakeout truck and we just sit and wait until she shows up to get rid of it? It's the one thing that can really burn her. She won't wait long."

"Give me three minutes to get dressed."

When I came out of the bedroom, Martin and Charlie were in the kitchen. They weren't looking at each other, nor speaking. Charlie was humming something.

"I've got to go out, Martin," I said. "Business. I don't have time to explain right now."

Charlie opened the door and held it for me.

Martin said, "If you leave with that man, the wedding is off."

Charlie laughed.

I said, "Good-bye then, Martin."

TWENTY-SEVEN

∎

Charlie and I sat in the back of the van with the lights out. The Toyota was across the street under an overhanging tree. I'd put a homing device under the rear bumper, so we were all set to follow Mrs. Holmcroft if she picked it up. We wanted to catch her in the act of dumping it.

It was a quiet street. Just after 1 A.M. I was tired, but I was excited, too. It was like fishing, waiting for the big one to strike.

I had a lot of time to think about Martin, too, and I was feeling glad it was all over with. He and I would never have made it, I would have just been one more notch on his divorce belt. He loved his work and there wasn't any room in his life for anyone else.

And I loved my work, too. It wasn't all Martin's fault. It wasn't all my fault. I was just feeling good it was over.

Charlie had not made a pass at me. If he did, I was ready to bloody his nose. Just because Martin and I were finished did not mean that I was ready to rekindle the flame of passion with a slime like Charlie Gore.

He munched on potato chips. He sipped beer.

In the dark, I could smell his aftershave. It provoked memories: How we fought on the floor. How we made love with blood running down his forehead. I felt a flicker of desire, but I extinguished it by remembering the wife he never told me about, and his blackmail scheme, and his little tryst with Holmcroft's maid.

I could feel his blue eyes on me in the darkness. I could feel his wanting me and it made me edgy. We were both quiet for a while, then he said: "I gave the money back to Mrs. Holmcroft. The whole two hundred thousand."

"Why would you do that?"

"I didn't want to lose you."

"I don't believe it."

"Believe what you like. I gave back every dime. I swear to God I did. My wife will have to quit drinking on her own; I've just been kidding myself that a clinic could help someone who doesn't want to be helped anyway."

Strange, but I believed him. So he wasn't a complete slime. The flicker of desire for him was becoming a flame. The old animal attraction. I could master that. People quit booze. Smoking. Even drug addiction. I could quit him. All it would take was a little willpower.

"One of us should get some sleep," I said.

"I'm going to have another beer." He reached over into the cooler and grabbed one.

"I know about you and the maid," I said.

"Angelica? What about her?"

"I know, that's all."

"You're acting like a wronged woman."

"I thought we had an arrangement."

"You think I banged her?"

"Well didn't you?"

"No, I didn't."

"You didn't?"

"No."

The wind rustled the leaves of the tree over the Toyota. Charlie moved his leg. I could feel his *presence*. It was as if his body had a kind of gravitational pull. I felt desire rising in me again. I told myself no. This was so absurd. I'd never felt this way about anyone. Damn it, I would beat it.

I said, "What business did you have with the maid?"

"She found the wig and the trench coat Mrs. Holmcroft put into the trash. I showed them to Mrs. Holmcroft, she almost fainted."

"But it could have been the boy's."

"Yeah, that's what she said. That was okay with me, she wanted to cover for him, she said. I believed her. She was going to pay me to shut up about the boy. But that doesn't explain the car. She was in on it, you can bet on that."

"I thought so all along."

We didn't say anything for a long moment. Then he said, "I've never felt about any woman the way I feel about you."

"Let's not talk about it," I said.

"I mean it. When I'm around you, my throat gets this itch in it."

"Really? You should see a doctor. Maybe you're allergic."

"Don't be cruel," Charlie said. "When I'm not with you, I'm hurting."

I wasn't going to believe him. I didn't believe him about the maid, either. I was going to be rid of him.

"Let's talk about something else," I said.

"Like what?"

"I don't know, anything."

"The only thing I want to talk about is us."

"I refuse to talk about us. There is no us."

"There could be."

"No, there couldn't be."

"I want to hold you," he said. "Just hold you. I've missed you."

I said, "So what do you think, are the Giants going to win the pennant?"

"Sure."

"They'll never get by the Dodgers or the Reds," I said.

"The Reds'll fold, and so will you."

227

"Pardon?"

"I want to run my tongue over every inch of your body."

I sang: "I'm not listening, Charlie."

"You're the greatest thing that's ever happened to me."

"I won't listen," I said. I could feel my skin warming. "Is there any bottled water in the cooler?"

"I don't know."

I got up to go to the cooler. Charlie's leg was in the aisle; I fell over it. He grabbed me as I went down and pulled me onto his lap. I slapped him and scrambled to my feet.

"What the hell was that for?" he said.

"For getting grabby!"

"I only tried to catch you."

"The hell you did!"

He grabbed my belt and pulled me onto his lap again. I slapped him again and again. He pulled me in close and I felt his lips on my neck.

"Let me go, you son of a bitch!" I yelled. I put my knuckle into a pressure point on his chest and he let out a "Yeow!" and let me go.

I stood up and tucked my blouse in.

"You want me as much as I want you," he said.

"A relationship is more than just sex, Charlie."

"For the first time in my life I would agree to that."

I sat down on the couch. I could hear his labored breathing in the darkness. The heat rising up in me was strong now. Suddenly, I was aware I was breathing heavy, too. I felt a great pressure building up inside me.

"I hate your guts, Charlie Gore."

He moved over onto the couch next to me. "You don't hate me, you hate wanting me. Don't fight it." He touched my hand, gently; it was like a spark. Something let go inside me, some explosion, and the next thing I knew we were kissing hungrily and undoing each other's clothes in a frenzy.

That's when we heard a car start up. We froze.

Charlie looked up. "Shit. It's her."

We scrambled to get our clothes back on. The Toyota pulled

out of the parking space, turned around in a driveway, and headed down the block. She was driving slowly and cautiously.

I got the van started. Charlie clicked on the homing device. It beeped away. He took out an infrared camera and started snapping pictures.

"Is it her in there?" I asked.

"I didn't get a good look, but I think so."

At the end of the block the Toyota made a right.

"She's heading toward the ocean," I said. "Dumping the other car into the bay didn't work well. What do you bet she's going to dump this one in the deep water."

We were on Geary Boulevard, heading west. We stayed back two and a half blocks. The traffic was light at that hour of the morning.

The driver was obeying every traffic law, keeping well under the speed limit.

I was feeling calmer now. Passions cooling. Reason taking over. How could I let myself get involved with this man again? What a dumbo.

As the fog thickened closer to the ocean, I closed the gap between us and the Toyota. The Toyota took a right onto Point Lobos Avenue. We were a block behind it. Suddenly the fog was much thicker and I lost her taillights. I sped up, going downhill toward the Cliff House, where the road horseshoes back down to the Great Highway.

Charlie said, "She turned off back there someplace."

I swung the van around and headed back up the hill, then made a turn onto Merrie Way, which runs parallel to the ocean.

Charlie's face glowed red in the reflection of the homing device.

"She's below us," he said, "we must have come back too far."

I made a quick turn on the narrow street and headed back to Point Lobos.

"There's a hiking trail over there," I said. I swung up over the curb. We started down the trail. I could see tire tracks on the damp ground ahead of us.

"She'll see the headlights," Charlie said. "We better hoof it."

I shut off the engine and we got out. Charlie had a flashlight, but he didn't switch it on. I asked him if he had a gun.

"Hell yes."

We made our way down the trail. It was cold and windy and the fog swirled around us. We could hear the surf crashing against the rocks below. A foghorn sounded. Charlie clicked on the light and we saw the tracks go around into Lincoln Park, down to the beach below the cliffs at Lands End.

"I've hiked here," I said. "There's a terrific riptide and undertow. Anything that goes in there is gone forever."

We came down onto the beach. I could see headlights in the fog ahead of us. We ran along the path. I pulled out ahead of Charlie, who lumbered out of breath.

Suddenly the fog broke. A three-quarter moon hung over the Pacific at the other end of the small grove of trees. We could see where the Toyota had crushed some brush. She must have had some trouble getting over a stump, because there was a place where the dirt was disturbed. At the end of the path on a small outcropping of rock she was just getting out of the car.

Mrs. Holmcroft had the door open and was gunning the engine and spinning the wheels but the car was hung up on something right on the lip of the outcropping.

"Halt!" Charlie yelled, pulling his gun. "Don't move!"

I clicked Charlie's flashlight on her. She looked strangely calm. She wore a long coat, opened in the front, and a white scarf around her neck which ruffled in the wind. The surf crashed against the rocks just below, sending a spray up around her that shimmered in the light of the flashlight.

Charlie and I were only a few yards away from her. She said something to us, but it was lost in the sound of the surf.

We came closer, just a few feet from her. She kept her hands away from her body as if she wanted to make sure we could see she wasn't armed.

She said, "Miss Gallagher, you are indeed becoming a nuisance."

"Your son didn't kill all those people. You did."

230

"Did I? I beg to differ with you. I have never killed anyone."

"Then why are you dumping this car?"

She had to think a moment, then said: "So I wanted to get rid of the car my son used in his crimes. Perfectly natural a mother would want to do that. What's the penalty for that? A hundred-dollar fine for illegal dumping?"

"This car was never your son's."

"Go ahead and file your charges. You have no proof. My son confessed, remember?" She started to walk away.

"Don't move," Charlie said, motioning with his gun.

"What are you going to do, shoot me?" Mrs. Holmcroft asked. "I hardly think so. You are a blackmailer, but you didn't even have the guts to keep the money. I doubt you have it in you to kill anyone. It takes a very special kind of person. You're not it."

"There is proof," I said.

"There is?"

"Charlie told you where Rachel was. There's no way Conrad could have known."

"My son must have overheard on the extension. He was always skulking around, listening to everyone's conversations."

"But he loved Mr. Elroy—the cat. It belonged to a little old lady near Conrad's school. Her name's Mrs. Keller. Conrad loved him and brought him home, didn't he? You drugged the cat with Amytal before you slit its throat. Conrad wouldn't have killed that cat."

She stiffened, but said nothing. Then she turned to Charlie. "Either shoot that gun or get out of my way."

"Your son didn't buy this car," I said.

"No, I bought it for him. It was insured for him. Check with our broker, if you like. His name is Walt Kaiser."

"You're a murderer," Charlie said.

"Not unless a jury says so." She started walking again, circling around us. We maneuvered to stay in front of her.

I said: "You know what's really weird about all this? It wasn't Rachel Collins your husband was in love with."

She stopped and seemed to turn to stone. Mist, glowing in the yellow beam of the flashlight, swirled around her. "What are you talking about?"

"He wasn't going to leave you for Rachel Collins. He was through with her."

"No he wasn't," she said. "He loved her. He was selling everything and going away with her. He pretended to be through with her, so I wouldn't suspect."

"Sorry, Mrs. Holmcroft. He really was through with her. It was the mousy little secretary he was nuts about. Hillary Hoyle. He was going away with her forever."

She gulped some air.

Charlie said, "It's a fact, lady, you went and burned the wrong woman."

Mrs. Holmcroft stood frozen for a long moment, her eyes fixed on me. They seemed to glow with almost demonic intensity. I could see the killer in her at that moment. Then, without saying a word, she walked straight ahead, between Charlie and me. I reached out and spun her around and hit her square in the face. She dropped unconscious like a puppet with its cords cut.

I stood over her. "You're under citizen's arrest." My hand hurt like hell, but I didn't rub it because I didn't want Charlie to know.

Charlie said, "Nice punch. Elegant, really."

"There are certain moments in life when you find out who you are," I said. "I just had to let her have it, just once."

"I know who I am," Charlie said. He grabbed Mrs. Holmcroft by the coat and picked her up and dumped her into the Toyota. He slammed the door closed and started to push.

"Charlie!" I yelled.

He stopped pushing. "You believe in justice, don't you? She killed my pal Fingers. She's got to pay for that."

"Not this way."

"Listen for once in your life," he said. "We haven't got anything on her her million-dollar lawyers couldn't shoot down in ten minutes." He went back to pushing.

"Still, her guilt or her innocence is not for us to decide."

The car started slipping forward. "Stop it!" I said.

He didn't stop. I kicked him on the side of his knee, knocking him to the ground. "Shit," he gasped. "We haven't got time for fun and games," he said, "she'll be waking up in a minute."

"We're turning her over to the cops, Charlie."

"Not a chance."

He leaned against the trunk of the car and pushed with all he had. The car jerked forward. I felt a jolt of fear that made me tremble.

"You don't get it, do you, Odyssey?" he said. "You just condemned Hillary Hoyle to death. You saw that look in her eyes, she'll kill her!"

"We'll protect Hillary. We'll get the law to protect her."

He just kept pushing. The car jumped suddenly closer to the edge.

"No, Charlie, damn it! Stop it!"

I kicked him in the ribs.

"Yeow!" he cried. "I've had it with you."

He turned and came at me. I went into my defensive stance and tried to catch his hand as it grabbed at my jacket. Suddenly my feet went up in the air and I felt myself flying through space. I crashed into a bush, rolled, and came up on my feet.

The marines teach a move like that. Crude, but effective.

Charlie was already pushing the car again. It moved forward, almost to the edge, but it wouldn't quite go over. Charlie bent his back to it and pushed with all he had, grunting, but it wouldn't go those last few inches.

"Come on, Genius, help me! We got to hurry, before she wakes up."

The car was teetering.

I ran at him and gave him a kick in the rump. "No!" He turned and took a swing at me, missed; I grabbed him by the wrist and sent him somersaulting onto the ground. A pretty nice *shiho-nage*. He got quickly to his feet and came at me again. I braced myself, he caught my arm, I twisted against his strength; he kicked my feet out from under me and sent me sprawling into some bushes. I untangled myself. He was already at the car. I could see Mrs. Holmcroft rising up in the front seat. Charlie gave the car a shove; the front wheels dropped over the edge.

"Wait!" she cried.

Charlie gave the car another shove and over it went. A hollow scream was swallowed up in the crashing surf below.

Charlie and I stood there for a long moment, watching the waves wash over the car, and then it was gone. Charlie reached for my hand; I refused to let him have it. I was feeling sick.

On the way back up the hill, Charlie said, "I took you pretty easy."

We stopped walking and turned back toward the sea.

"You let me win, didn't you?" he said.

I listened to the waves crashing on the rocks far below. "Did I?"